"JACK FL... ...n Post

Praise for Doug Swanson's
Dreamboat

"Gruesomely funny . . . [As in] Swanson's endearingly demented first mystery . . . you don't so much follow the plot as trot alongside, giggling in horror, while it sniffs its way home." —*New York Times Book Review*

"Full of memorable lines, laugh-out-loud-funny—and [Swanson's] ability to use those lines to create characters who are both bizarre and believable."
—*Dallas Morning News*

"Swanson makes you glad he knows every last thing about these guys and where they live and what they're gonna do next." —*Kirkus Reviews*

"[Swanson] does for Dallas dialogue what Elmore Leonard does for the criminalspeak in Detroit . . . Jack Flippo remains [a] thoroughly human hero, and he clearly has more adventures to come." —*Albuquerque Journal*

continued . . .

Big Town

"Detective fiction at its finest—fast, fun, and full of surprises. The characters are exuberantly dirty and the dialogue is pricelessly funny and true."   —Carl Hiaasen

"Snappy, funny, and worldly-wise . . . Mr. Swanson's feel for the pulse of everyday minds marks the caliber of this book."   —*Dallas Morning News*

"Rich in characters, seamless plotting, evocative in detail. Doug Swanson does the underbelly of Dallas to perfection . . . and on-the-skids attorney is the ideal guide, finding humanity and humor in the lives of the hustlers, hookers, and con men scrabbling for the last crumbs of the American pie. This one will haunt you."   —Lee Standiford

MORE MYSTERIES FROM THE
BERKLEY PUBLISHING GROUP . . .

THE HERON CARVIC MISS SEETON MYSTERIES: Retired art teacher Miss
Seeton steps in where Scotland Yard stumbles. "A most beguiling protagonist!"

—New York Times

by Heron Carvic
MISS SEETON SINGS
MISS SEETON DRAWS THE LINE
WITCH MISS SEETON
PICTURE MISS SEETON
ODDS ON MISS SEETON

by Hampton Charles
ADVANTAGE MISS SEETON
MISS SEETON AT THE HELM
MISS SEETON, BY APPOINTMENT

by Hamilton Crane
HANDS UP, MISS SEETON
MISS SEETON CRACKS THE CASE
MISS SEETON PAINTS THE TOWN
MISS SEETON BY MOONLIGHT
MISS SEETON ROCKS THE CRADLE
MISS SEETON GOES TO BAT
MISS SEETON PLANTS SUSPICION
STARRING MISS SEETON
MISS SEETON UNDERCOVER
MISS SEETON RULES
SOLD TO MISS SEETON
SWEET MISS SEETON
BONJOUR, MISS SEETON
MISS SEETON'S FINEST HOUR

KATE SHUGAK MYSTERIES: A former D.A. solves crimes in the far Alaska north . . .

by Dana Stabenow
A COLD DAY FOR MURDER
DEAD IN THE WATER
A FATAL THAW
BREAKUP

A COLD-BLOODED BUSINESS
PLAY WITH FIRE
BLOOD WILL TELL
KILLING GROUNDS
HUNTER'S MOON

INSPECTOR BANKS MYSTERIES: Award-winning British detective fiction at its
finest . . . "Robinson's novels are habit-forming!"

—West Coast Review of Books

by Peter Robinson
THE HANGING VALLEY
WEDNESDAY'S CHILD
INNOCENT GRAVES

PAST REASON HATED
FINAL ACCOUNT
GALLOWS VIEW

CASS JAMESON MYSTERIES: Lawyer Cass Jameson seeks justice in the criminal
courts of New York City in this highly acclaimed series . . . "A witty, gritty heroine."

—New York Post

by Carolyn Wheat
FRESH KILLS
MEAN STREAK
TROUBLED WATERS

DEAD MAN'S THOUGHTS
WHEN NOBODY DIES
SWORN TO DEFEND

JACK McMORROW MYSTERIES: The highly acclaimed series set in a Maine mill
town and starring a newspaperman with a knack for crime solving . . . "Gerry Boyle is the
genuine article."

—Robert B. Parker

by Gerry Boyle
DEADLINE
LIFELINE
BORDERLINE

BLOODLINE
POTSHOT
COVER STORY

UMBRELLA MAN

Doug Swanson

BERKLEY PRIME CRIME, NEW YORK

UMBRELLA MAN

This is a work of fiction. Names, characters, places, and incidents are either the product of the author's imagination or are used fictitiously, and any resemblance to actual persons, living or dead, business establishments, events, or locales is entirely coincidental.

A Berkley Prime Crime Book / published by arrangement with the author

PRINTING HISTORY
G. P. Putnam's Sons hardcover edition / 1999
Berkley Prime Crime mass-market edition / May 2000

The Penguin Putnam Inc. World Wide Web site address is http://www.penguinputnam.com

ISBN: 0-425-17464-6

Berkley Prime Crime Books are published by The Berkley Publishing Group, a division of Penguin Putnam Inc., 375 Hudson Street, New York, New York 10014.
The name BERKLEY PRIME CRIME and the BERKLEY PRIME CRIME design are trademarks belonging to Penguin Putnam Inc.

PRINTED IN THE UNITED STATES OF AMERICA

10 9 8 7 6 5 4 3 2 1

*For Jules Swanson,
the original*

ACKNOWLEDGMENTS

My thanks to filmmaker Bill Guttentag of Los Angeles, to Detective Kim Sanders of the Dallas Police Department, and to Stacey Loizeaux of Controlled Demolition, Inc., Phoenix, Maryland, for generously sharing their time and expertise. And I offer heartfelt appreciation for the hard work of incomparable agent Janet Wilkens Manus and peerless editor Jeremy Katz.

UMBRELLA MAN

1

The twenty-second day of November came with brilliant sunshine and perfectly clear skies, a beautiful slice of fall in Dallas, Texas. Eddie Nickles said, "Let you in on a little secret, my friend. Snipers love weather like this."

As he spoke, a midnight-blue 1963 Lincoln convertible limousine made its way down Main Street, engine purring, paint glinting in the sunlight. Christ, it was a beautiful car. Two flags rippled from small staffs above the Lincoln's headlights. One was the Stars and Stripes. The other displayed the seal of the President of the United States.

A radio newsman described the scene. Big deep voice, trying to paint a picture for all the listeners: *The crowds are six deep here along the sun-splashed streets of downtown Dallas, a colorful sea of Texans. It's a warm, friendly Lone Star welcome for the President and Mrs. Kennedy.*

"Everybody's happy, everybody's feeling good," Eddie said over the radio cheers. "Especially the dudes with the guns. Notice I said dudes, plural. Notice I— Hey, champ, do me a favor, don't spill no coffee on the upholstery."

The Lincoln moved now toward the old schoolbook depository, a red brick box of a building. The grassy knoll loomed ahead. Eddie glanced at a window on the book depository's sixth floor. He said, "Here's where we get down and get funky. Like the man says, Gentlemen, start your carbines."

From the radio newsman: *President Kennedy's motorcade has entered Dealey Plaza. The President is smiling and waving to the delighted crowd. He seems to be saying something to Mrs. Kennedy.*

"You got that right." Eddie nodded and licked his lips. "He's telling his old lady they should get the hell out of this burg right now."

The Lincoln crept downhill, into the sweeping curve toward the Triple Underpass. Now the radio guy was confused: *There seems to be some problem . . . A sound . . . Could have been a motorcycle backfire . . . Something has gone terribly wrong.*

"Shots fired!" Eddie shouted. "Hear that? Shots fired! The President has been hit! President Kennedy has been—" Eddie broke off his shouting when the Lincoln became hard to control. Saying to himself, the hell is this? He gripped the wheel with both hands and steered the limo toward the curb, like bringing a big boat to dock in rough water.

"You believe this?" Eddie said. "This is nuts. I think we just blew a tire."

The radio newsman was at fever pitch now. Jabbering about gunshots and Secret Service agents and Mrs. Kennedy on the trunk of the car—going full tilt until Eddie pressed the eject button on the Lincoln's tape player. The newsman's voice went silent and a cassette came sliding out. On its label: YOU ARE THERE, DALLAS, NOV. 22, 1963. Copyright 1999 by Edward T. Nickles, Grassy Knoll Productions.

"Goddamn piece-of-garbage used tires." Eddie shifted the Lincoln into park and slammed a hand against the dashboard. "Supposed to be a twenty-thousand-mile guarantee."

Traffic backed up behind the Lincoln. A driver in a delivery truck hit his horn twice. Eddie gave him the finger as he got out of the car and checked the damage. The right front tire was nothing but shredded rubber.

Eddie said, "We're talking lawsuit now."

This should have been his biggest day of the year, the anniversary of the JFK rubout. There would be people all over Dealey Plaza—all over the world, it seemed to Eddie—wanting to take the Assassination Re-creation Tour in Eddie's authentic replica of Kennedy's limo. People who would think nothing of paying twenty-five dollars a head while Eddie drove them along the exact presidential death route, playing the *You Are There* tape and providing expert commentary as needed.

"The sons of bitches will not get away with this." Eddie leaned against the hood, his hands flat on the shiny new paint job that still hadn't been paid for. The presidential flag stirred in a light breeze. "These tire company bastards are gonna cough it up big, believe that. Major damages."

From behind him a man's voice said, "Pocklin?"

Eddie turned. The tourist who had been in the back seat of the Lincoln stood on the sidewalk now, still holding his coffee cup. Eddie tried to remember what country the guy was from. All he could come up with was one of those places where they wore leather shorts and yodeled all day.

"Now what?" Eddie said.

The tourist set his coffee cup on the sidewalk, unzipped his fanny pack and found one of Eddie's brochures for the Grassy Knoll Experience. He pointed to the section labeled *Exciting Finale*. Eddie had written the text himself: *Join in the exciting thrill of a high-speed dash to Parkland*

Hospital, where gallant doctors worked feverishly in a vain effort to save the mortally wounded President's life!!!

"Go now?" the tourist said.

That was the best part of the tour, Eddie had to admit. Doing eighty up Stemmons Freeway, the limo's top down, while the *You Are There* tape gave the sound of a siren over moans and screams. Then roaring into the Parkland entrance and hitting the brakes in front of the emergency room.

Some of the customers liked the Parkland run so much they tipped Eddie a ten-spot. One night it even got him laid, right on the Lincoln's JFK death seat by a thin, bucktoothed girl with a Jacqueline fixation.

"To Pocklin now?" the tourist said.

Eddie pointed to the dead tire. "Hey, ace, you see this? Maybe in Slobovia you drive on a flat. Not in this country."

The tourist frowned and said something about money back. Amazing, Eddie thought. The guy could barely speak English but had the concept of refund down cold.

"Hey, if it was up to me, sure. But refunds are against federal law. Tell you what I'll do, though. Right up the hill here"—Eddie pointed up Elm—"is a place called the Conspiracy Institute. Go up there, say Eddie Nickles sent you, they'll let you in free."

"Say Eddie Neekles sent you."

"In Dallas, Texas, them words is magic."

When he hesitated Eddie told him, "They might even throw in a free T-shirt." That sealed it, and the tourist walked away, leaving Eddie to deal with another problem: No spare tire in the trunk, and not enough ready cash for a tow truck.

A small crowd had gathered near the Lincoln, which happened whenever he brought it anywhere near the assassination site. Eddie got ready for the question somebody was sure to ask: Is that *the* car? If I tell you that, Eddie always answered, the Secret Service will have me *and* you killed.

He found some Grassy Knoll brochures in the glove box and handed them out to the people gawking at the limo. Saying, "Have it up and running in no time, folks. Then you can take the death ride of your life."

An old man with a video camera wandered over. He taped the Lincoln from a couple of angles, finally asking Eddie, "What happened?"

"Somebody sabotaged it. Slit the sidewall."

The old man knelt and studied the flat tire. "Looks like it just wore out to me."

"No, somebody cut it," Eddie said, loud enough for everyone to hear. "Wouldn't be surprised if it was the CIA. Could have been the Cuban mob, they're around." He gazed toward the Triple Underpass. "They don't like what I'm doing out here, I can tell you that, the things Eddie Nickles is uncovering. They don't like it one— Hey, no more pictures. Who you working for anyway? You with the FBI?"

2

Jack Flippo parked in front of Big Dee's Adult Books & Videos on a hideous stretch of Dallas named Harry Hines Boulevard. Thinking as he got out of his car, the things I do for lust.

Big Dee's filled a windowless building between Stag's Topless Lounge and a discount mattress outlet. Jack opened the door and walked into low-ceilinged, overlit fluorescence and the smell of disinfectant. He saw rows of videotapes arranged by persuasion—traditional, bondage, groups, amateur. Half a dozen male customers wandered the place, hands in pockets, not making eye contact.

Jack found what he was looking for on a shelf along one wall, near the edible underwear and just above a display of picture books called *Hot Knockers & Humongous Butts*. He took four boxes from the shelf and carried them to the cash register. Each contained one life-size blow-up woman, Vinyl Venus, $12.95 apiece. Jack checked his wallet to see if he had enough.

The clerk looked bored, chewing gum. He started to ring up Jack's purchase, then stopped. "For the same price you can get Party Gal and Party Pal. Better grade of plastic."

"Sure." Jack shrugged. "Go for quality. Where do I find them?"

The clerk pointed. "Aisle two. Next to the inflatable sheep."

Jack paid cash and drove toward home with two Party Gals and two Party Pals boxed and bagged on the seat beside him. Traffic was heavy as the late-afternoon light drained away. He called Lola from the car, telling her as soon as she picked up, "Okay, I got what you wanted."

"You're my man," she said.

"Be there soon."

"I'll be waiting."

Lola was twenty-seven, ten years south of Jack, with business cards that identified her as a Next Wave Artistician. Her dark hair had purple and green streaks. There were two silver studs in her nose and a ring in her left eyebrow. Her parents called her Jennifer, but she had renamed herself after hearing the old Kinks song. Lola stayed out of the sun and slept only about four hours a night. She had more tattoos than a merchant seaman.

She had been living with Jack in his East Dallas bungalow for two months. Lola liked to refer to it as a fact-finding mission among the indigenous peoples of the bourgeoisie. Jack would unlock his front door each evening and call out, "Hi, honey, I'm home." Cracked Lola up every time.

Tonight Lola was in the kitchen. She wore a black shirt, black tights, black boots and some kind of short-sleeved, knee-length coat, black. "Johnny Cash just phoned," Jack said, walking in. "He wants his clothes back."

She kissed him on the cheek and said, "How was your day, dear?" Another joke.

"It was—" Jack stopped. "Something's wrong here. I smell food."

Lola beamed. "Yes, you do."

"You cooked? You're kidding me."

"Special occasion. Just for tonight."

Jack opened the oven and saw six TV dinners bubbling in their trays.

"You want fried chicken," Lola asked him, "or meat loaf?"

Jack chose meat loaf and choked down as much as he could, a couple of bites. Bland and hard to swallow, just like his new job. He had shuttered the one-man detective agency known as Flippo Associates. Now he was drawing a check at the downtown law firm of Lennard & Ratliff, wearing a dark suit every day: the prodigal attorney, allowed back in the club.

Lola said, "You think you'll like it? That would be cool. Then it becomes like a daily Stockholm-syndrome hostage thing, you know?"

"No, I don't know. Listen . . ." Jack was ready to give a speech, tell her what she and her friends, irony-dripping artsy-fartsies straight out of trust fund land, didn't understand about making a living.

But Lola, pushing back her chair, said, "Pictures, remember? You promised."

"What? Oh, baby, not tonight. I'm beat. I had a long day cheating widows out of their pensions."

Lola put a box on the table, reminding Jack that her gallery show was only two weeks away and there was no time to spare, tons of work to do before then. She cracked open the box and breathed out as if she'd just glimpsed King Tut's tomb. "Oh . . . awesome."

Jack took a handful of old black-and-white photographs and spread them on the table. "What are you talking about?"

"These are beautiful. I mean, look at the history here."

Jack didn't see history. All Jack saw was a bunch of old shots of the Flippo family from when he was a kid. Lola stood behind him, looking over his shoulder. She said, "I think it's so cool that you grew up in the sixties."

"Check this one, the old man in a suit and tie. Must have been a wedding or a funeral." He held up a shot of his father: Tall and thin, with a big handle of a nose, just like Jack. "Guarantee you," Jack said, "somewhere outside the frame there's a Pall Mall going and a can of Schlitz making a ring on the coffee table."

Jack remembered a man who had two modes of dress around the house, his jumpsuit from Flippo Bros Welding or his underwear. A man who, if he had a few beers in him, might break wind at the supper table. Then ask while the kids laughed, Somebody hear a spider bark?

"Hey, check this one," Lola said.

It was another black-and-white, a little fuzzy and under-lit. Jack studied the whole Flippo family: Mom, Dad, big brother Jeff and one gawky teenager with zits and a bad haircut—Jack.

"That's it." Lola reached for it. "That's the one I want."

Jack gazed at his mother's smiling face. "The woman was sad every day of her life."

"It's perfect." Lola took the picture from him and moved into the living room. She began unboxing the Party Gals and Party Pals. Asking Jack, "Aren't you going to help me blow these up?"

He helped for a while, inflating the two plastic women before retreating to the back of the house. Jack took a shower, then looked for something to read, going through a stack of magazines but not finding what he wanted. He checked a drawer of the nightstand and turned up only a dirty sock and a bound copy of Lola's master's thesis, "The Slaughter of Arnold Ziffel: CBS Television's Embrace and Subsequent Abandonment of the 'Rural' Comedy, 1965–71."

He called out, "What the hell happened to my *Sporting News*?"

"In here," Lola answered.

Jack walked back toward the living room and stopped at the edge. "It's a joke, right?"

Lola swept the room with an open palm. "I'm moving this whole tableau to the gallery. When you walk into my show, this will be the first thing you see."

The blow-up dolls were seated on Jack's furniture. One held a newspaper, one had its face toward the television, one had knitting in its lap and one had its hands inside its pants.

Lola said, "I'm calling them the Nuclear Love Family."

They were dressed in thrift shop clothes and bedroom slippers, and had blond wigs taped to their plastic heads. They dined at fold-up trays holding the TV dinners that Lola had heated up. The picture of Jack's family, now framed, rested on a lamp table.

Jack bent to get his *Sporting News* from the coffee table. "Wait," Lola said. "You can't do that. The magazine is part of the scene."

He sighed and glanced at the clock. Time for working stiffs to get some rest anyway. "Fine," he said. "Now how about something real? Something like you, in bed with me, and all that black shit you're wearing on the floor."

Lola fussed with the wig on one of the Party Gals. "In a minute maybe. I've got some touching up to do."

"Or"—Jack smiled—"we could do it right here on the floor. With the Nuclear Love Family watching."

She turned toward him, gave him a look. "I like that," Lola said. "I really do." She took her coat off and began to push her tights down, keeping her eyes locked on Jack's. Man, she was twisted. Jack loved that about her.

From Jack's driveway there was the sound of a car door slamming. Lola pulled her tights back up. She went to the living room's big picture window and parted the curtains, looking across the front yard. "Wow," she said. "Cool car."

The doorbell rang twice, followed by three quick knocks. "Whoever it is," Jack said, "I'll kill him." He opened the door and stared into the porch light at a face he hadn't thought about lately.

"Hey, Jackie," Eddie Nickles said. "You got a minute for an old friend?"

3

Jack and Eddie had drunk beer together a couple of times over the years. And Eddie had done a motel room stakeout for Jack last winter. They weren't big pals, but they would stop and talk if they passed on the street.

The way Jack first heard it, Eddie had been a cop in New Jersey, got laid off, came to Dallas and joined the department in the early eighties. Eddie started by patrolling deep nights in South Dallas, busting every bootlegger and dice game he could find. Earned a nickname in a hurry, Bent Nickles.

Within three months everybody had a story about him. Like the time he arrested a transvestite hooker. Eddie tells the man in a dress, You're going down. Hooker says, Go down on you, baby? That'll cost you twenty dollars. Eddie lets his nightstick slip, knocks out two of the he-she's teeth.

He had a few problems, but Eddie logged some high-profile arrests. He made detective and before long was plain-clothes vice back on the same South Dallas streets he had patrolled as a uniform. Some of his drug pops were big ones.

Jack, working as an assistant district attorney, had met
Eddie in court on sales and possession cases. Eddie wasn't
a bad witness, but you wanted to make sure he didn't take
off on his own speculations. Keep him reined in, that was
the book on Eddie Nickles.

One night on a raid, Eddie was kicking a door in when
his gun went off and put a bullet through his left knee, bad
enough that he left the department on disability. But before
all that Eddie had saved Jack's life. That's the way Eddie
told it.

It happened after Mineola Watts, a five-foot-one piece of
dog, arrived back in town, having done a couple of years in
state prison. Jack had sent him down for selling crack, just
another case, nothing special.

But Eddie had heard that Mineola was planning payback.
Eddie came to see Jack, said Mineola had put out the word
he was going to get the motherfucking white lawyer who
nailed him.

Help me help you, Eddie said. Give me some names,
some numbers. Telling Jack, Maybe I can figure out where
he's laying right now. Jack pulled his file from the old case
and came up with some friends and relatives of Mineola
Watts.

A couple of days of poking around and Eddie learned
that Mineola was spending his days in a dive apartment
south of the river. The way Eddie described it later: He went
there, knocked, heard nothing and turned the doorknob. The
place was unlocked, so Eddie walked in.

Mineola lay on the couch watching *Wheel of Fortune*
with his gun in his hand, and started blazing as soon as he
saw Eddie. Eddie stiffed him with one shot to the gut. In the
back of the apartment he found the body of Mineola's wife,
Shauntelle. She hadn't been dead long, a bullet in her head.
A bullet, as it turned out, from Mineola's gun.

That night Eddie called Jack. Saying, "I took care of him for you, man. The little fuck had deceased his old lady and was about to rain on you next. Well, you don't have to worry about him no more, because Eddie Nickles covered you."

With history like that, Jack could at least show up. That was the favor Eddie had said he needed when he stopped by Jack's the night before. Eddie had stood in the middle of the Nuclear Love Family and told Jack he wanted a friendly face at his side. Back me up tomorrow, he'd said, while Eddie Nickles knocks this town on its ass.

So Jack left the Lennard & Ratliff offices at noon and walked five minutes to the John F. Kennedy Memorial. The memorial had its own downtown block, with a green lawn that needed mowing and a border of sidewalks plastered with bird shit. In the middle some high walls surrounded an empty platform. This was supposed to make people contemplate the missing man, the lost innocence, the murdered hopes and all that. You didn't know better, Jack thought, you might think the county had run short of funds and pawned the statue.

Eddie's Lincoln limo was parked in a towaway zone on Main. The Channel 4 Eyewitness News van was behind it. Just outside the memorial's wall Jack saw a rectangular table topped by a battered wooden lectern. Eddie was taping a banner along the front of the table. The banner said, in big red letters, "ALL LIES."

"Finally," Jack said, "truth in advertising."

Eddie stood. "You're not gonna believe this. I'm painting the sign last night, but I run out of room on the paper I'm using. So I have to make it in two sections. Understand what I'm saying?"

"So far. But that could change."

"So when I'm driving here this morning, the second part, which says 'must end,' it flies right outta the back seat. Wind catches it. Before I can pull over and pick it up, a dump truck runs it over. You believe that?"

"And is there ever a dump truck around when you really need one?"

"Asshole was following way, way too close."

Eddie looked into the distance, working his jaw, still hot about the truck. Jack studied him: lounge act hair going a little thin, puffiness around the eyes, skin showing some sag. But it was more than age pulling on Eddie. He was starting to act and talk like a guy whose wiring had been gnawed by rats.

"Almost forgot." Eddie snapped his fingers. "My Zapruder snuff shots are still in the car."

Five minutes later Eddie had them propped on the table for display: grainy eight-by-ten freeze-frame enlargements from the home movie of JFK's death. There were shots of Kennedy in the limo, of Kennedy clutching his throat, of pieces of Kennedy's brain spraying from him.

Eddie leaned into the microphone on the lectern, tapped it twice and said, "Let's get started before the CIA scrambles its surveillance teams onto the surrounding rooftops."

He cleared his throat. Then: "I want to thank all of you for being witnesses to the history that will be made here today." Jack looked around. Not counting him and the Channel 4 crew, the crowd had swelled to seven or eight.

"One score and sixteen years ago, a President came to Dallas." Eddie was reading from a sheet of paper now, rolling the words out flat, using terms like "a malignant collusion of sinister forces." Jack envisioned Eddie the night before, bent over a thesaurus. "And what of the citizens of this great republic"—Eddie pounded the lectern, a couple of beats late—"whose heritage has been befouled by the whitewash?"

Jack stepped away to call his office on his cell phone. While he talked he looked toward Eddie's JFK limo. He wondered if tourists ever went to Abraham Lincoln's box in Ford's Theater and pretended to be shot in the head by John Wilkes Booth.

"There is a film," Eddie was saying when Jack got off the phone, "from the twenty-second day of November, nineteen hundred and sixty-three. A film that was lost to the ages. Or so everyone thought. Everyone but Edward T. Nickles, premier assassinologist of our times."

Jack half tuned out as Eddie went on about the film, how he'd picked up some information that it had surfaced. There was something about a second umbrella man, whatever that meant.

"It shows," Eddie said, "another gun. Do you hear me out there? Proof positive of a massive conspiracy operating on that fateful day in Dallas."

More interesting to Jack was the reporter from Channel 4—short skirt, tall and thin, with thick blond hair, couldn't have been more than twenty-three. Heather something or other. He remembered seeing a report she had done not long ago, a sweeps week exposé on poodle puppy mills.

Eddie got louder: "The film is out there. I'm offering two hundred and fifty thousand dollars for it. That's right, a quarter-million for the lost film of the second umbrella man."

Jack's phone was ringing with a call from a client who wanted to sue a neighbor because leaves from next door kept blowing onto his tennis court. Just as he hung up, he looked to the lectern and saw Eddie pointing at him. "And to help," Eddie said, "I have retained the services of noted investigator Jack Flippo. Wave to the crowd, Jack."

The next thing Jack knew, the Channel 4 camera was in his face, with the blond reporter shoving a mike, coming at him as if he had sold somebody a sick poodle. Asking him, "And just how are you going to find this film?"

Jack stammered and cleared his throat. Finally he managed to say, "I don't know. I guess you just start kicking over rocks."

"That's an answer?" Heather said.

Jack saw Eddie heading their way. In two seconds Eddie had Heather by the elbow, telling her, "This is exclusive to you, all right? I got CNN begging for a live remote, but I told them to go screw themselves, I'm giving everything to you guys."

One of the Kennedy freeze-frames, the one showing the President falling into his wife's lap, blew off the table. Eddie was saying to Heather, "That's a cool quarter-million from the personal account of Eddie Nickles. I think that's putting your money where your mouth is, don't you, honey? You don't mind I call you honey? Some chicks get all frosted about that for some reason. Especially the skanks, which makes no sense to me whatsoever."

Jack caught Eddie's eye and waved, then started to walk up Main, trying to generate some enthusiasm for the afternoon. Six months on the lawyer job and the days already had a coat of boredom.

There was a voice from behind him. "Hey, Jackie, wait up." Jack turned to see Eddie coming his way, moving as fast as he could on the bum knee. Eddie reached Jack and gave his shoulder a light slap. "Thanks for coming, man."

"Happy to help. Good luck finding whatever it is you're after."

"Hope you don't mind I mentioned your name, Jackie. Just trying to put some juice in the goose."

"Sure. But you know I'm out of the detective business." Jack rubbed the lapel of his suit. "Gone disrespectable."

Eddie winked and pointed a finger. "I got you."

"I don't mind being a prop for your speech, but I can't do any snooping for you."

"Hey, Jack, it was just to get the machinery in place. Know what I'm talking about, my friend?"

Jack thought about telling him, Not one clue in the world. But he said, "Gotta go, buddy."

"And hey, listen, one more quick thing, you don't mind." Eddie looked away, then brought his eyes back to Jack. "You got maybe fifty bucks I could borrow till Monday? Or if you could spare it, a hundred would be great."

4

Weldon Chaney said, "What I'm trying to tell you is, we always had a crew and a plan. None of this seat-of-the-pants bullshit. When we took down a store, when we beat a bank, we knew what we were doing."

He rode in a Ford pickup, seated between the Gillich half brothers, Roger and Rodney. Roger drove while Rodney smoked Red Kamels and stared out the window, talking to himself.

"And we stuck together," Weldon said. "All right, give you an example. One Friday night—I'm talking thirty, thirty-five years back—in Red Wilson's Pool Hall, Idabel, Oklahoma, somebody hit Tom Fossey over the head with a beer mug. Killed him dead. Who cares why they did it. The boy needed killing."

They had stopped at a light. Roger glanced to his left. "Check the bitch in the Toyota."

Rodney craned his neck and looked. "Like to go to Tongue Town with her."

Roger nodded, chewing on a toothpick. "Like to do the backdoor chocolate store."

Rodney said, "Like to have lunch at the Y."

Weldon waited. Then picked up with, "So Tom Fossey's laid out on Red Wilson's floor with a dozen men in there drinking beer and playing pool around him. Sooner or later somebody gets around to calling the sheriff. Sheriff comes in and feels up Tom Fossey—"

"Feels him up where?" Rodney said.

"—and the sheriff says, 'This s.o.b. is stone cold. What the hell took you so long to call me?' And Red Wilson looks at the sheriff and tells him, 'We had to get our story straight.'"

Weldon glanced from Roger to Rodney, getting nothing back. "Point of what I'm saying, boys, is we stuck together."

After a moment Roger reached for the radio knob with, "This song sucks."

Rodney lit another cigarette. "Hey, man, when we gonna get some beer?"

Weldon looked at Roger: long blond hair like the hippies wore and a dangling earring, the kind Weldon used to see only on fruits and old ladies before the world went to hell. Roger had a tough-guy stare he liked to practice in the mirror. Hadn't held a steady job for two years, since his dishonorable discharge from the Army, where he had lasted just long enough to learn how to blow things up.

His half brother Rodney had a grown-out buzz cut dyed red, two gold teeth in front and fingernails chewed to the nub. He jittered all the time, not the kind of man Weldon would put behind the wheel of his getaway. "Anything you need to know," Weldon said, "about what we've discussed so far?"

"Yeah." Rodney flicked his cigarette butt out the window

and began to crack his knuckles one by one. "What's harder for you, Roger? Being dumb or being ugly?" Rodney shook with hooted laughter.

Roger said, "Better than being a candy-ass like you."

Weldon sighed and rubbed his eyes. Eight in the evening, he should have been home, drifting into sleep with the Golf Channel at low volume. Instead he was riding in a pickup truck around south Dallas County with two boys he never would have wasted half a thought on.

The problem was, his twin daughters—Brandi and Mandi, beautiful little girls, Weldon would do anything for them—had made the Gillich half brothers his sons-in-law. Weldon tried to remember how many fights had broken out at the double-wedding reception. At least five, not counting when the Gillich boys' mother threw a drink at her fourth husband. Of course Weldon got stuck with the bill, seven hundred dollars for damage to the Elks Lodge furniture.

Brandi and Mandi had come to Weldon one Sunday afternoon—Weldon in his La-Z-Boy, eating salted peanuts and watching the Cowboys game on his new big screen—and asked him to teach Roger and Rodney the business. Both girls looked as if they had been crying.

The Gillich half brothers could use some coaching. Both of them had already done time: Roger six months in county, and Rodney almost two years at Texas Department of Corrections. While Weldon, forty years in the trade, had never been convicted of anything.

The girls had kissed Weldon on the cheek and asked him please, Daddy.

Now Weldon told Roger and Rodney, "We'll talk details later. Things like how to watch a place, stake it out before you hit it, whether to go in through the door, the wall or the ceiling. Main thing I want you to hold on to right now, boys, is the importance of planning." Blank faces from both of them. Weldon said, "Any questions so far?"

"My question," Rodney said, "is am I gonna have to kick Roger's sorry ass to make him stop this truck for some beer?"

Ten minutes later Roger pulled into the parking lot of a Howdy-Mart somewhere between Balch Springs and Seagoville. Weldon said, "Take this place as an example. Nothing on either side of it, but a car lot across the way. And a pretty busy highway out front with no side streets. You were gonna do a gun-and-go here, what's the first thing you'd look for? Rodney?"

"First thing I'm looking for right now is a place to piss." Rodney opened the door and stepped from the truck. "'Cause I'm like this close to wetting my pants."

The half brothers walked across the gravel lot to the store, with Weldon waiting in the truck. Rodney said, "I have to listen to that geezoid ask me any more questions, the top of my head's gonna go off like a Roman candle."

They went into the store, no one else in there but a clerk. Roger headed for the magazine rack. Rodney beat it to the beer cooler and got a twelve-pack of Bud. The clerk, a little dark guy, was frying chicken wings in some deep vats at the end of the counter. Rodney said, "Where's your bathroom, Punjab?"

The clerk wiped his hands and moved to the cash register. "No public rest room," he said.

"That's cool. I'll use the private one."

The clerk shook his head. "No public rest room."

Rodney looked past the clerk to Roger at the magazine rack, caught his eye and gave a nod. "Then I'll just have to let it loose"—he unzipped—"right here."

The clerk went for something under the counter. Roger came up from behind him, had his knife to the man's throat in a flash.

Rodney began to urinate on the floor, but stopped after five seconds. Asking, "Ever seen wiener brakes that good?"

Roger said, "Hold this." Rodney leaned across the counter to take the knife and a handful of the clerk's hair. He pushed the point of the blade just far enough into the man's neck to draw a pearl of blood. Roger jerked the phone from its jack and wrapped the cord around the clerk's wrists, then put him on the floor and hog-tied him, wrists to ankles.

Rodney climbed onto the counter and stood, looking down at the clerk. "This is fucking America, asshole. That means when an American needs to use your toilet, you got to say yes." He left his cock dangling and pulled the lining from one of his front pants pockets, letting it hang out too. Saying, "Hey, Roger, ever seen a one-eared elephant?"

Roger was busy taking bills from the cash register and stuffing them in a paper bag. Rodney began to pee again, this time on the breath mints display.

When Roger had all the cash from the register he said, "Let's roll."

Rodney moved down the counter to the deep-fry vats. He pissed into the grease, making it crackle and spatter. "Here's where I give new meaning," Rodney said, "to the term golden fried chicken."

"Two seconds"—Roger headed toward the door—"or you'll have to thumb it on home."

Rodney, still standing on the counter, saw a security camera hanging from the ceiling, not five feet from his head. "Hey, check it out." He leaned toward the lens, stuck his tongue out, showed the camera his gold teeth, did a little cock-wave dance. Then said, "I'm not really a crazy-ass motherfucker. But I play one on TV."

Just past nine at night, Weldon was in his easy chair in front of his big screen, drinking sangria and eating some Chex party mix. Thinking, what a day. Wondering if they came any dumber than the Gillich boys, who would slice up a store clerk in plain view of the parking lot, just to steal fifty-eight dollars.

The news was on: a bleach blonde and a black guy at a shiny desk, telling Weldon what was happening. Brandi and Rodney sat on the couch, not talking. Weldon looked over and saw Rodney trying to lick Brandi's neck. Weldon closed his eyes. He was tired of thinking. His back hurt. He let sleep settle over him, moving in like gentle rain on a hot day.

And then the black guy on TV said, "When we come back, the search for what they're calling the lost film of the JFK umbrella man."

Weldon sat upright and stared at the screen, mouth open, finger digging in his ear as if to clear a path.

Brandi came to him. "What's wrong, Daddy? You all right?"

Rodney stayed on the couch. Saying, "Damn, Mr. Chaney, that's the first sign of life I seen out of you all day."

5

Jack sat on his couch, next to the Party Pal who had his hands in his pants. Lola was styling the blond wig of another. Jack had worked up some low-wattage dread for the next day, and was trying to drown it with his fourth beer. Telling Lola, "Maybe this was a mistake."

"What's that, Jack-man?"

"Going to work for Lennard and Ratliff." Jack backhanded some air. "I mean, the place is full of guys talking about their golf games and what kind of Lexus to buy. Apprentice fat cats, Lola. And they've got me sitting at a big wooden desk. All my life I've been a metal desk man, know what I'm saying? Sheet metal with a Formica top. Linoleum floors, bad coffee in a Styrofoam cup, that's me."

Lola stared at the television, watching a *Beverly Hillbillies* episode she told Jack she had seen at least twenty times. She said, "If I ever have a kid, know what I'm going to name it? Jethro Bodine."

"Did I tell you about one of the partners? The one with paintings of English fox hunts in his office? Hey, the guy grew up in Grand-fucking-Prairie. I know for a fact his father worked the line at the GM plant."

"Sit up straight now," Lola told one of the blow-ups. "That's the way."

The credits were rolling on the hillbillies. Jack used the remote to flip to the Channel 4 Eyewitness News. "Let's see what Heather the poodle protectress made of the day's events."

He watched the world's woes between commercials. Finally Heather's piece rolled, starting with some old footage of JFK's ride through Dallas, then dissolving to Eddie's limo. "Mission accomplished," Jack said. "Free publicity."

Heather laid out the bones of the story, followed by her interview with Eddie: Big conspiracy, Eddie said, almost four decades of cover-ups. Quarter-mil reward. Next came a reaction shot of Heather nodding gravely.

Jack laughed. "You believe this? She's taking him seriously."

He stopped laughing when Heather's talking head said, "A private investigator, Jack Flippo of Dallas, vowed to do everything it takes to find the film."

Jack on the couch said, "Say what?"

On the screen was a close-up of Jack—his big nose, his messy blond hair, wrinkles starting to show at the corners of his eyes. His voice telling everyone, "You just start kicking over rocks." Then Heather came back, doing a stand-up from Dealey Plaza, talking about lingering mysteries and hidden answers.

Jack had leapt from the couch. "That's a bunch of crap!" He was pointing at the TV, shouting at it like a loony coot in the day ward. "What she said I said, that's not what I said. I mean, I said that. But that's not what I said."

Lola gazed at him. "You don't have a face for television, you know that?"

"Completely out of context. Get me the phone book. I'm calling these low-rent assholes."

"No, I mean it." Lola shook her head. "You look much better in real life." She seemed disappointed.

For dinner Eddie Nickles had a can of beef stew. He couldn't find a clean bowl so he ate the stew straight from the pot, cooling his tongue with instant iced tea from a jelly jar. Two cellophaned saltines, saved from yesterday's diner lunch, were the side dish. And for dessert, vanilla wafers.

When he was done he reached for the portable radio above the sink and turned up the volume. Oldies rock filled the room: Ricky Nelson, then Sam Cooke, followed by Elvis. Mysterious deaths, every one. Some d.j., Eddie thought, was sending a message.

He sank onto a black leatherette couch whose holes had been patched with electrical tape. His phone was on the coffee table. He stared at it and thought about dialing up his ex-wife, Iris.

Eddie punched in her number and got the answering machine. "Hey, lay-dee!" Eddie, doing Jerry Lewis. Then: "It's me, pick up the phone. Hello? Anybody home? Hey, I know you're there. Goddamnit, Iris, pick up the phone."

He slammed the receiver down. Roy Orbison was singing from the radio. Jesus, another dead guy. Eddie killed the music and took a bath, reading a checkout-stand tabloid in the tub. What he learned: Woodpeckers don't get headaches, Dolly Parton was having problems with her man and a race of giants was living at the center of the earth. Hard to believe, Eddie thought, that a stacked babe like Dolly could have love troubles.

When news time rolled around, Eddie settled in front of the TV, which had a snowy picture despite foil balls on the rabbit ears. It was clear enough, though, for Eddie to see himself interviewed, to hear himself talking, to take in the beautiful shot of his car.

Finally, at last, and just in the nick of time: a break for Eddie Nickles. His long run of bad luck might have come to an end; the TV bim had swallowed his story whole. Eddie began to dance around the room, lifting his one good knee and swinging his arms. Chanting, "Yes, yes, yes!"

He planned to get the limo out extra early tomorrow. Eddie could imagine customers lining up to take the ride. He might even boost the price a couple of bucks.

But why stop there? Chances like this didn't come along very often. How, Eddie asked himself, to make the most of this?

Jack was in bed when the first phone call came. He said hello and heard a voice that sounded like someone talking through a thick sock: "This is a warning. Stay away from that Kennedy shit." With Jack thinking, boy, the cranks weren't moving so fast these days. The news had been off for a couple of hours.

He hung up without a reply and walked up the hall to the dark living room. He could hear Lola talking. She lay on the floor, lamps off, curtains of the big window open. She was bathed in dim milky streetlight, with the blow-ups in their seats around her. "You coming to bed?" Jack asked.

"We're all having a conversation right now."

"Maybe you could come talk to a live person."

"Be there soon."

Jack sighed and trudged back to the bedroom. As he settled back under the covers, the phone rang again. The same odd voice told him, "Back away now, or your life may be in danger."

Jack said, "Is that you, Eddie? Or some other lunatic."

After the third call he took the phone off the hook. Jack tried reading but gave up. Something was bothering him but he wasn't sure what: some small worry, zinging around the inside of his head like a bird trapped in a house, banging into a window each time it thought it had found a way out. Not to mention the stirring he felt in his pajama pants. He considered trying to summon Lola again, but he could hear her in the living room, saying, "I'm really starting to feel close to you." She wasn't addressing him.

He closed his eyes, and was sinking into sleep when shots began ripping into the house.

They came in quick succession, five of them over the space of a few seconds. There was a scrambled burst of noise: the pop of gunfire from the street, the breaking of window glass, the thud of the slugs into the living room wall. And then Lola's screams.

Jack had jumped from bed at the first shot. Now he ran up the hallway. Lola's wails washed over him, as if he were swimming against a current of sound.

She was on the floor, on her knees. Jack pushed her down and lay on top of her as her screams melted down to whimpers. It took him a while to see that she had not been hit. But all around her the dolls were nothing but deflated heaps of plastic.

The Nuclear Love Family was dead.

6

Nothing good, Jack thought, ever comes from TV. They show your face for maybe ten seconds and you're easy meat for any psycho with cable and ammunition.

The morning after the shooting a reporter from the paper phoned, some young news ferret addressing Jack as Mr. Flippo and wanting to know what happened. Jack had to laugh. Asking, What's the matter, Dallas running low on mayhem? You people reduced to writing about a couple of broken windows now?

The reporter wondered if it had anything to do with this Kennedy film Jack was looking for. I'm not looking, Jack told him, for any Kennedy film. That's not what we were told, the reporter said, and what about the threatening phone calls? Who told you that? Jack asked. The reporter couldn't say. Well, Jack said, I got a prettty good idea who it was, and he told you wrong.

The morning after that, Jack opened the Metro section and got a smack in the face from a headline: "Search for

Phantom JFK Film May Have Sparked Shooting." With
Jack's name in the story practically jumping off the page at
him, along with some quotes from "self-styled assassinologist" Eddie Nickles. The paper had Eddie saying, "Someone
tried to murder my investigator. But we're going to find that
film, no matter what they do. Because $250,000 in cash
makes things happen."

Jack had to take deep breaths, calm himself down. He
left early for the office, to give himself some extra time to
cruise downtown on the hunt for Eddie Nickles. Eddie, who
hadn't answered his phone for two days. Who was going to
find his ass in front of a judge, if he didn't stop dragging
Jack into this.

For the next half hour Jack breathed rush hour fumes in
Dealey Plaza—doing his version of the Lee Oswald skulk,
waiting for the presidential Lincoln. The plaza was a green
half-bowl. Traffic flowed on three streets that came together at the bottom of the hill, passing under railroad
tracks like water through a chute. At the borders of the plaza
were some cream-colored masonry walls put up during the
Depression and a scattering of live-oak trees. The schoolbook depository anchored one corner at the top of the rise.

Dealey Plaza wasn't much to look at on its own terms.
But it had plenty of holy sites for the conspiracy pilgrims:
the Triple Underpass, the Grassy Knoll and the Sixth Floor,
which contained the Sniper's Perch. Even at this hour
clumps of people gathered along the sidewalk, pointing at
windows and the motorcade route, trying to pull from the
air and the bricks the knowledge that Oswald was alone on
November 22, 1963. Or wasn't. As Jack walked up the hill,
a small greasy man handed him a leaflet that claimed Joseph
Mengele, the Nazi doctor, had been in the plaza just before
the bullets flew. "He worked," the greasy man said, "with a
woman named Mrs. Krebs."

"Hey, everybody knows that," Jack said. He kept walking; he had his own lone nut to deal with. What he planned to tell Eddie, if he found him: I have a wacko shooting at me and I just got popped for a five-hundred-dollar glass repair job, all because you decided to get cute on TV. And now this newspaper story . . .

He also had a question or two. Like where the hell was Eddie when all this shooting was going on? And could he prove it?

But Eddie never showed. At eight-thirty Jack walked the six blocks to his office and took the elevator, a noiseless chamber of recessed lighting and teak paneling, to the twenty-seventh floor of the MercBank Tower. He walked into the law offices of Lennard & Ratliff, into the steady low hum of billable hours, still muttering about Eddie.

On his desk, phone messages were stacking up already, and he had a long deposition—267 pages of professionally typed lies—to read before noon. And then his assistant buzzed in: Senator Lennard wished to see Jack. Right away.

The senator—he liked to be called that after two terms in the state legislature twenty-five years back, fighting Marxist infiltration of local schools—had the big corner office. His was the first name on the firm's letterhead. He was a strutting little guy with a frequent look of annoyance, like a rooster whose chickens had dried up.

"Curious about this thing in the paper," the senator said when Jack sat down. He was scowling.

"Yes sir." Jack shifted in the chair and cleared his throat. "Which thing, exactly?"

"The Hints from Heloise." The senator paused a beat. "What the hell you think I'm talking about?"

Jack started talking fast. "That JFK stuff? I put the lid on it already, Senator. Big misunderstanding, all taken care of now."

The senator folded his hands, silent. "And the broken windows," Jack said, "came from kids in the neighborhood, I'm pretty sure. Now all that crap about a Kennedy investigation and me, I'm calling the paper today to—"

The senator held up his hand, his signal to stop talking. He was showing a thin smile now; the man changed moods the way some people switched radio stations. "Ever notice," the senator said, "my little fishbowl out in the lobby?"

Hard to miss, Jack thought, a 550-gallon aquarium. Telling the senator, "It's very striking."

"All those beautiful fish in there, they didn't just fly in through the window."

Jack didn't know what to say.

"I collected them all," the senator said. "Six trips to South America, two to Africa. I swam rivers in Ecuador you won't see on any map. Damn near got eaten by crocodiles twice, but I got my fish. What do you think of that?"

I think, Jack thought, you have too much money. He said, "That's very impressive."

"Some of the rarest in the world, right here in my tank. Probably twenty-five, thirty thousand dollars in fish right outside that door." The senator leaned back in his chair. "Think that'd make a good newspaper story?"

"Uh"—Jack blinked a few times—"sure."

"Think the reporters wouldn't eat that up like roaches on a meat loaf at midnight?" The hand went up before Jack could answer. "Moot point," the senator said. "Because at this firm we stay out of the media. Our clients like it that way."

Jack nodded. "It won't happen again."

"We stay out, and they stay out."

"Consider it done. Or not done, as the case may be."

The senator sipped some coffee from a bone china cup and brushed lint from his regimental tie. Then he drilled his glare into Jack. Saying, "My son Danny talked me into hiring you. You know that."

His old law school roommate. "I'm grateful," Jack said.

"Frankly, I had my doubts. Still do. I looked at your record and I told Danny, 'This boy's hauling baggage like a drunk skycap.' Danny says, 'Dad, his past is all behind him. All those fuckups,' Danny says, 'they're all dead and buried.'"

"I'd like to think I've learned from them," Jack said. Telling himself, man, that's one lame answer.

"Mistakes dead and buried," the senator said again. He shook his head, seemed to be talking quietly to himself now. "Been my experience it's not that easy."

"Let's get a plan for this," Weldon Chaney said. "A plan that's good."

"That last I had was good," Rodney Gillich said. He showed a smile of gold caps.

"You boys listening now?" Weldon watched Roger Gillich pet his long blond hair. "Very important that you pay attention here."

"It was good, good, good," Rodney said. "But hey, who's ever had bad quim? Except maybe a homo. Right, Roger?"

"Kiss my ass, freak."

"Boys, listen. We gonna do this or not?" Weldon rubbed his temples and checked his air supply. For a year now he'd been breathing from a clear hose connected to a steel oxygen bottle, the reward for a lifetime of Chesterfields. "Now," Weldon said, "what we're doing here is trying to break the chain. And a chain is only as strong as what?"

"As steel," Rodney said.

Roger barked a laugh. "What about plastic chains, dumb fuck?"

"Hey, shithead, he ain't talking about fake chains,"

Rodney said. "I mean, if he was, what about gold? You can snatch one of them right off somebody's neck no problem. Right, Mr. Chaney?"

Weldon swallowed hard, trying to keep himself under control. "The weakest link, boys, was the answer I was looking for."

"Told you," Rodney said.

"Now I've given this some thought and I think the weakest link in this particular case is the investigator." Weldon paused to go over some notes. "That's the first place we ought to go."

"Upside his head, is where we ought to go." Rodney pushed his chair back and stood. "You ready, Roger? You and me, let's do it."

"Do it the quick way," Roger said, "and blow his sorry ass up."

"Whoa now." Weldon smiled. "I admire your spirit, boys, but let's talk to the man first. Talk to him, tell him what the stakes are, let him know what's in it for him. Maybe he's willing to cooperate. And if he's not, well, that's where you two come in. Are you listening, Rodney?"

"To what?" Rodney said.

Jack's assistant had gone for coffee. He had one phone line on hold and a client waiting out front. Then Lola called on his cell phone to tell Jack about her latest plans for the blow-up dolls. She would patch them and inflate them again but would use some red paint to make the bullet holes into bloody wounds. New name: the Nuclear Love Survivors. "Or maybe the Nuclear Love Victims," she said. "What do you think?"

Jack noticed a memo on his desk that needed a response right away. "That's nice," he said.

"Which one?" Lola said. "Victims or survivors?"

"Hey, Lola, you're the artist."

"*Artistician.*"

"Exactly. So maybe you should be the one to make the call. I mean, if they needed estate planning or something, I'm your guy, but—"

"Retrofuturism, Jack, is not the easiest thing in the world to pull off, okay? All I'm asking for is like a minute of your oh-so-valuable time."

Jack checked his watch. He was ten minutes late for his client meeting. "Lola, you sound a little bit on edge."

"You know what? Screw you."

Jack's other line was ringing. He told Lola, "Hold on a sec," and answered. An old man with a voice like a can of rusty nails said, "Mr. Flippo, we need to talk."

The man wouldn't give his name and wouldn't leave his number. All he said was he had an important case to discuss with Jack. "Tell you what," Jack finally said. "I'll be in my office late tonight, probably way past midnight. Call me back tonight, I'll talk to you then."

"You'll be up there that late?"

"Just me and the fish," Jack said.

Weldon put the phone down. Rodney was smoking and watching cartoons on TV. Roger was reading an old copy of *Soldier of Fortune.* "He'll be in his office late tonight. All alone," Weldon said. "That's absolutely perfect."

Rodney looked up from *The Jetsons.* Telling Weldon, "That last I had was perfect."

7

Christmas Eve, 1963, the way Weldon remembered it: She had come to him across the smoky dance floor of the old Gator Lounge on Samuell Boulevard in East Dallas. A young, beautiful woman in a tight midnight-blue dress, with every man watching her walk. A lynx among the back-alley cats, there at the Gator. She headed straight for Weldon, like special delivery of a dream come true.

She took the empty stool next to him, beneath a shabby string of colored lights hanging from the ceiling, the Gator's weak stab at holiday spirit. Brenda Lee sang "Rockin' Around the Christmas Tree" from the jukebox. Weldon was drinking Johnny Walker Red to celebrate.

The woman asked Weldon if they could talk privately. "Honey," he said, "we can talk any way you want." Two minutes later they were in the parking lot, in the front seat of Weldon's Plymouth, shivering. Bitter cold outside, the wind blowing so hard it rocked the car.

She spoke of a man named Sylvan Dufraine. "Sylvan

Do-what?" Weldon said. "What kinda silly name is that?" He gave her a grin, trying to loosen her up a little.

The woman didn't seem to be in the mood for loosening. "Sylvan Dufraine," she said, the words coming out like hammered tin. "He takes pictures, and he makes films."

"You mean movies?" The night before, Weldon had taken his old lady to see Van Heflin in *War Is Hell.*

The woman turned toward him. The light from the Gator sign had dipped her in green. "He needs—" She stopped and looked all around, waiting while a car passed. "Sylvan Dufraine," she finally said, "needs to be killed."

Weldon lit a Chesterfield, cracked a window, blew smoke out into the cold. He looked her up and down, wondering if she was the law, out to set a trap. You didn't see many cops with shoes that nice. He said, "Honey, this is crazy, you walking into the Gator and two minutes later you're talking about getting someone dead, like you looked in the Yellow Pages under rubout services and saw my name. And on Christmas Eve, for goodness sake." With Weldon trying not to stare at her chest the whole time he was talking.

She took one of his Chesterfields and lit herself up. "I've been following your case."

"Little lady, I walked that. Charges dismissed, not that anyone paid attention. Everybody's so caught up with who shot Kennedy, it's Kennedy this, Kennedy that, they don't notice that meanwhile Weldon Chaney's skating a murder indictment. Three paragraphs way inside the *Times Herald* that nobody saw."

"I saw it."

Weldon didn't mention that the DA had to drop the case because his star witness took a powder. A powder that cost Weldon ten grand. In the old days people charged three, four thousand to get lost, but the price of disappearing was going up. Between that 10K and the bills his lawyer was sending, there wasn't much this year under the rotating aluminum Christmas tree back at the Chaney house.

And the job—putting a hole in a liquor wholesaler who had scammed his partners—hadn't even paid cash. All Weldon got out of it was a 1961 Plymouth, the one he and the woman were sitting in now.

Weldon decided to make conversation. "What'd this Sylvan Do-what do that he deserves to get it?"

The woman showed a small, unhappy smile. "He pointed his camera the wrong way. He made a movie he shouldn't have made."

"That's it? That's all?"

"That's enough."

"What's your name?" Weldon said.

"Alice."

"That's your real name? Alice?"

"Real enough."

"Alice, on a night like this shouldn't you be back at the house? Maybe trying to assemble your kid's new bicycle with the instructions some Jap wrote? Mixing the egg with the nog, all that?"

She reached into her purse and removed an envelope. "Here's five thousand dollars," she said.

Weldon loved the feeling of cash money in his hand. Funny how it worked like the finest grease known to man. Anything that was stuck, cash could unstick it.

He took the envelope from her, opened it and fanned the bills. Telling her as the cold wind rocked the car, "And a Merry Christmas, Alice, to you too."

8

They were packed into the cab of the truck again, just before midnight in downtown Dallas. Roger Gillich drove, Rodney smoked and Weldon droned on about his plan. Rodney thought if he had to hear it one more time, his brain would start to drain out his ears.

"You're the advance man, Rodney, you're the point," Weldon kept saying. "Get us inside, and we'll go upstairs and talk to this investigator in a persuasive fashion. We'll light a little fire under him, one way or the other."

"I got you, Mr. Chaney," Rodney said. But no matter how many times Rodney told him that, the old man kept yakking.

Finally Roger pulled the truck to the curb. Rodney got out as fast as he could and walked away, with Weldon leaning from the window and saying, "Now remember what I told you."

"I got you, Mr. Chaney," Rodney said.

Rodney wore a blue smock, which was supposed to make him look like a custodian, with a phony ID card clipped to the pocket—Weldon's doing, part of the big scheme the old man had spent all afternoon doping out. Rodney carried a white rag and a plastic spray bottle full of some sort of liquid cleanser. Pretty stupid to fill the bottle, he thought, because Rodney Gillich don't clean nothing but his plate.

Except for right now. He walked to the big revolving doors at the front of the MercBank Tower. The only person in the lobby was a security guard at the desk near the elevators. Rodney sprayed cleanser on the push bar of one of the doors and wiped it with his rag.

He turned the door and moved inside, still spraying and wiping. Rodney caught the guard's eye and said, "How's it going?" Spraying and wiping, singing to himself a little bit. Thinking, do this janitor scene for eight hours a day? Shit, he wouldn't do it for eight minutes.

What was supposed to happen now; Rodney would walk past the guard—giving him some working-class hero crap like, Hey, is it Friday yet?—to the elevators. Go down to the second level of the parking garage and let Weldon and Roger in through a service entrance. Then all three would ride to the twenty-seventh floor.

But as Rodney made his way past the desk the security guard said, "Where you headed, man?"

Rodney turned and looked at a smallish black guy in a white shirt and gray pants, little rent-a-cop badge on his chest, no gun showing. "Got lots more cleaning to do," Rodney said. "Place is just nasty as hell." He watched the guard's hands, and was ready to nail him if he went for the phone.

The guard said, "Hey, man, that can hold." He was smiling. "Do me a favor, sit here while I run to the bathroom."

Rodney squinted, then glanced about the empty lobby. He said, "You got it."

The guard went around the corner, and Rodney checked the desk drawers. Because you never could tell when someone might leave some cash about.

Three drawers gave him nothing but Styrofoam cups, Pepto-Bismol tablets and an old copy of *Road & Track.* But the fourth held a ring of keys, and on one key was a green strip from a labelmaker. It said MASTER.

Rodney took that key and scampered for the elevator. It wasn't in Mr. Chaney's plan, but so what? Mr. Chaney could stay in the parking garage and talk to his air tank about the plan while Rodney handled the situation the Rodney way. Show the man how it's done.

The elevator opened on 27 with the double glass doors to Lennard & Ratliff just across the hall. Rodney slipped the master key into the lock and turned it. The bolt slid free with a happy metal smack. Rodney cracked the door, peered in and chirped, "Housekeeping."

He stood in the reception area and listened, hearing nothing but the bubbles of the filter in the fish tank. Unbelievable, the size of that thing, bigger than a bathtub. It had fish of all colors and shapes.

He unscrewed the top of his spray bottle and poured cleanser into the aquarium. Saying, "Some refreshments for the little fishies."

Then he had an even better idea.

Jack let the phone ring twelve times before hanging up. This late at night, even girls with green hair and tattoos should be home, but Lola wasn't answering.

He rose from his chair and stepped from behind his desk. His body was sore and weak, his brain having a flickering brownout. Jack tried doing some stretches, but his heart wasn't in it. He gazed out the window at the glass box across the street. A few lights were still on in the cages of other pin-striped wage apes. With Jack thinking, lawyers working overtime, how scary was that? Plenty of midnight oil being burned at the town's screw-job factories.

Jack turned back to his desk and a stack of paper at its center. He had been preparing a long list of questions for the opposing party in a particularly nasty lawsuit. He remembered his big brother Jeff's term for such a list: sewer lights.

Until cocaine blew every fuse in his heart, defense lawyer Jeff Flippo was one of the greats at getting criminals back on the streets. Jeff didn't so much defend his clients—How do you defend, he'd ask, a bunch of bottom-feeding assholes?—as attack the opposition.

It's the perpetual search, Jeff said, for one thing they've done that they don't want anyone to know about. Ask the right questions, and you find out what's been stuffed under the shed out back.

Everybody's got it, Jeff told Jack long ago, and all you've got to do is keep asking until you find it. But unless you're knee-deep in slime and maggots, you're looking in the wrong place.

Well, Jack thought as he closed down the memory, that's enough cheeriness for one evening. He leaned over his desk and picked up a pressurized can with a nozzle top: BK-12 spray-on solvent. His client, a fifty-two-year-old woman, had tried to use BK-12 to take off her makeup one night. Because it was more suitable for the removal of axle grease and paint, it burned the woman's face. Now she wanted to sue the manufacturers.

Jack decided to give it a test. He rolled up his sleeve and sprayed some BK-12 on the inside of his forearm. He yelled, "Shit!" His skin felt as if it had caught fire.

He needed to wipe the solvent off fast. Jack headed out of his office and down the hall, making a quick dash to the coffee room for a towel. But when he turned a corner into the lobby, he stopped cold.

A red-haired man in a custodian's smock stood on a chair, his pants unzipped. He was singing as he urinated into Senator Lennard's aquarium.

9

Jack had seen a lot of strange things in his life, but never this. He said, "What are you doing?"

"Giving the fishies something to drink," the man said.

Jack looked at the man's spiky red hair and low-spark eyes. His expression reminded Jack of a childhood friend, Johnny Fowler, who blew up toads with firecrackers.

"Do you work here?" Jack moved sideways toward the receptionist's desk.

"Watch this." The man made a high sound from his throat like skidding tires as he stopped pissing. "Ever seen wiener brakes that good?" He left his uncircumcised penis dangling. "You Mr. Firpo?"

"Flippo."

"Both of them is stupid fucking names, you ask me." A hand went into his pants pocket. "Hey, ever seen a one-eared elephant?"

"Who are you?" Jack picked up the handset of the receptionist's phone and set it on the desk.

"I'm Rodney." He seemed to be shaking all over.

"Rodney who?"

"Rodney who don't take no shit, no way. Hey"—he pointed to the phone—"don't be calling nobody."

"Just the Psychic Hot Line."

Rodney pulled his hand from his pants. He held a large black-handled pocketknife. "You and me need to talk."

Jack pressed 9 to get an outside line. He could hear a dial tone from the distant earpiece. "Talk about what?"

The man smiled, showing gold caps. "About what you've been doing that you ain't supposed to be."

"What would that be?"

"Don't you know?"

Jack pressed 9 again. "I lose track."

"Something about a movie, that's what I know. Something about— Hey, I already told you once, stop screwing with the phone." Rodney opened the knife, showing a six-inch blade.

Jack hit 1 and 1 again on the phone, then raised his hands shoulder-high. He was still holding the can of BK-12. "All right, let's talk."

"I said hang up, goddamnit."

Jack studied the man's eyes. He'd seen dozens of faces like that when he was with the DA, factory-second badasses staring across the courtroom at him, guys with beaten girlfriends or dead liquor store clerks in their recent pasts. To send them to prison had been a joy. Now Jack said, "Got your pocketknife out and your johnson hanging, you must mean business."

The man gave him a goofy grin. His head vibrated as if it were on a spring. "Damn straight I do."

Jack started to ask what that business was when he caught the voice of the 911 dispatcher from the phone. He couldn't make out what she was saying, but he could hear her talking.

That's when Rodney jumped.

The guy seemed to take flight from the chair, coming with some kind of mental-ward yell. He swept the knife in front of him as he dropped.

Jack tried to move aside but wasn't fast enough. Rodney landed on him and knocked him into the wall. The back of Jack's head slammed into the wood paneling.

They fell together and rolled three times on the Berber carpet. Jack gripped Rodney's wrist, pinning the knife arm across his chest. The guy was scrawny; Jack had him by at least twenty-five pounds. But Rodney had plenty of fight in him, and Jack didn't know how long he could hold the clench.

The two of them lay on the floor, grunting and squirming against each other, then rolling over twice more, back to where they began. Rodney started to work his way free.

He had managed to turn himself sideways and was jamming an elbow into Jack's throat. Jack tried to breathe, and was about to lose his grip on Rodney's wrist, when he saw the can of BK-12 on the floor.

Jack's first idea was to go for Rodney's eyes. But their faces were too close together. He might douse himself.

Plan B: Somewhere to the south, Jack figured, the guy's cock was still nosing its way through his zipper. He grabbed the can, aimed it toward Rodney's crotch and pressed the button.

It took three or four seconds for the screaming to start.

"Talking about TV programs," Eddie Nickles said. "My family, when we had things going right, before everything turned to shit, it was a beautiful scene. Just like that old show—what's the name?" He snapped his fingers when it came to him. *"My Three Sons."*

"A classic," Lola said.

Eddie glanced around the coffee shop on Elm Street, just east of downtown. The postmidnight crowd of losers and studded-leather street reptiles was starting to filter in. You had to wonder, he thought, how these people made their money.

"The first five seasons were especially primo," Lola said.

"The Nickles house? Just like that show, honest to God. Except, you know, I only had one son, Eddie junior, plus I had Iris, my wife. But other than that . . ."

"Because the first five, that's when it costarred William Frawley as Bub." Lola was nodding, serious. "The crusty but lovable old codger. Then five years out, Frawley dies."

"No kidding?" Eddie looked Lola over. She wasn't bad at all, you lose the green hair and the studs in her nose. "That's a tragedy."

"They needed a new lovable codger, right? I mean, a show like that has to have one."

"Sure it does." Eddie tried to flag a waitress. "Get a refill over here?"

"So they bring in William Demarest to play Uncle Charley."

"Exactly."

"Meanwhile, they can't say Bub's dead, right? Come on, get real, it's a sixties sitcom."

"You better believe it."

"So they tell everyone Bub's gone to Iceland. *Iceland.* You know that some writer had the laugh of his life with that one."

With Eddie telling himself, I got no idea in hell what this chick is talking about. "You know what, Lola? I'm glad we got this chance to have a conversation."

She reached across the table and touched his hand. "You were really sweet to help me move my exhibit to the gallery."

"I'll tell you, all them blow-up dolls reminded me of a perv we took down once when I was on vice. He had about twenty of 'em around his bedroom. Big fat guy liked to put on a turban and pretend he had a harem."

Lola shook her head, looking away. "It's such typical Jack. I mean, I rent a van, I tell him the whole tableau has to move tonight. And where is he? Somewhere else, as usual."

"The guy we popped. Selling kid porno mail order. Last I heard *he* was part of a harem, serving state time."

She touched his hand again. "I'm lucky you stopped by."

"Hey, I was in the neighborhood, so thought I'd drop in and see how my good friends Jack and Lola were doing." Eddie poured sugar in his coffee. "Can't have enough good friends, Lola."

After Rodney ran from the office, cupping himself and yelping like a scalded dog, Jack staggered to his feet. He felt a stinging across his chest. He looked down and saw that his shirt had been sliced open. Jack parted the fabric to reveal a thin pink crescent, with some blood seeping along it, from collarbone to nipple. Rodney's sweeping blade had caught him, but barely. An inch or two closer and Jack probably would have been down for good.

He picked up the phone; the 911 operator was still there. Jack gave the address and told her what had happened. Next he called building security and repeated the story. Then he sank into the receptionist's chair—his legs a little shaky—and thought for a while about fate, luck and close calls.

Jack also wondered, as he checked the hole his head had

made in the wall paneling, if he would be able to keep his job after this. He imagined trying to explain everything, and wondered if the senator would buy any of it.

He got his answer with a glance toward the aquarium. The senator's fish were beginning to go belly-up.

10

ey, I think getting fired is kind of cool," Lola said.
"Then I'm the coolest guy around," Jack said.
They stood on the sidewalk outside the entrance to
Greenie's Office Building, which sat atop Greenie's 24 HR
Coffee Shop. Jack pointed with, "Ready to go on up?"

The stairs still creaked when he climbed them, and the
unraveling carpet hadn't lost its stains. The hallway lights
were as dim as he remembered, as if sufficient power
couldn't quite make it to the second floor, like hot water in
an old hotel.

The second door on the right said FLIPPO ASSOC in
white letters, though someone had colored over the last O
and the C with a black marker. Jack unlocked the deadbolt
and walked into familiar drabness. The room smelled of
cramped air and old papers, and of the bacon frying one
floor below. There were dead flies on the windowsill and
cobwebs in the corners.

"Spooky-town," Lola said.

He raised the shades. The brightness didn't do the place any favors. Jack opened the window and dropped into his old chair, sending dust motes swimming in the sunlight. Just outside, Greenie's neon frog hung as always from the side of the building.

"Feels like home," Jack said. "Glad I kept paying rent on this old place."

The phone lines were dead so he used his mobile, calling to see if his check had cleared. It had. The recorded voice gave him numbers he had never heard connected to his own account. For the first time in his life he was a man with decent money.

Two days before, he had strolled into Lennard & Ratliff to see the senator, knowing as soon as he glimpsed the drained aquarium—nothing but a glass tank with some rocks in it now, a fish apocalypse—that the conversation would not be happy. It was the perfect position for a reluctant lawyer: They wanted him to leave, and he wanted to leave for the right price.

After Jack mentioned his concerns about poor building security—armed lunatics disguised as custodians, wandering the halls at night—and how it almost cost him his life, they had worked a deal in five minutes: He wouldn't sue the firm, and the firm would give him a year's salary plus benefits to walk away. For the moment, failure was tasting pretty sweet.

"Back in the snoop business," he said to Lola from behind his old desk. "All I need now is a client."

"Something to poke your big nose into," she said.

"Right." Jack stood and said, "Which reminds me . . ."

Once he found the key he needed, he left his office and walked down the hall with Lola behind him. They went past Jarrell's Collection Agency and Astro Beeper Repair, past the water cooler that had never worked, to an unmarked door.

The lock needed oil, and the door was warped. Jack put his shoulder into it; the door groaned as it scraped across the floor. He flipped on the overhead light and saw everything as he remembered: a dozen cardboard file boxes stacked like tombs.

"The records of wrecked lives," he said. "Including mine. A copy of every case I ever worked with the DA."

Lola wrote her name in the dust on a box top. "You're the sloppiest anal retentive I know."

"You throw dirt on these things," Jack said, "but some of them bubble up in the strangest places."

The boxes were arranged in order along one wall, beginning with sketchy records of misdemeanor trials he had handled. The last box said STATE VS. LAMONT on its side: Jack's final case, in which he found himself having an affair with the wife of a cocaine dealer. A cocaine dealer, as it turned out, he was supposed to prosecute. Thus was Jack's employment with the DA's office quickly ended.

The file he wanted now lay somewhere in the middle. Jack moved to the boxes and removed a couple of lids. Telling himself it was like wading into a toxic waste dump and prying open fifty-five-gallon drums, just to see what's inside.

He ran a finger over the names on the file tabs. There was Antoine Lewis, who habitually stole cars, but only red Pontiacs. Jack nailed him for five years in prison, where Antoine died in a fight over whether the dayroom TV should be tuned to *Hollywood Squares* or *The Price Is Right*. The last words Antoine Lewis heard: "Come on down!"

He spotted the file of Walter Brinkley Thornton, who raped dozens of women and laughed about it in court. Walter had rotten teeth and was missing part of one ear. After the sentence of ninety-nine years was read, Walter's girlfriend tried to kick Jack in the balls.

Next Jack saw the name Alfred Boyette, but couldn't put
a face to it. After half a minute or so it came to him: the
Famous Penhead. A molelike guy in a brown suit who kidnapped a Waffle House waitress. When they caught him he
tried to kill himself by jamming a Bic ballpoint up his nose.

"Precious memories, every one," Jack said.

Finally he found the case he wanted. He pulled it from
the rest, closed the lid of the box and relocked the storeroom
door. Back in his office, he put the file on his desk. Case
number 91-4328, State vs. Mineola Watts.

Jack opened the file and paged through a stack of indict-
ments, judge's orders, lawyers' letters and a presentencing
report. Halfway through he saw what he was looking for, a
fishhook that had stuck in him all this time. It was an inter-
nal memo, written by Jack. Seven years old by now, half a
page single-spaced.

He held it to the light and read the title: "Questions
Concerning Fatal Shooting of a Suspect by Dallas Police
Detective Edward Nickles."

11

L ast but not least," the salesman said, "the *coup de résistance* of novelty items." He turned the pages of a catalog. "Introducing the Chungco Remote-Control Severed Hand. State of the art and selling like hotcakes."

"I got to admit," Mr. Marty said, "those Chinese commie creeps do some amazing things with latex nowadays." He glanced at the front of the store when the door opened, watching as a stooped woman with four battered shopping bags shuffled in. Mr. Marty's wife, Nita, left her stool behind the counter to wait on the woman. With Mr. Marty thinking, that old broad won't spend ten cents in here.

"Two double-A's, plus a nine-volt in the remote. So whenever you move one, you get the battery sales too." The salesman tapped the photo of the Chungco Hand. "Hey, tell me you saw that baby lying in the middle of the room, you wouldn't haul butt the other way." He cut loose with a couple of big laughs, his Salem-menthol breath washing over

Mr. Marty. "Listen, we got a report of a woman in Tulsa actually passing out, she saw one of these."

"I got to admit," Mr. Marty said, "it looks good in the picture."

"One glance, she was out cold."

"All right, I'll take one."

"One? Molberg Novelty took a dozen, for Christ's sake. And they sold out in a week."

"Molberg Novelty is in a mall," Mr. Marty said. "We're not. Which you might have noticed. Which even damn Mr. Magoo would notice, he was brave enough to make the trip to my store. If he had himself an armed guard and a tank."

"Come on, it's not that bad." The salesman looked toward the front window. "Is it?"

"Dalworth Novelty Supplies," Mr. Marty said. "Know what our slogan is? 'Forty years at the same location, while the neighborhood rots around us.'"

The old woman shuffled out; all she had wanted was change for the bus. Nita returned to her stool and her crossword puzzle book. While the salesman wrote on his order pad Mr. Marty surveyed his store: rubber masks, party favors, balloons on plastic sticks, cat posters, cat coffee mugs, cat figurines. Jesus, he hated cats.

He cut his gaze to the other wall and saw decks of cards, magicians' supplies and *Star Trek* paraphernalia. And the joke shelf, with the whoopee cushions and fart pills.

All of them, Mr. Marty thought, nothing but dust collectors now. And burglar magnets. The store had been hit twice in the last four months by after-hours thieves who took every piece of electrical equipment in the place, including six battery-operated back scratchers.

Several weeks ago someone had tried to set the building on fire. It wasn't much, just a scorch of the back door, but the timing couldn't have been better. It would deflect suspicion from Mr. Marty when the whole place went up in flames. Which it would as soon as he had a chance to bump up his insurance coverage.

He imagined the little brick building on Haskell Avenue on fire, and added numbers in his head. One last score, he thought, for this poor country boy.

The salesman left; time for lunch. Nita sliced his tuna fish sandwich in half, and put a couple of celery sticks on the side of his plate.

"They should warn you when they give you that triple bypass," Mr. Marty said. "The rest of your life you'll eat nothing but shitty food.'"

"Don't be silly."

"They oughta rip out your taste buds while they're working on your chest, make the rest of the way easy on you."

Mr. Marty found a copy of the *Morning News* from a few days back and paged through it while he ate. He was about to throw the paper away when a headline flew at him. Mr. Marty read the story, and read it again.

Someone was offering big money for what was being called the lost film of the second umbrella man. Mr. Marty said, "Jesus Christ in a black Cadillac Seville."

Nita looked up from her crosswords. "Is something wrong?"

"Nothing." He tore the story from the paper. Telling himself, did I say one last score? Maybe I meant two.

Jack drove past Fair Park and kept going south. He found himself well into what was, for plenty of people in Dallas, foreign soil. That went for him too. Twice he had to stop and check his map. He passed a couple of small motels, some liquor stores and a shopping center that Neiman-

Marcus wouldn't be coming to anytime soon. Then he cruised through a neighborhood of neat but tired frame houses. A few older people waved from their porches, while some of the younger ones gave him the fisheye. It wasn't hard to figure why. In this part of town, driving his Chevy Caprice, he looked like a plainclothes cop.

A couple of wrong turns and he found what he was looking for, the government-issue slums known as the Lipscomb Homes. Red brick, two-story, with torn screens and scuffed yards. Women sat on kitchen chairs on concrete-slab stoops and watched small children playing. At the corner half a dozen teenage boys in droopy pants had gathered in a circle, smoking and laughing. Across the street music poured from the open door of something called the Pup Club.

Jack felt as if he had just beamed in from the Ice Planet of the White People. He parked at curbside and went looking for an address that had been good ten years ago. Apartment 244 was just like all the rest except for a pot of flowers next to the front door. Petunias. Or pansies, maybe. Jack didn't know flowers. He opened the screen and knocked four times on the metal door.

Curtains parted and a face appeared in the adjacent window. A few seconds later the door opened and Jack faced an elderly black woman who wore a robe and slippers. She had thick glasses and her bony hands shook. The woman smiled. "They told me you would be stopping by."

"They did?"

"Please come in."

"Thank you," Jack said. Telling himself he could figure out later what she was talking about.

The front room was clean but near bare, with an old couch and a couple of banged-up chairs. An oval braided rug covered part of the linoleum floor, and a few family pictures hung on the walls in dime-store frames. Jack recognized the young man in one of them.

The woman stood at the bottom of the stairs and shouted up. "Treena, the man's here." Then to Jack: "She'll be right down. Would you like some coffee?"

"That would be great."

"Treena!"

Jack said, "You're Verdis Watts, is that right?"

"I certainly am." She climbed one stair.

"I don't know if you remember me."

"Treena! Don't make the man wait." Mrs. Watts stepped unsteadily to the floor and walked toward the kitchen. "Take your seat now. I'll get that coffee." Jack sat on the couch and studied the seven-year-old memo he had exhumed from his files: Verdis Watts, grandmother of Mineola Watts, had phoned the DA's office days after her grandson was shot and killed. She claimed that the police weren't telling the truth, that she had a witness who would talk. But when a DA's investigator went out to see her, the old lady had nothing to say, couldn't remember a thing, slammed the door on the investigator's nose.

"Do you take cream and sugar?" Mrs. Watts called from the kitchen.

"Black," Jack said. He thought of his prosecution of Mineola Watts—just another crackhead, nothing special—and saw Mineola's face in his grandmother's. Then he saw it again in the young woman coming down the stairs.

She wore a red tank top and was zipping up her jeans as she came into the room. Tall and thin, late twenties, bare feet, dark brown skin that had a luster to it. Her hair was short and dyed blond—wavy, plastered to her scalp, reminding Jack of the wiring on a circuit board.

Her eyes were puffy and bloodshot. She rubbed her face as she crossed to one of the chairs, stumbling a bit before she sat. Saying, "How the hell I'm supposed to get by on three hours' sleep?"

Jack smiled. "Tired, huh?"

Treena looked up, staring at Jack a good five seconds before saying, "And what was your first clue?"

Jack waited. Treena went back to rubbing her face, muttering, "Night shift's about to kick my ass." Then: "All right, it's not gonna get any better. Let's talk about insurance."

Jack squinted. "Why?"

"These letters you been sending to my grandma about her policy? Buncha crap, man."

"Wait a minute—"

"She's been paying every damn month. On time."

"You got the wrong guy."

"Don't tell me you ain't been getting them—"

"I'm not from the insurance company."

"—'cause I watch her write the checks." She stopped, twisting her face in annoyance. "Not from the insurance company?"

"What was your first clue?"

They stared at each other. Treena said, "Then who the hell are you?"

Mrs. Watts walked in from the kitchen with two coffee mugs. Saying, "This gentleman's from the insurance company, Treena."

"No, he's not," Treena said.

"Of course he is."

"No," Jack said. "I'm not."

They were all quiet until the young woman said, "Not getting enough sleep tends to put Treena in a bad damn mood. You getting the picture, man?"

Jack turned to Mrs. Watts. He told her his name, said he

had come to see her on a matter from some years back, hoped she could help him. "When I was with the district attorney's office," Jack said, "I handled the case against your grandson Mineola."

"I know you. I *know* you." Treena was standing and pointing. "You're the motherfucker sent Mineola down. Excuse my language, Grandma." Then to Jack: "Don't try to say you're not."

"Mrs. Watts," Jack said, "after Mineola was killed, you called our office. You wanted to tell us something about his death. Do you remember that?"

"Here's what Treena has to tell you, chump." She was standing between Jack and the grandmother now, shouting. "In ten seconds your sorry white ass better be out that door. Think you can remember *that*?"

Jack managed to hand a business card to the grandmother before he left. Then he drove back to his office and spent the afternoon putting the place in order. By five he was ready to leave, thinking he might stop by the gallery and see how Lola and the Nuclear Loves were coming. He was locking up when the phone in his pocket rang, Greenie from the coffee shop below. Saying, "Guy down here asking for you, Jack."

Greenie pointed him out when Jack walked in. An old man with slicked-back gray hair, whistling quietly and watching the waitresses go by. He wore the sort of thin mustache and loud plaid jacket they gave to sharpies in dinner theater comedies.

Jack approached the booth. The guy had a sunlamp tan and a nose that looked as if it had been stuck on his face in the dark. The man extended his hand and said, "You can call me Mr. Marty."

"Fine. You can call me Señor Jack."

They shook, and Jack watched this Mr. Marty check him over, head to toe and back. "Take a load off," the man said.

Jack slid into the seat across from him. "What can I do for you?"

"I called your law office and asked to speak to the famous lawyer that's been in the newspaper. They said you're hanging out here now."

"I like the smell of hash browns."

"Have to say, I didn't expect you to be so tall and skinny." Mr. Marty slurped his coffee. "I was expecting somebody that you can hear their *cojones* clank when they walk. Know what I mean?"

Jack waited.

"Like big steel bearings," Mr. Marty said, "down there in the scrotal sac."

Jack looked at his watch. "It's late," he said, "and I have someplace to go."

"All right, hey, we got off on the wrong foot. Don't take it personal." Mr. Marty reached into the breast pocket of the plaid jacket and came back with a spoon. He immersed it in his cup of coffee. "Watch this," he said. When he pulled it from the cup, half the spoon was gone. "Now that's some strong joe."

Jack wondered if he would ever again talk to someone who wasn't a wack job.

"Dissolving flatware," Mr. Marty said. "Think that won't crack them up at dinner parties? The soup course'll never be the same."

"I can imagine." Jack slid to the end of the booth. "I believe I'll leave before the fake vomit makes an appearance."

"Now you're talking the novelty classic."

"Good to meet you." Jack stood.

"Before you go, I seen in the paper where you're looking for some lost film."

"Don't believe everything you read."

"I think," Mr. Marty said, "I might know where you can find it."

12

The sun was setting as Eddie Nickles jaywalked Main Street, downtown Dallas. As he crossed toward El Centro College, Eddie was thinking of a man who had called himself Bill Gilbert.

The six-story building that housed El Centro was once a department store. Bill Gilbert had worked there, a clerk in menswear. When the big JFK motorcade rolled down Main in 1963, store management let the help go outside and watch. Eddie had seen a photo from that day. It showed the long, thin face of Bill Gilbert, who was a tall man, looming above the other spectators. They're looking at the motorcade and waving happily as it passes, but Bill Gilbert's narrowed eyes are aimed to the right, where—within a minute—the President would be shot.

Days after the assassination FBI agents went to the Hotel del Comercio in Mexico City, a cheap dive near the bus station. Lee Harvey Oswald, down in Mexico to make contact with the Cubans, had stayed there two months before the big day in Dallas. Room 18. The agents checked the guest register and discovered that an American had rented the room next door to Oswald's at the same time. He was Bill Gilbert of Dallas, Texas.

The investigators wished to learn more about this. They went back to Dallas, to the department store on Main, up to menswear on the second floor. What they found: no Bill Gilbert. What they learned: He had walked out of that store on the afternoon of November 22, 1963, and vanished forever.

None of this appeared in that whitewash the Warren Commission called a report, naturally. But Eddie Nickles had it, courtesy of a retired FBI agent he'd bought a drink for once. What it meant, Eddie wasn't sure. All he knew was that his customers on the Grassy Knoll Productions Assassination Re-creation Tour ate it up with a knife and fork and asked for second helpings.

Now Eddie entered El Centro through the same doors he imagined Bill Gilbert had used for his quick exit, and crossed the lobby to the elevators. Both of them were out of service. So Eddie climbed the stairs, never an easy trip for a guy with a bad knee.

He walked down the second-floor hallway until he saw a sign taped to a door: black felt marker on red construction paper, "Conspiracy Institute Seminar on Who *Really* Killed JFK?" Eddie opened the door slowly. The lights were off in the classroom, and an overhead projector cast a display on a screen. It showed a photo of Dealey Plaza from above.

A man with a pointer stood in the shadows next to the screen. Eddie knew him, a short little putz named Monroe Beets. Founder of the Conspiracy Institute who thought he was God's freaking gift to assassinology. Who insisted that everyone, including his wife, call him Dr. Beets.

"And right here"—Beets used his pointer—"behind this wall, is where police detained the so-called three tramps.

Three hobos, who just happened to be hanging out right next door to the murder of the President of the United States."

Eddie sat at a schoolroom desk in the last row. He counted the house; there were maybe a dozen. And no wonder: Beets's high, whiny voice scraped against his eardrums like a nail file.

"The police set the so-called tramps free," Beets said. "Never booked them, never fingerprinted them, never ID'ed them, set them free as birds. And now, we know who they were. Are you ready for this? One was a professional Mafia hit man, one was a Cuban national and one—hold on to your hats, folks—was a United States Secret Service agent."

Eddie couldn't take any more. He said, "That's a complete load of crap, midget man."

"What?" Beets shielded his eyes and looked toward the back of the room, like an actor trying to peer past the stage lights. "Who said that?"

"They were CIA," Eddie said. "All three of them, CIA. Why don't you tell the true facts for once?"

"The only confirmed CIA sighting"—Beets cleared his throat—"was that of an agent in a storm sewer on Elm Street. A sharpshooter in the sewer, armed with an Italian rifle. Which, I might add, he never fired."

"You're still peddling that?" Eddie stood, addressing the class now. "I mean, the dude's in a *sewer*? With an Italian rifle? From that angle he might as well use an Italian sausage."

A few people laughed. Someone was standing next to him, a woman. "Hello, Eddie," she said. Vivian Beets still had the body to make an accountant skim pension funds and skip to Mexico if she promised to come along. Why she stayed with Dr. Schmuck, Eddie couldn't understand. He said, "Tell your husband to stop foaming at the mouth. Tell him I'm a paying customer. He's put on some weight, by the way."

Beets moved to the wall and flipped a switch. The fluorescent lights stammered on. He pointed to Eddie and said, "I knew it was you. Get out."

Eddie waved a small piece of paper, his receipt for a new tire for the Lincoln. "See this?" He stuffed it back in his pocket before anyone could get a good look. "My proof of payment from the adult education office. It says I forked over twenty-five dollars cash money to attend this little session. Which, based on what I've seen so far, is a twenty-five-skin rip-off." He turned to the woman. "Viv baby, let's ditch the short man and go dancing."

She almost smiled, Eddie was sure of that. But movement caught her eye and she turned to the front. So did Eddie, in time to see Beets huffing toward him on stubby legs. The man had his wallet open, pulling out bills. Saying, "Here," and slapping two tens and a five on the desk. "There's your refund. Go crawl back in your hole now."

The class had turned to watch. Eddie picked up the money and said, "You think you can just buy off the truth? The truth don't come that cheap." Eddie folded the bills and slipped them into his pocket.

Beets went back to the front and put a new transparency on the overhead, this one a photo of the schoolbook depository. "Now let's take a look at the position of the so-called sniper's nest. If someone would get the lights, please."

Eddie said, "The truth ain't no whore."

Beets slapped his pointer against an open palm. "Do I need to call the police, Eddie?"

"Speaking of the Dallas police," Eddie said. "Who here wants to hear about why they let Jack Ruby pull off a mob hit on Oswald?"

Vivian stepped forward. "Dr. Beets, if I could make a suggestion . . ."

"By all means," Eddie said to her. "Especially if it involves you, me and some hot massage oil."

"Our old friend"—she gestured toward Eddie—"seems to want to address the class."

Eddie applauded. "Beets, the pretty lady's still the brains of the outfit."

"Why don't we allow him to make some brief remarks, and then I'm sure he would be happy to be on his way."

Beets fumed for a moment, then said, "For thirty seconds, then he leaves."

Eddie walked to the front of the room, shaking his head. "The truth don't watch the clock. The truth takes its own sweet time."

"One minute," Beets said. "That's my final offer."

"Three. And I get to pass out brochures for the Assassination Re-creation Tours." Eddie spotted a couple of granny types in the front row. "Ladies, it's a beautiful, respectful tribute to our late, beloved, tragically slain President. Plus, every customer's eligible to win a free 'I Survived the JFK Death Ride' T-shirt."

Eddie turned. He and Beets had their backs to the class. "Let me guess," Beets said, low enough so only Eddie could hear. "You want to talk about that great lost film you're chasing."

"Maybe."

"I'll admit it, you got some TV play out of it. Fine, congratulations. But there's no such thing. You know that. Every credible researcher agrees, that film absolutely does not exist."

Eddie moved in close enough to track the broken veins in Beets's nose. Whispering, "Why not let the suckers dream a little?"

• • •

Hey, the asshole just about burnt my manhood off." Rodney Gillich sat at the kitchen table in Weldon Chaney's house
in south Dallas County, talking to his fat wife and her fat sister. "So, to answer your question, hell yes, I'm gonna kill
him. Track him down and kill him way past dead."

"Honey, I think you should sue," Brandi Gillich said. "I
bet you could get all the money in the world."

"Shit, more money than that." Rodney shook his head
and looked at his crotch. "I don't care what's happened to
you in your life, I don't care what you been through, there
is no goddamn pain in the whole goddamn world like somebody spraying poison on your pecker."

Brandi touched her sister's arm. "Mandi, he couldn't
even get hard last night, it hurt so much."

Rodney said, "Hey, shut up, bitch."

"Well, it's true."

"Maybe I'd of gotten hard if there was anybody around
the house worth being hard for. Ever thought about that?"

That sent Brandi running from the table in tears. Mandi
got up to follow her sister but said to Rodney before she left,
"Way to go, Mr. Smooth."

Rodney didn't even answer. Fuck both of them. The
dumbest thing he and his half brother had ever done, mar-
rying those two, who set the state record for complaining
about money.

Weldon Chaney walked in a few minutes later, hauling
his air tank. Asking, "Why's Brandi crying?"

Rodney wiped his nose with the back of his hand. "She's
just having her period, Mr. Chaney."

"I don't like it when my girls cry."

"I been trying to cheer her up all day. It's just one of
them female things."

"No sir, don't like it when my girls cry." Weldon went to the window. Roger was outside, about fifty yards away, kneeling next to an old tin shed. "What's he doing?" Weldon said.

Rodney stood, winced and moved to the window. "Friend of his that owes him money paid off with some explosives."

"What kind of explosives?"

"Liberated from a construction site. So you know Roger, like a kid with a new toy now."

They both stared into the dusk, watching Roger for a while, until Weldon cleared his throat and said, "After what happened to you the other night, that business in the law office, I've been giving a lot of thought to what our strategy should be now."

With Rodney thinking, please, God, do something to shut the old fart up.

"Son, I hope your accident makes you understand the need for a plan. I hope—"

Weldon stopped talking when the door opened and Roger came in, breathing hard. Saying, "Come on out. Less go. Come on and watch this shit."

Roger, Rodney, Weldon and the girls gathered outside. "You plan to blow that shed up?" Weldon said.

"I'm gonna smithereen it," Roger said.

Weldon drew air from his hose and nodded. "Good thing there ain't a neighbor for half a mile."

"Now watch this shit." Roger held something that looked like a TV remote control. "Two sticks of dynamite in there. Got a radio ignition operation with a chip in the explosive that gives a five-second warning before she blows. And get this. It's a fucking musical warning."

He aimed the remote toward the shed, punching the numbers and saying, "Six and nine and six and nine."

From the shed came faint digital music. "That's 'Candle in the Wind,'" Brandi said. "I love that song."

Then the blast, lifting the shed off its foundation. When the smoke cleared and the dust settled, all that was left was a snarl of tin.

Roger melted into a lawn chair as if he'd had an orgasm.

Rodney whistled in appreciation. "Blew that shed all to shit. Didn't he, Mr. Chaney?"

"Well," Weldon said, "it does take care of business pretty good. . . . How much of that stuff you got left, Roger?"

13

"Pure torture, watching that go by," Mr. Marty said. A Greenie's waitress scurried past with a full tray. "Can't tell you how good that plate of bacon and eggs looks. Nothing like forbidden fruit, is there?"

"So have some," Jack said.

Mr. Marty put on a mournful look and waved the thought away. "The old lady'd smell the grease on my breath when I got home."

"Sorry I mentioned it."

"Ever since my bypass she's got this boy eating like a goddamn parakeet."

Jack shrugged and looked at his watch. "What did you want to talk to me about?"

"Friend, it'll happen to you too, live long enough. Remember when you was twenty-five? What was the only thing you thought about then?"

"Can we get to the point here?"

"Pussy, that's what. Well, that's the way I think about eggs now."

"You said you knew something about the JFK film."

Mr. Marty gazed toward the fry cook and asked, "You hungry?"

"No."

"I was thinking you might order a Denver omelette, and old Mr. Marty could have just a nibble or two."

"I'm not hungry."

"Not the whole thing. Just a taste."

Jack sighed and waved a waitress over. Telling her, "One Denver omelette."

"With plenty of onions," Mr. Marty said. "Don't scrimp on those darlings."

When she was gone Jack sat back and folded his arms. The guy had thirty seconds.

"All right." Mr. Marty clapped his hands once and kept them together. "Let's talk business. I hear you're looking for that film."

"So everyone seems to think."

"The newspaper said you're offering one quarter of a million."

Jack shook his head. "Someone else is offering that money. Which, you should know before you get too excited, I seriously doubt he has."

"Quarter-mil sounds low-ball to me. I'd of thought—" He stopped, closed his eyes and sniffed the air. "Smell that? One Denver omelette, coming up. Anyway"—he opened his eyes and came back to Jack—"seems to me a film like this, I mean one that really got the worm can open, could be worth twice that on the open market. Hey, maybe more. Depends on the quality of worms."

Mr. Marty looked quickly from side to side, as if checking for spies. He leaned forward, dropping to a whisper. "Imagine you're there. November twenty-second, nineteen hundred and sixty-three. The fateful day, and you're in Dealey Plaza with your movie camera."

"Like Zapruder."

"No. Hell no. Zapruder's on the other side of the street. The wrong side, you want my opinion." Waving one arm and raising his voice: Mr. Marty must have stopped worrying about eavesdroppers. "Know what really burns my ass?"

"A flame about ass-high," Jack said.

"Every time anybody talks about this stuff, it's Zapruder this, Zapruder that. Like he was the pro's pro with the camera. Crying out loud, the man made dresses for a living. A goddamn dressmaker, and everybody acts like he's the Cecil B. De-fucking-Mille of the Grassy Knoll."

Jack drank his coffee and watched while the guy flared. The scent of Old Spice poured off him.

"Zapruder? The little bastard didn't know what he was doing," Mr. Marty said. "He got lucky, that's all. Hey, I've seen better film on an old dog's eyes." The little man didn't stop complaining until the omelette arrived. Then: "Look at that, mortal sin on a plate. Mind if I have just a taste?"

Jack shoved the oval platter across the table. Mr. Marty coated it in Tabasco sauce, grabbed a fork and moved in for the kill. Saying as he chewed, "All right, imagine you're there, Dealey Plaza, camera rolling. Green grass, blue sky."

"You're shooting in color?"

"No. Uh-uh. Who said anything about color? Black-and-white, sixteen millimeter, Bell and Howell camera with a zoom. You look up Main Street and here comes the motorcade. Lead car takes a right on Houston, then a left on Elm. Right there in front of the Texas School Book Depository, the one with the Hertz rent-a-car sign on top. With Lee Harvey Oswald on the sixth floor, getting his Italian rifle ready to go. Texas School Book Depository, where all the action is. Right?"

"I suppose so."

"Completely wrong. And you call yourself an investigator? Who are you, Shitouttaluck Holmes? Look." Mr. Marty held an imaginary camera to his eye. "All right, you're pointing toward the motorcade, your right eye on the camera lens. But your left eye is open. You *are not squinting*." He slapped the table three times, with each word. "Damn amateurs squint the free eye. Zapruder was squinting, take my word on it. But you, you got yours open. Very important, know why?"

Jack drank more coffee.

"Because"—Mr. Marty paused to shove egg into his mouth—"in the corner of your left eye you catch some movement. You lower your camera and you turn to look. Across the street, up the grassy knoll, above the wooden fence, you see a man with an open black umbrella. And you just know something is not right."

"The President of the United States is about to roll by, and you're distracted by a guy up the hill with an umbrella?"

"Let's get one thing straight. This is *not* the umbrella man everybody already knows about. That's umbrella man number one, he's standing on the knoll and he's sending signals to Oswald. Common knowledge—I mean, shit, you can read about him in all the goddamn books. But this one you're looking at, that ain't him. You're looking at umbrella man number two. And nobody knows about him but you. Got that?"

"All these umbrellas," Jack said. "Must have been a convention of British bankers in town."

"Stay with me now." Mr. Marty locked on to Jack with brown, watery eyes. "Here comes the motorcade. It's about to pass right in front of you. History, close enough for you to spit on. JFK's waving and smiling. Jackie's in her pink suit, little pink hat, holding her roses. But something's telling you to keep your camera on umbrella man number two."

"Who's telling you that?"

Mr. Marty looked annoyed. "Telling me what?"

"Who's telling you to keep your camera on umbrella man junior?"

"There ain't no *who*. It's instinct. A little voice in your head."

Jack sighed and rubbed his eyes. Voices in the head again. Someday, if he lived long enough, he'd meet a lunatic with a more original explanation.

"So you're rolling." Mr. Marty raised the imaginary camera again. "You put Kennedy's limo in the frame, then you pan up the knoll to your man behind the fence. Next—and here's where we get to the short strokes, beloved—the man lowers the umbrella. He puts the butt end against his shoulder and the barrel end on the top of the fence. You zoom in."

"Where's the babushka lady?" Jack said. "All my life I've been hearing about the babushka lady on the grassy knoll."

"You zoom in, you're rolling film. And from the tip of the umbrella, there's a flash of light and a puff of smoke." Mr. Marty paused, watching Jack's face. "Bang."

"But of course," Jack said. "The famous umbrella-gun trick."

"Everyone knows Kennedy got shot from the front."

Jack nodded. "I think the Penguin used one of those on *Batman*."

"Imagine you got that on film. That flash of light, that puff of smoke. You know what you got then? You got what everybody in the world believes in but nobody's been able to prove, all these years. My friend, you got the goddamn second lone gunman. You got lone nut number two." Mr. Marty let that sink in. Then: "How much you think that would be worth now?"

Jack shook his head. "Are you saying this actually exists? Are you saying you have it?"

"I'm saying imagine it does. How much?"

The guy talked like a graduate of Billie Sol Estes State. Jack said, "How the hell should I know?"

"Maybe you could inquire around, find out."

"Why would I want to do that?"

"For a piece, a broker's fee. Ten percent of the sale, if you find the buyer. How's that?" The omelette was gone. "Hell, make it fifteen. What do you say to that deal?"

"Thirty-six years after the fact, this thing just magically appears? I have a hard time with that."

"Well, there might be a reason."

"And what would that be, exactly?"

"Son of a bitch, look at the time. I gotta pick my wife up at the beautician's." Mr. Marty slid to the end of the booth and stood. "All right, twenty percent, my final offer. Here's what you do. Ask around the right places. Tell them you've got the Sylvan Dufraine umbrella man film. Say Sylvan Dufraine, watch their mouths drop open." He nodded, winked and shot a finger gun at Jack. "You and me, we'll talk soon."

Mr. Marty turned and headed for the front: all plaid and aftershave in a quick, splayfooted water bug skitter. Jack watched him go, saw him make a left out the door, cross before the plate-glass window and disappear around the corner.

"Not so fast," Jack said. He went to the rear of the dining room and into the kitchen, past busboys yelling at each other in Spanish. A screen door opened onto Greenie's back parking lot. Jack peered through it and saw Mr. Marty getting into a white Cadillac with Texas plates. He wrote the number on a paper napkin as Mr. Marty drove away.

Jack pulled his phone from his coat pocket and dialed the county. See if Augie Newton was still around at this hour. Or if he was still around at all. Augie was a three-pack-a-day man when Jack worked for the district attorney. Augie the Almanac, forty years with the sheriff's department, couldn't remember where he put his coffee cup five minutes ago but never forgot a name.

A secretary tracked him down while Jack held. "Jackie boy," Augie said when he picked up the phone. "What kinda trouble you in now? You still make it your business to put your business where you got no business?" Augie laughed, then coughed for a while. Jack waited as the busboys kept their argument at top volume. Something about *dos mujeres* and a twenty-dollar bet; Jack's Spanish was rusty.

"The hell is that?" Augie said when he caught his wind. "You calling from Matamoros?"

"Need to run a name by you," Jack said.

"Hit me."

"This guy would have been around town about the time of the Kennedy assassination."

"Way back. All right, I'm ready."

"Sylvan Dufraine."

"Let me think about it, I'll call you."

Ten minutes later Jack was upstairs with Augie phoning back.

"Sylvan Dufraine," Augie said, "was an asshole that probably deserved what he got."

"You know him?" Jack said.

"Everybody knew Sylvan."

Jack got his napkin with the license number ready in case he needed to take more notes. "Lay it on me."

"Wormy little bastard, always around crime scenes taking pictures. Vulture stuff. Like a double homicide out in Red Oak, Sylvan'd be there to nab a shot of the bodies coming out in bags. Every now and then one of the papers might buy one." Augie coughed a few times. "I'm a little fuzzy here, but the word was he made bachelor-party movies too."

"Movies. That's our man."

"Have to check the records, but I think Dallas PD took him down on a morals charge, early sixties. Something about underage models with no clothes."

"Any idea where he is now?"

"Sylvan Dufraine, if memory serves, died behind the wheel of his car."

"A traffic accident."

Two more coughs from Augie. Then: "Jackie, when your car's been burnt to a crisp, and so have you, and you got shot in your head to boot, and they find you and your car on a lonely dirt road outside a landfill in south Dallas County—hey, *accident* is not the first word that springs to mind."

14

Four hours after she sent the man packing, Treena Watts still felt the heat rising in her face. Her heart was banging with anger, her blood pressure way up. She could forget about getting back to sleep.

Some skinny prosecutor ships her brother Mineola to prison, then shows up years later claiming he wants to look into what the police did. Talk about being just a little late.

Treena was quick to blow these days anyway. Two months now she had been living with her grandmother, back in the Lipscomb Homes again, waiting on her divorce decree. Waiting on the death certificate for her six-month marriage to an all-night R&B d.j. known professionally as the Truckload of Love. Treena filed on him when she found out he was making after-hours deliveries all over town.

Now Treena said, "Taking a walk."

"You'll miss some good music," her grandmother answered. Accordion sounds wheezed from the TV. Verdis Watts had to be the only black woman in America who watched Lawrence Welk.

Treena grabbed her jacket and bolted outside. The night was cool and clear, with a full moon floating just past the rooftops. She walked past the empty clotheslines and full garbage cans, past the apartments of people she had known since she was sixteen.

There was Mrs. Young's place, the windows dark except for the blue light of the TV leaking around the shades. Mrs. Young had raised two sons in the Lipscomb Homes. One got a scholarship and found work as a computer programmer in Houston. The other died at nineteen, stabbed by his girlfriend while he was slapping her around. Treena remembered him as a tall, shy, soft-voiced boy who once took her to a high school dance. Then they all grew up.

When she was younger Treena had lived in the projects for three years, she and Mineola moving in with their grandmother after their mother had some troubles. Treena finished high school and then did two years of community college. Mineola dropped out and hung out. He snatched purses and stole cars, was in and out of jail so many times Treena lost count. He walked a rape charge when the victim wouldn't testify, and got six months on an assault.

Then came Mineola's arrest for selling crack. He was sentenced to ten years and served three, was out only a month before the cop shot him. Shot him and tried to spread the story that Mineola had killed his new wife, Shauntelle. The grand jury had no-billed the cop, but Treena never bought it. Mineola had loved Shauntelle, had said she was the one who would turn his life around. Shauntelle had put him straight. She was going to save Mineola from himself.

Treena thought about them now as she walked, seeing their faces and hearing their voices, wondering why they died. Wondering if she could have done more to find the truth.

She walked fast, talking to herself for fifteen or twenty minutes, not paying attention to time or where she was going. When Treena finally stopped and looked around, she didn't know where she was.

Everything had changed since she was a girl. Where houses should have been, she saw only dark weedy lots. Apartments had been abandoned, plywood over their broken-out windows now. Big pieces of the neighborhood had died and fallen away, like branches of an old, sick tree.

Treena tried to read a street sign, and retraced her steps in her head. The only landmark she remembered passing was the True Word Pentecostal Tabernacle, maybe ten minutes back. Her grandmother had taken her there a few times, made her sit with the big-hatted ladies who sang about the help they were going to get someday from Jesus.

Now she turned and moved along the buckled concrete of the sidewalk, headed in what she thought was the direction of the Lipscomb Homes. No one else was in sight, as if the city had emptied while she turned her back. Her feet crunched broken glass that caught the dim sparkle from vapor streetlights. Slum emeralds.

After a few blocks the street dipped and crossed under railroad tracks. Treena didn't remember this from the first leg of her walk. The concrete tunnel had enough curve that she couldn't see the end. Caged lightbulbs hung along its ceiling. Treena plunged in.

Halfway into it she saw them. Two long-legged boys on the sidewalk, coming toward her. Fifteen or sixteen years old, maybe. Tall and thin with loping walks and huge baggy jeans slung low. Both of them wore sweatshirts with hoods pulled over their heads, their faces in shadow.

When they spotted Treena they quit talking. She glanced over her shoulder, saw nobody in the tunnel but them, heard nothing but her shoes on the concrete.

Treena froze. The boys kept walking, hands in their pockets. Hard to tell in the dim light, but she thought one of them was smiling.

Street hyenas: she saw them all the time in her job at ABC Bail Bonds. The ones who moved as if they were worn out from a double shift of carjacking. Grabbing their crotches and laying the thug-life stare on her as she typed up the bond sheets for whatever aspiring habitual felon they wanted to cut loose. Treena gave every one of them the stare right back. Letting them know she'd lived where they'd lived, only she was smart enough to get out.

But it was different out here in a tunnel at night. A stare wouldn't stand a chance. Two questions only as they closed in: How near would she let them get? And how much of a move would she let them make?

She slipped her right hand into the side pocket of her jacket, going for her gun. It was a .32 Remington, fully licensed under the conceal-and-carry laws of the state of Texas. Fired only on the range, but always with the thought that she could pop it on live flesh when the occasion arose.

The occasion was arising now. The boys were less than ten feet from her.

Treena pushed her hand deep into her pocket, her fingers slightly curved, ready to grip the handle of the .32. But she found nothing. The other pocket then. Left hand in, fast as she could, and coming up empty. The gun was not there either.

Panic raced through her, with one image flashing sharp and clear: She saw her hand placing the gun on the top of the toilet tank in her grandmother's apartment. Putting it down but not picking it back up.

"Lose something, sister?" one of the boys said. The other one laughed.

And then they were past her, one going by on either side

of her, like water flowing around a rock. She turned and watched them walk up and out of the tunnel. They were talking again, elbowing each other, just a couple of kids. She looked at their backs and saw her baby brother, Mineola.

Treena was still shaking when she reached the Lipscomb Homes. She opened her grandmother's door and sank into a chair with, "God, what I almost did."

Verdis Watts looked up from Lawrence Welk. Smiling and saying, "You're just in time for that cute couple that dances so nice."

Treena climbed the stairs on shaky legs. She retrieved the gun from the top of the toilet tank and put it in her purse. Then she showered and dressed for work.

Back downstairs, she found her grandmother in the kitchen, blowing on a bowl of soup. Treena sat across the table and took her grandmother's hands, knotty with arthritis, in hers. Asking, "You remember that man who was here this afternoon?"

Verdis Watts frowned. "I don't care what he said. That man was *not* from the insurance company."

"That's true. Listen, Grandma." Treena leaned forward but tried to make it sound casual. "He said you might know something about what really happened to Mineola."

The old woman pulled her hands back and picked up her spoon. "This soup is just too hot. Burns my mouth."

"He said you wrote a letter after Mineola was shot. You had something you wanted to tell the district attorney."

"Oh, honey, who can remember that long ago?"

Treena watched as her grandmother closed her eyes and said a prayer of thanks for her can of chicken and stars. After the amen Treena said gently, "You can tell me. What did you want to say?"

Verdis Watts's face clouded over and she shook her head.

"Honey, ain't nothing good would come from digging all that up."

Treena patted her grandmother's hand. "You never know."

"Oh yes, I do," the old woman said.

15

Jack hoped to surprise Lola at the gallery. Give her a big
kiss, tell her how great her display was, take her to dinner, take her home. Spend some time with her for a change.
They hadn't been in the same bed together for a week.

He drove to Deep Ellum, just off downtown, and finally
found a place to park so secluded and dark he imagined the
car thieves considered it holy ground. He had to walk five
blocks to reach the gallery, a place called Glen-or-Glenda.
"The hell does that name mean?" he'd asked Lola once. She
had looked at him, shook her head and said, "You're hilari-
ous, Jack."

Now he passed a brew pub and a taco bar. The gallery
was next door, in an old brick building that used to be full
of wholesale plumbing supplies. Back when, it seemed to
Jack, the world knew what it was doing.

Jack walked in the gallery door and waved to the owner,
Frank. Frank was all right, considering. He said, "Lola's in
the back. Not to mention over the top."

The entry to Lola's exhibition was through some yellow plastic shower curtains onto which she had stenciled small white mushroom clouds and tiny hearts. Jack parted the curtains and looked in. A department store mannequin stared back with eyes that had been whited out like Little Orphan Annie's. It was a bald plastic woman wearing nothing but a pair of red cotton briefs so old that tiny elastic worms protruded from the waistband.

Jack stepped closer. "Hey," he said, "that's my underwear."

The mannequin held a sign in her frozen hand: "THE NUCLEAR LOVE SURVIVORS/INTO THE MILLENNIUM." Fluorescent-green shoe prints on the concrete floor marked a path down the hallway and around a corner. Jack followed, hearing the sound of hammering as he drew closer.

He was thinking that maybe he should have brought Lola some flowers. Something she could mock as a bourgeois mating ritual, which usually got her pretty hot for action.

Jack took the corner and saw, in a dimly lit room, the Party Gals and Party Pals, reinflated and sitting on his furniture. His TV was there too, with a tape of the O.J. Bronco chase going.

The hammering continued; he could make out someone bent over behind the couch. Give Lola this, she worked hard. Jack called out, "Hi, honey, I'm home."

The figure straightened up, and a face turned toward him. Jack smiled big until he saw that, Jesus Christ, it was Eddie Nickles.

"Hey-hey, Jackie." Eddie struggled to his feet and limped to the middle of the room. "Been wondering when you'd show up."

"Where's Lola?"

Eddie motioned over his shoulder to some black velvet curtains. "She's working on the Chamber o' Death. Man, wait'll you see that. You step in there, complete darkness, utter fucking silence, right? Then we pipe in the odor of spoilt meat. Think that won't blow some people away? You know what she said to me, Jackie? She said, People are gonna leave here knowing that it's love or die."

"I left you five messages, Eddie. I'm still waiting for a callback."

"Jackie, this Lola, she's a very talented young lady. Not to mention very attractive, especially if you eighty-six the scorpion tattoo."

"Five messages, Eddie."

"On my answering machine? I shoulda told you, that thing's been broken for days. No telling the calls I missed. Probably some excellent opportunities right down the drain."

Jack was close enough to him now he could smell the stale coffee on the guy's breath. "Eddie, I'm going to ask you a question now."

"And this Nuclear Love stuff is just incredible. She explained the whole thing to me, Jackie. It's all about love, plain and simple. I take one look at this"—Eddie waved a hand at the blow-up dolls—"and believe it or not, I can see where it went wrong with me and Iris."

"One question, and I want the straight answer. Nothing but."

"Hey, what else you gonna get from Eddie Nickles?"

"Did you shoot out my windows the other night?"

"Jackie, it ain't that simple."

"Yes or no, Eddie."

"I was gonna pay you, man. Soon as the business came rolling in, you'd be the first name on the list. You wouldn't be out one red cent for them windows. Honest to God. I just needed to generate a little publicity."

Jack stared. Eddie said, "And let me remind you that Eddie Nickles is not the only man in Dealey Plaza with a Lincoln and an assassination tour. The Grassy Knoll, Jackie, is a very competitive marketplace."

"You pull the trigger or you hire someone? Because I want to know who to kill now."

"Jackie, listen. I took every precaution. Before I shot I did a creep on the house, even peeked in the window to make sure nobody was in the room."

"Lola was in the room, Eddie."

"I would never harm one hair of that lovely girl's head. So I'm just sick about the whole thing. Which is what I told her myself not two hours ago. You know what she says to me? Get this. She says thanks. You believe that? On account of me, she says, the Nuclear Love exhibit got a whole new dimension. Tell you something, my friend. That is one super lady."

With Jack shaking his head. "This is ridiculous."

Eddie said, "You want to hit me, don't you?"

Sure, Jack thought, beat a man who's almost on crutches.

"I don't blame you." Eddie pointed to his chin. "Go ahead, put a good one right there, whammo. Then everything'll be square between me and you."

Jack turned away, swallowing his anger. He backhanded the head of one of the Party Pals and sent its blond wig flying.

Eddie hustled over to set the doll straight. "Jackie, please. Don't take it out on the art, for Christ's sake."

The velvet curtains parted, Lola walking in. She wore black stretch pants and a black leather bra, and let her glance fall off Jack as if he were a piece of used furniture.

She carried a rectangular Tupperware container marbled with blood and fat, like a take-out box from the slaughter-house. "Eddie," she said, "I'm going to need more meat."

"You got it. Beef or pork?"

She studied one of the dolls. Its bullet hole had been patched, and Lola had painted drops of red flowing from the wound. "He's not sitting right," she said. Then back to Eddie: "There's some steak in Jack's freezer. Could you go get that for me?"

"On the double."

"Wait a minute," Jack said. "You're talking about *my* steaks?"

"If we let them sit out overnight"—Lola looked at Eddie as she spoke—"we'll have just the right amount of spoilage by tomorrow."

"The nose knows." Eddie gave two thumbs up. "That, Lola, is why you're the artistician."

"You're both nuts." Jack was close to shouting. "That's thirty dollars' worth of T-bones."

Lola gave him a look that lowered the room temp about twenty degrees, then went back behind the velvet curtain. Eddie took Jack's elbow. Saying, "Jackie, you don't mind my telling you this, you got some making up to do here. The lady is extremely cheesed at you, my friend."

Jack rubbed his temples. "Jesus, what a day."

"Come on," Eddie said, "let's go get them steaks."

Roger and Rodney Gillich had left before he was finished talking again. Weldon Chaney had watched as his sons-in-law carried guns and dynamite to Roger's truck. He didn't have the energy to try to stop them. Strength seemed to be draining from him as if he leaked, each day a little bit worse than the one before.

Now Weldon lay in his La-Z-Boy and closed his eyes.

Breathing from his bottle. Thinking that life was a big web stretching among people and across the years. Every time you did something, you were pulling one little strand. And later—decades later, maybe—another strand on the far side of the web might vibrate in return.

Weldon remembered again the woman outside the Gator Lounge on Christmas Eve, 1963. Remembered how she gave him five thousand in cash and asked him to take care of someone named Sylvan Dufraine, a guy who pointed his camera the wrong way.

Back then Weldon Chaney had strength to spare. None of this oxygen-bottle, tired-all-the-time shit. The men he robbed banks and armored cars with had a name for him: the Big Chain. When he was in his prime, the Big Chain could have turned punks like Roger and Rodney Gillich into dishrags. In 1954, outside a bar in Gladewater, Texas, Weldon beat an ex-boxer to death with his bare hands.

The funny thing about Weldon, though, was he prided himself not on his muscles but on his brains. Like with this Sylvan Dufraine. Most guys would have walked into his place of business, put a couple of bullets in his head and walked out.

But Weldon didn't care for the risk of the spontaneous hit; there was always the chance of witnesses. So he watched the man for a couple of days, learned his habits, got to know him in a way. Saw that he liked young ladies and college football. Weldon struck up a conversation with the man at a lunch counter, talking the TCU-SMU game. Next thing he knew, he had an after-hours invitation to Sylvan Dufraine's studio to watch some game film.

Weldon took the opportunity—the two of them alone in the studio—to pull his gun. And the man said, "You gonna kill me? Let's talk about this. Maybe we can make a deal." Calm as he could be when he said it.

Weldon liked that calmness, respected it. That somehow made everything different. And because of it, thought Weldon, almost forty years later an old, weak man who could barely breathe was hoping for one more pull of the web.

Eddie had the JFK limo parked near the gallery, so they took it, even though the night was cool for riding in a convertible. When they were rolling Jack said, "I was thinking about Mineola Watts today."

"No kidding? That jerk-off ain't crossed my mind in years. What's the occasion?"

"Nothing special." Jack watched the scenery, then turned to Eddie. "I don't know, I was just thinking about that grand jury. The one that looked into your shooting of Mineola."

"Took them jurors about thirty seconds to no-bill Eddie Nickles, Jackie. Same-day service. Hey, they let grand juries give out medals, I woulda walked outta there looking like General Patton."

Jack nodded, watching the traffic. Then: "Just out of curiosity, did Mineola's grandmother ever testify?"

"Shit, I don't know. I can't remember what I had for breakfast yesterday. How'm I supposed to know what some old lady did way back?" Eddie found a cigarette in his shirt pocket and lit it. "Why you asking me about this now, anyway?"

"Just crossed my mind, that's all."

"You wanna get a hard-on about some seven-year-old case, Jackie? Here's what I remember. Mineola aced his old lady and was coming for you next, except Eddie Nickles took care of him first. That's what I remember."

"Debt of gratitude, Eddie."

"Guy was a piece of shit, Jack. Case closed."

Jack let it drop. They spent the rest of the ride talking

sports. When they got to the house they both gazed into the freezer at packages of beef wrapped in white paper.

"Some stew meat in here," Jack said. "Let's take that instead."

"Lola said steaks."

"Cheap stuff rots just as good as expensive." Jack closed the freezer. "Want a beer?"

"Does the Pope crap in the woods?"

Jack got two bottles, set them on the table next to the meat. "Eddie, you ever heard of a guy named Sylvan Dufraine?"

"Jackie, about that window . . ." Eddie was looking toward the living room. "I'm gonna pay you, man. Next week, the latest."

"Forget about it." Jack popped the caps on the beers. "This film you're supposed to be looking for—"

"Hell of a stunt, you gotta give me that. Even if you're still pissed about the gunshots. For two, three days I had those news guys eating out of my hand."

"But the movie itself—that's why I mentioned Sylvan Dufraine—you think you're any closer?"

Eddie drank some beer and wiped his mouth with his wrist. "Closer to what, Jackie?"

"Jesus, Eddie, finding the umbrella man movie. The one you've been flapping your lips about."

"Hell of a stunt."

"This whole thing you dragged me into. The reporters calling, the wack attack showing up at my office trying to muscle me—"

"What are you talking about? I didn't come nowhere near your office."

Jack took a breath, then drank some beer. "Let's start over. Do you know where this movie is?"

Eddie coughed a couple of times. "I had cash flow problems, all right? I'm looking to churn some customers. Then one day down in the Plaza I'm talking to one of them JFK fruitcakes, he starts jabbering about umbrella man number two and the missing film. Fine, that rumor's been around for years, every asshole with two ears has heard it. Right?"

"I suppose," Jack said.

"So later I get to thinking, hey, why not say I got some new dope on its whereabouts? Offer a reward for it. Which me and you know I'll never have to pay."

Jack nodded slowly. "Right."

"Like I said, Jackie, it was a stunt. That's all." Eddie finished his beer. "And everything worked out fine. Hey, nobody got hurt, did they?"

"Hell with messing around with guns," Roger Gillich said. "I got the stuff right here in the truck. Let's just blow their asses to Venus, Texas."

Rodney shook his head, watching the house. He was sitting in the passenger seat of Roger's pickup. "Motherfucker almost melts my dick off? His last act on earth is gonna involve suffering."

Roger got a comb from his pocket and groomed his long blond hair. "Takes five minutes to plant a charge under that car. Better yet, wait till your man leaves again, we sneak in and put a blow-pack under his bed. Then when he comes home and hits the sack, it's one push of the button and he's gone, no forwarding address."

Rodney had a .357 between his legs, the barrel like a steel erection. He turned to his half brother. "You know what I'm sick of, Roger? All my life people like you been treating me like I just opened a fresh can of dumbass."

"Imagine that."

"Well, I'm smart enough to know this. Me and this gun is going into that house, and I'm gonna make the dick-melter eat the barrel while I slice on him awhile. Only question I got is if you're coming with me or not."

"Well, genius, the point is moot." Roger pointed to the two men walking from the house. "'Cause they're leaving."

"Boogie time." Rodney opened the truck door. "Hit the mothers with the high beams."

16

Jack locked his front door and walked across the yard toward the curbside limo. He carried a package of stew meat. Eddie had the car started. Saying, "Hey, Jackie, how about I play the *You Are There* tape for you now?" Pushing the cassette into the player as he spoke.

"I don't think so," Jack said. He was three or four steps from the Lincoln when he felt lights on him. He stopped and looked to his left, into the high beams of a pickup truck half a block up. Its engine raced and someone shouted. The truck burned rubber as it began to move. "Neighborhood's going to hell," Jack said.

The truck was about thirty yards from him when it jumped the curb. Jack saw a flash and heard a blast. He stood still for a second or two, thinking that the truck had blown a tire. Then he saw someone roll from the truck, stand and point a gun his way.

Jack ran and dove for the limo, like a fullback going over left tackle. Something ripped the package of meat from his arm just before he hit the seat. He was shouting to Eddie,

"Go! Go!" The car began to move. Jack flattened himself against the upholstery as fife-and-drum music blared from the speaker near his ear. A man's voice over the music said, "Welcome to the Grassy Knoll Experience." Jack heard another gun blast as the car gained speed. Then from the speaker: "You're sitting in what has come to be known as the presidential death seat."

Rodney saw the dick-killer frozen in the headlights. His plan was to get out of the truck and approach the dude, telling him not to move and keeping the gun on him. Get close enough to say, Remember me? Then take the guy's knees out from under him with the first shot. Let him roll around on the ground in pain, thinking about what he did.

"This'll be sweet," Rodney said as he opened the truck's door.

Only problem with his plan was he forgot to tell Roger about it. Roger had his own idea: give the truck major gas. Which he did just as Rodney opened the door. With Rodney shouting, "The fuck you doing?"

Roger looked over to see Rodney hanging on to the inside of the door, running with the truck. He leaned across to pull Rodney back in, trying to steer the truck straight at the same time but having some trouble. It banged over the curb. As Rodney slammed into the door his gun went off. Roger hit the brakes as Rodney screamed.

The truck came to a stop in someone's front yard. Rodney rolled, stood and fired. He got off another shot as the Lincoln began to pull away from them. "Hey, fucknut," Roger called. "Get back in. Unless you want to chase 'em on foot."

Jack had a friend in high school named William who loved the old wooden roller coaster at Fair Park. William would go to the park late at night, a few minutes before closing, when no one else was around to ride the coaster. He would pay his admission and get in the tenth car, at the very end.

Then as the train began its climb into that first steep hill, William would leap from the last car to the one in front of it. And from there to the next car. And to the next. All through the wild drops and turns William would jump, trying to reach the first car by the time the train made its circuit.

Jack's thoughts flashed on William now as he rolled from the back seat of the limo to the middle one, and from the middle one into the front. The Lincoln was up to sixty on straightaways, taking corners at a scream, the truck still behind. William might have been the thrill man in his day, but Jack was taking the title now. Because William never made his leaps with bullets flying.

By Jack's count, four shots had been fired at them since the chase began. One of the sideview mirrors shattered. Make that five.

Jack raised his head just far enough to see where they were: headed east through a residential section of Mockingbird Lane. To Eddie: "The hell we going?"

"Just watch." Eddie's hair was blowing wildly in the wind, and he wore an escape-from-the-nuthouse smile. "Jackie," he shouted, "if I'd been driving JFK in sixty-three, they wouldn't of touched the son of a bitch."

They took the exit off Mockingbird so fast that Jack wondered why his life wasn't flashing before him. The truck stayed with them as White Rock Lake came into view. Park land surrounded the lake. A two-lane road hugged the shore, full of sharp turns. Eddie said, "Now let's see the bastards catch us."

This time of night the park was empty except for a few back seat lovers parked under the trees. A full moon and a stiff breeze gave the water milky scales, lovely but for the gunshots. Eddie killed the car's lights; they were flying by moonlight now. He yelled, "Watch it!" The limo went airborne, then bottomed out hard with an oil-pan-to-asphalt scrape. Eddie accelerated, shouting, "A car chase with speed bumps. Is that fucking sad or what?"

The truck rattled over the same bump and stayed close, maybe a hundred feet back. Jack heard another shot but nothing hit. From the *You Are There* tape came the sound of sirens. It made Jack remember—asking himself how the hell he could have forgotten—the phone in his jacket pocket. He pulled it out and dialed.

"The big's one coming up," Eddie yelled. He was gaining speed on a bumpless stretch. "Jackie, we're exactly where we want to be."

"Fucked us up, going over that curb," Roger said. The truck had a bad shimmy, hard as hell to keep it on the road, especially when you're doing sixty. "We're gonna have to pull over, let 'em go."

"No way, dipshit." Rodney was sitting on the sill of the passenger-side window, head and arms outside, firing when he could. When they hit the speed bump he almost fell out of the truck. He shouted at Roger to floor it.

One last try, Roger thought. And if that doesn't work, we go plant some dyno. He punched the gas, gaining on the limo now in a nice long piece of straight road. With Rodney screaming something about a little bit closer and he could nail them.

Roger was close enough to the Lincoln to read the license plate, the truck's steering wheel about to jump out of his hands, almost doing seventy. He glanced at Rodney, then back to the road, and the limo was gone. Then so was the pavement. He hit the brakes, the truck sliding sideways off the road, across the dirt. Like slo-mo in a way, until the rear quarter panel banged into a tree. Rodney flew from his perch as if a big hand had yanked him out the window.

The truck stopped sliding a couple of feet before the water's edge. Roger got out and followed moans in the dark. He found Rodney in a heap in the dirt. "I think my leg's broke," Rodney said.

Roger loaded him into the bed of the truck. Telling his half brother over the moans, "Look at my front end, asshole. And how much you think a new back fender'll cost?"

Rodney was crying. "Goddamn, this hurts. Oh, Jesus . . ."

Roger shut the tailgate. "Next time, fucknut, we do it Roger's way. Next time, nothing but boom."

Eddie said, "I don't think they made it, Jackie. I think the curve did the trick. . . . Who'd you piss off, anyway?"

The Lincoln was backed into a blind spot behind some brush, lights off. No sign of the truck. With Jack on the phone to the police dispatcher, trying to tell her where they were and what was happening.

"Hey, when I was a uniform?" Eddie lit a cigarette. "I did three months in Northeast Division, and we had calls all the time, people wiping out on that curve. Worst hairpin in the park. Good thing I remembered it, huh?"

Jack said to the phone, "I don't know the block number. Somewhere on the west side of the lake."

"And half the wipeouts ended up in the water," Eddie said. "Tell you this, when cars go into that lake, it takes a crane to get them out. It ain't deep, but that silt is like quicksand."

Jack put the phone back in his pocket. "The police are on their way."

Eddie snorted. "Hey, one time I jump in to grab some lowlife, right? Don't ask me why, I mean where's he gonna go? He's gotta get out of the water at some point. But for some reason I jump in after him. And right away, both of us are sinking in mud up to our armpits, no shit. A Tarzan movie in there. I'm like, 'Cheetah, go get help.' My partner was laughing his ass off. . . . At least he was till I said that Cheetah thing. Guy was one of those black dudes always with the chip on his shoulder. I'm neck-deep in quicksand, I ain't taking time out to insult some guy's color."

Jack, watching the road, said, "If they were still tailing us, they'd have come through by now."

Eddie put the car in gear. "Let's go see what happened." He kept the headlights off, creeping along the road. They reached the curve and saw no truck. Eddie took a flashlight from under the seat and swept the shoreline. Saying, "Well, Jackie, that's two."

"Two what?"

"Two times now Eddie Nickles has saved your sorry-ass life." Eddie stepped from the car. "But hey—who's counting?"

"Hard to get a good look when you're running for cover." Jack got out too. "But the dude with the gun looked like the redheaded loon who came after me the other night."

"Took a hit on the mirror here." Eddie inspected the car with his flashlight.

"The same one who was after the Kennedy film. Any idea what's going on?"

"Somebody don't want you to find something, Jackie. Simple as that. . . . Oh boy, look at this."

Jack walked over. Eddie was shining his light at the last seat in the car, at upholstery spattered with blood. Jack reached in and touched one of the red spots. It was icy. "So much for Lola's stew meat," Jack said. "He shot it right out of my hands."

Eddie grinned in the moonlight. "Bloodstains in the death seat. Man, I should have thought of that years ago."

17

By the time Jack retrieved his car from its dark spot—the thieves must have taken the night off—dawn had started its seep. He drove to his office above Greenie's and climbed the stairs with dead legs. The old couch took him in like home; he slept until three in the afternoon.

Lola had a gallery party at ten, and even by the standards of Glen-or-Glenda Jack had some cleaning up to do. Or maybe not: The bits of old stew meat clinging to his shirt might make him the hit of the party, a portable Chamber o' Death.

Until then he thought he might try to discover why people were out to kill him. He started with the napkin, still in his shirt pocket, with Mr. Marty's plate number on it. Five minutes at his computer and he had the registration: a 1995 Cadillac, owned by Dalworth Novelty Supplies.

A quick check of state incorporation listings showed that the president of Dalworth Novelty was one Anita T. Dufraine. Dufraine as in Sylvan. Even Shitouttaluck Holmes would notice the last name.

After a brief stop home for a shower, with a loaded shotgun across the toilet in case his visitors returned, Jack drove to North Dallas. Nice rambling brick houses by the thousands out here, exuding order and prosperity, every block just like the next. For people whose eyes didn't demand much excitement, this was the place.

Anita Dufraine's address was a little more overgrown than most. The brown grass had a raggedness to it, and shaggy bushes obscured the windows. Leaves spilled from the roof gutters. The doorbell had a piece of tape over it, so Jack knocked.

Ten seconds later the door swung open, and Jack gazed down at a short man who looked stunned. Mr. Marty swallowed once, then said, "I'll be damn. The boy's not as dumb as he looks."

"Some days are better than others."

Mr. Marty peered past Jack, scanning the street. Then: "Come on in, let's talk. Unless you're here to sell Amway."

The house looked as if it had been furnished from the Roy Rogers estate sale. There were wagon-wheel chandeliers, ceramic horse-head lamps, couch cushions with a cattle-brand motif. A coatrack made from horseshoes was mounted near the front door, with Mr. Marty's plaid jacket hanging from it.

Clashing with the Ponderosa theme were photographs in black frames arranged on the yellow living room walls. Jack studied them as he crossed the room: black-and-white city street scenes, with cars and clothes not seen since Ike was President. But good use of light, taken by someone with an eye. "Nicely done," Jack said. "Yours?"

"Somebody else took those." Mr. Marty sat on the cattle-brands couch and crossed his legs, showing some hairless old-man skin between the cuffs of his slacks and his thin black socks. He wore fuzzy brown bedroom slippers. "Listen, how'd you find me?"

"Computers do amazing things nowadays." Jack sat down and took two sheets of paper from his coat pocket, but kept them folded. "A name here or a number there, you can unlock all sorts of doors."

"Like what?" Mr. Marty stared at Jack's papers, not happy. When Jack didn't answer, Mr. Marty said, "What kind of doors, exactly?"

They sat looking at each other until a woman walked into the room. She was short and plump, in her late fifties. Gray hair cut above the shoulders, pink sweatshirt over loose jeans. Pale skin, and green eyes behind oversized glasses.

Jack stood. With Mr. Marty saying, "This is the famous Mr. Flippo, the one everybody's been reading about in the newspaper. My wife, Nita."

She stepped forward to shake hands. Saying, "I haven't seen the paper in a few days. What did you do that I missed?"

"Nothing that I meant to do."

"He's looking to broker a deal," Mr. Marty said.

"Really?" She was smiling toward Jack, but with her eyes on her husband, unsure.

"Involving the missing film of umbrella man number two." Mr. Marty said it as if making an announcement. "The famous Sylvan Dufraine film. If it exists. If it can be found." He and his wife locked eyes.

Jack thought about passing a hand between them to break the beam. But Mr. Marty took care of it with, "The man and I need to talk, hon."

The woman turned to Jack. "Very nice to meet you." Talking to him as if he were Charlie Manson dropping by for tea.

Then she was gone, into the kitchen. Mr. Marty clapped his hands once and rubbed his palms. "Well, what can you tell me? We got an offer yet?"

"Couple of questions first." Jack unfolded his papers.

"I'm not answering nothing till I talk to my lawyer."

"Do what?" Jack shook his head. "Who's your lawyer?"

"Don't have one. You available? Let's talk terms."

Jack took a breath. Talking to this guy was like driving a car with electrical shorts—try to blow the horn and the wipers come on. "All right," Jack said, "let me explain to you why I'm here. Somebody shot at me last night. Not once but a number of times."

Mr. Marty looked him over. "I'm no doctor but I'd say they missed."

"Best I can tell, the same asshole firing the gun came to my office a couple of nights ago. Said he was there because of a movie. Have any idea who that might be?"

"Not even a hint. But now you see my point."

"I wouldn't go that far."

"They're shooting guns at you? What do you think they'll do to me, they find out what I might have? They'll be scooping my damn eyes out with a melon-baller."

Jack felt a headache coming on.

"You see my position here?" Mr. Marty leaned forward, hands out. "I need all the help I can get. Even yours."

"Answer some questions, then we'll talk about what I can do for you."

Mr. Marty shook his head, looking at the wall, talking to himself. "Everybody wants their pound of flesh."

Jack glanced at the two sheets of paper from his computer search. "According to this, Martin Dufraine, age sixty-six, lives at this address. I'm assuming that's you."

"Man, you're sharp."

"And"—Jack cleared his throat—"your relationship to the late Sylvan Dufraine is what?"

"We're brothers. Or were."

Jack read from the paper. "This is from the State of Texas Department of Vital Statistics. Sylvan Dufraine married Anita Tipton in April 1962, Dallas County."

"I wasn't invited. But go ahead."

"And in December 1963—that right?—Sylvan was murdered. A homicide that remains unsolved."

Mr. Marty scratched his ear, looked away, then came back to Jack. "Maybe you have some spare time you can wrap that case up too. You and your computer."

Jack, reading again: "January 1971, Dallas County. Anita Tipton Dufraine, widow of Sylvan, married you, Martin Dufraine."

"Glad to know the state's keeping all this straight."

"Two brothers, one wife?"

Now it was Jack's turn to stare. With Mr. Marty asking, "You got a problem with that?"

"A man with my marital history passes no judgments."

"Nothing to pass judgment on, junior. Listen, Sylvan and me? We barely knew each other. We didn't grow up together, we wasn't even in the same state. While Sylvan was at home with Mama and Daddy, I was raised by my aunt and uncle in Monroe, Louisiana."

Mr. Marty had a look on his face as if to say, And that explains it all.

Jack said, "And . . ."

"What I'm saying is, far as Anita's concerned, Marty Dufraine didn't make the scene until after Sylvan Dufraine ran into his big trouble."

Jack looked over Mr. Marty's shoulder, toward the kitchen. He could see the woman's shadow falling across the floor. She was listening.

Mr. Marty was out of his chair, moving toward a table. He took a framed photograph from beneath a horse-head lamp. "Tell me you wouldn't go for this girl."

Jack gazed at a black-and-white portrait of a striking young woman. A studio shot, from the midriff up. She had thick dark hair tumbling over her shoulders and a sweater tight enough to stir impure thoughts.

Mr. Marty said, "Nita Dufraine, twenty-two years old. Tell me that wouldn't start your car."

Jack didn't even have to lie. "Very beautiful." When Mr. Marty kept the picture in front of him he added, "As she still is, of course."

"Oh, please. Spare me the bullshit." Mr. Marty put the picture back on its table. "Listen, you want to work for me or not?"

With Jack thinking, that's the last thing I want to do. He said, "Maybe. If you answer the rest of my questions."

Mr. Marty sighed. "Ever seen one of those dogs that's just got to sniff everybody's crotch? Who do you think that reminds me of?"

"Why was your brother killed?"

"Come on, the boy makes a film that shows somebody shooting the President. A few weeks later he's dead. What kind of picture I have to draw for you?"

"Who killed him?"

"Who killed the President? How the hell should I know."

"I'm asking," Jack said, "who killed Sylvan."

"Guess what. Whoever did it didn't keep me informed."

Jack glanced toward the kitchen. The woman's shadow hadn't moved. "Where's the umbrella man film now?"

"Here we go again." Mr. Marty fanned the air as if he were clearing smoke. "You and I have to make a deal here, junior. Anything I tell you is between you and me. When you go out to ask around, to find out how much our little commodity is worth, my name is never, ever mentioned."

"It's okay to mention Sylvan Dufraine, just not Martin?"

"You got it."

Jack watched the little man smooth his eyebrows with his fingertips. Finally Jack said, "All right."

"All right what?"

"Your name stays out of it."

Mr. Marty smiled. "We're in business, then."

"Where's the film?"

"I don't have it on me right now. But maybe I can get it."

"*Maybe* you can get it?" Jack waited.

"The right price can do a lot of things."

Jack had more questions, but they were for Mrs. Dufraine, whose shadow hadn't moved. He would get her later, alone. "I'll call you when I know something," he told Mr. Marty.

Before he left they shook hands. With Mr. Marty saying, "Forget all this stuff from your computer. You and me are making a business transaction, plain and simple. No reason to pick old scabs here."

"Maybe you're right," Jack said.

"Believe me"—Mr. Marty released his hand—"it's the only way to go."

18

No telling when the gun-toting truck boys might stop back by the house. So after the gallery party Jack and Lola spent the night at a Marriott—Lola's choice, a good place for more bourgeois field research. It was karaoke night in the motel lounge: traveling salesmen with a few drinks in them, murdering the Beatles. Lola stared, engrossed, like a scientist in a pith helmet watching a tribal dance.

"Enough torture," Jack said. "Let's go to the room. Hey, Lola? You coming?"

"Maybe later." She was drinking a frozen margarita with a straw from a thick glass that could have been a miniature birdbath. On the small stage a guy who looked like Al Gore was trying to sing like Al Green. "This is fabulous," Lola said.

Jack was thinking that the only way to get her out now would be to seduce her. He leaned close and said, "Fantasy time, baby. I'm a lonely district sales manager for a major plastic pipe manufacturer. And these pants I have on?

Dockers." She glanced his way, showing some interest, maybe. Jack waited, seeing if the fire would start to catch. Then he put his lips to the rim of Lola's ear, where she had rings spaced like shower curtain hooks. Telling her, "I drive a Taurus wagon and have a thing for the fried shrimp at Red Lobster. Let's get to know each other better."

The guy on the stage was trying to do Stevie Wonder now. Lola moved her hand up Jack's leg. Asking, "What do you have in mind?"

"Something to make this world a better place." Jack stood and took Lola's hand, raising her from the chair. "Let's go up to the room, see if we can get *Topless Brain Surgeons* on the pay-per-view."

ABC Bonding operated from a double-wide trailer half a block from the Frank Crowley Criminal Courts Building. With a big electric sign out front, so it could be seen from the windows in the jail.

This night was a busy one at ABC. In four hours Treena Watts had bailed three burglary suspects, a theft of services and two agg assaults. Plus a man who tried to steal a toilet from a restaurant. He had dressed himself like a plumber, figuring he could carry the bowl out of the place without raising suspicion.

For all this, Treena was getting no help from fabulous night manager Ralphie, who sat in his office drinking coffee and using his stubby fingers to pick lint off his Dallas Cowboys windbreaker. Treena planned to write one more bond and leave at seven a.m. on the nose, when her shift was done. Let Ralphie handle the filing and cleanup.

One more client to go. She looked at the woman waiting and said, "Miss, you're next."

The woman couldn't have been past thirty, but she rose off the couch as if gravity were stronger in that part of the room. The seven or eight steps to Treena's desk became a long trip. With Treena thinking, she moves any slower and moss will grow.

The woman dropped into a metal folding chair, slumping, her coat across her lap and her purse on top. She wore a red Bugs Bunny T-shirt and had skin the color of unwashed sheets.

Treena read aloud from a sheet of paper on her desk: "Twenty-four-year-old male, bond set at thirty thousand, charged with injury to a child." Then: "It'll cost you three thousand dollars cash. You got that much on you?"

The woman nodded and opened her purse. "Dwayne's mama gave it to me." She took a roll of old bills, secured by a rubber band, from the purse.

Treena didn't reach for the money. "This is your husband we're talking about?"

"We been living together off and on."

"What kind of injury to a child?"

The woman looked away. "Dwayne couldn't hear the TV 'cause she was making noise."

"What kind of injury?" Treena said.

"I told her, Honey, go to your room. But she just stayed right there in front of the TV. Sometimes she just don't listen to me."

Treena waited. The woman said, "The doctor at the hospital give her some medicine so it wouldn't hurt."

"Where's the girl now?"

The woman turned slowly toward the front. "That medicine was making her sleepy."

Treena rose and went to the front window, but couldn't see much, trying to peer between the "Se Habla Español" and "E-Z Terms" signs. Then she was out the door and into the morning cold. The sun was rising behind thin clouds, the sky a hammered gray. She saw a junker Monte Carlo in the lot, its engine running, with vapor puffing from the tailpipe. Treena opened one of the rear doors and the dome light flickered on.

Curled on the vinyl backseat was a girl, asleep, covered with a pink bath towel. Nine or ten years old, Treena guessed. There was a blue bruise the size of a quarter on her forehead and a cast on her left wrist.

Back inside the office Treena said, "Listen to me." She waited for the woman's eyes to find their way to hers. "What's your name?"

"Donna?" Saying it as if she weren't sure.

"Do you have someplace else to go, Donna? Any family?"

"I got a brother in Houston."

"How much money do you have?"

"You said three thousand dollars to get Dwayne out." The woman seemed to come alive for the first time, with fear running a small charge through her. "That's what—"

"Donna, how much money do *you* have?"

"I don't . . ." She shook her head and looked away.

Treena said, "You take that three thousand, and you get that little girl away from your piece-of-crap boyfriend."

Donna sat with her mouth open. Finally she said, "His mama give me that money. That was for Dwayne to get out."

Treena leaned into Donna's face. "I find you bailed him out? And he's around that child? I'll have the state on your butt, and they'll take that girl from you and place her in a safe home. Don't think I won't turn you in, 'cause I will."

The woman blinked a few times. Treena said, "You understand me, Donna?"

When the woman had left, Ralphie waddled out of his office to ask, "The hell happened to her?"

"She's gone," Treena said.

"You write her?"

"How I'm gonna do that"—Treena gave Ralphie a look—"when she's out there, and I'm in here?"

Ralphie took a moment to figure that one out. Then said, "Don't tell me you did your save-the-world bit again."

Treena got her coat from the rack. "Later, Ralphie."

"Where you going?"

"Wherever it is, you won't be there"—Treena opened the front door—"so the day is looking up already."

Ralphie followed her outside. "What do you think we got here, a fucking church? Second time in two weeks you've run off a client."

Treena unlocked her car and opened the door. The wind had picked up, and was starting to lift Ralphie's comb-over off his head. "Hey," she told him, "you know me."

She slipped into her car and shut the door. The last thing she heard was Ralphie shouting that she shouldn't bother coming back.

Fine with her. She had work to do. She'd been able to pry one small piece of information out of her grandmother about Mineola's death. It wasn't much, but it gave her a start. Now she had people to see, people to find. Not that they would all be happy to look up and see Treena Watts looking back.

Jack's grasp of assassination lore was a little weak once he got past the Oswald-Ruby basics. He couldn't deliver an off-the-cuff on the reliability of Mannlicher rifles, couldn't even fake cocktail party chatter on the shape of the President's throat wound. If he was going to play with the

big-league nuts he would need a quick tutorial. Eddie
Nickles said he had a friend who knew it all. Have to warn
you that the guy's kind of a dipshit, Eddie said, but let's
drop by and I'll introduce you.

So just after sunrise Jack left Lola asleep at the motel
and drove across town, listening to lame morning d.j.'s
yucking it up at their own jokes. He imagined fat assholes
in Hawaiian shirts. He tried to drink gas station coffee
but hit a pothole and spilled some on his pants. Traffic
ran thick and slow, and there was a new knocking from
under his Chevy's hood. Also, yesterday's headache was
back.

None of that mattered. Jack was after a scent: a bad
smell, the best kind.

He had thought about it after he left Mr. Marty's the
night before. No question that the little guy was lying, and
Jack loved being lied to. Lies meant someone was hiding
something. Lies put Jack on the hunt. That, he had finally
figured out, was what he wanted out of life.

Jack's life. He was acquainted with lots of people but
had no real friends. He knew himself well enough to see he
was a guy who had found out plenty and never knew what
to do with it. Made money but couldn't save it, got jobs but
couldn't hold them. Over the years he had pulled stupid, almost suicidal stunts for sex, while driving away every
woman, including two wives, who loved him.

His favorite part of the chase was the instant just before
the absolute end. As a prosecutor Jack had loved coming
after witnesses, loved ripping away their lies as if he were
tearing off their clothes, a layer at a time, until they were
naked on the stand. Finally, the moment of poison joy: he
could reach inside them, almost like putting a hand down
their throats, and yank out that last little treasure of knowl-

edge they had been keeping from him. Then walk away, leaving them for dead.

You know what you look like, another lawyer told him once, when you've really got somebody nailed? You get that expression on your face, like a grave robber pulling a gold ring off the finger of a corpse.

Now Jack drove Ross Avenue past Mexican bars and used-car lots, then took Fitzhugh into sagtown: old houses flaking paint, weedy yards, apartments that had gone up in a hurry now coming down slow.

Eddie's address begged for the wrecking ball. Jack parked at the curb and walked into the courtyard of a small apartment complex. Two floors, with rotting eaves and broken windows, lined a pool on three sides. The pool had been drained, with nothing in it now but a few inches of green rainwater, some dead leaves and an old roll of carpet.

The whole place had been abandoned. Jack glanced around at the kicked-in doors, at the old newspapers and trash building up in corners.

"Hey-hey, Jackie." Eddie's voice from above him. Jack looked up to see Eddie leaning over the second-floor rail. "Be right down."

When they were in the car Jack asked, "Are you squatting in that dump?"

"Government redo." Eddie slipped his wraparound shades on. "They're gonna rehab all fourteen apartments, owner's a friend of mine. Hey, I needed a place to live when Iris kicked me out. So I'm keeping watch on the complex while the work is done."

"I didn't happen to notice any work being done."

"Nothing gets past you, does it? Fucking alert, man." Eddie changed the radio to an oldies station. "They fixed up the unit I'm in, but that's about it. Tell you the truth, I'm guessing my buddy took his federal swag and boogied for the Caymans."

"Based on what?"

"Based on my knowledge of the way human beings love money, Jackie."

They crossed Gaston Avenue, catching a green light. "Need to drop by my office," Jack told Eddie, "to pick up some papers."

"So I called Heather from Channel Four last night." Eddie cleared his throat. "Loveliest set of cans on local TV, you want my opinion. Anyway, I gave her the real deal about the limo getting shot to shit. She's all hot to do another story, show what those assholes did to my beautiful car. I told her, 'Heather, whoever those assailants were, they will not obstruct the Eddie Nickles search for the truth.'"

Jack thought about the truck boys, and tried to wire a connection to Mr. Marty. But that didn't make much sense, Mr. Marty's asking Jack to broker a deal on the film and wanting him dead at the same time. So Jack tried a different tack: Maybe there really was an umbrella man film, and someone didn't want him to find it, even after all this time. It would help to know who killed Sylvan Dufraine, torching him inside his car. Jack had a feeling, nothing more, of a string running from that burned, shotgunned body to the red-haired crazy from the other night.

Eddie said, "Which I'm planning to have copyrighted, by the way."

Jack came back to the conversation, lost.

"Come on, Jackie, what I just said. The Eddie Nickles Search for the Truth Corporation, my new company name." Eddie reached into his pocket and found a bent cigarette. "Paint that right along the side of the limo. Think you could handle the legal end for me? Since we're sorta partners now."

"We're not partners."

Eddie turned away. Jack could tell by the clench of his jaw that he was fuming. "Cool off, Eddie. You need some papers filed, I'll take care of it."

"Some of us"—Eddie turned, pointing the crooked cigarette at Jack—"some of us has to work for a living."

Jack was sorry he'd said anything. "I know, Eddie."

"Grassy Knoll Tours, that's my bread and butter, Jackie. Not all of us got that free gift of a year's pay in the bank, you know."

Jack whipped around. "Who told you about that?"

Eddie shrugged and pushed in the dashboard lighter. "I hear things."

"Heard where? From Lola?"

"Tell you something about Lola, Jackie. You don't mind my saying, you could be a little more attentive to her. She's lonely."

Jack tried to remember what he had said to Lola about Eddie and Mineola Watts. "What else did you and Lola talk about?"

"TV, man." The lighter popped out and Eddie fired up. Took a deep drag and said, "The girl knows her programs. You got a question about *Petticoat Junction?* She's the one to see."

Jack pulled the car into a head-in space in front of Greenie's. Telling Eddie as he opened the door, "I'm gonna run upstairs and come right back."

"I'll be at the counter." Eddie got out and walked toward the restaurant, talking to himself and scratching his ass as he went. Jack watched him go, wondering if he was a real mental fry-job or just pretended to be.

The plate-glass door to Greenie's Office Building was unlocked. Jack opened it and headed up the stairs. He stopped when he saw someone sitting at the top. Jack took a couple of seconds to register the face. Then said, "The charming Miss Watts."

"About time you showed up." She stood. "What's the deal, man? You have trouble dragging your sorry butt out of bed this morning?"

19

Jack unlocked the door to his office and left it open for Treena Watts to follow him in. She looked around and said, "What's this supposed to be, some kind of haunted house? Maybe you heard, they got this new invention called a vacuum cleaner."

"The cleaning lady took the year off."

Treena inspected the room as if he were charging her rent. "You know you got spiderwebs hanging from the ceiling here?" She shook her head. "Man, the way you people live . . ."

"I'm on my way somewhere." Jack stood behind his desk, pulling some papers together.

"Good for you, big boy."

"So you've got about thirty seconds."

Treena gave the closest chair a couple of backhand finger sweeps, then sat. "Listen, you and me need to talk."

"Not right now we don't." Jack glanced at her black dress, her heels, the few pieces of jewelry she was wearing. A little racy for the office, but not enough flash for a big night out. You saw her on the street, though, you'd take a second look. Maybe think about getting to know her, think about it until she opened her mouth.

Treena said, "Are you telling me to come back later? Or are you telling me to fuck off? Hard to know with someone like you, because I believe I've seen more expression out of a grapefruit. Blink once for yes, twice for no."

"Some other time," Jack said. The woman had a good run of hostile patter going now, but without the pure hatred of the other day. For Jack it was like getting hit with the ax handle instead of the ax. He said, "You came to talk about Mineola?"

"No, I want some decorating tips. Who did this place, Lighthouse for the Blind?"

"Are you free later today?"

"And you, you ought to think about a massage. Go get laid or something. Anything to loosen up that face. . . . Yeah, I'm free."

"How does two o'clock this afternoon sound?"

"It sounds like the time I'm usually asleep. So I might not be my usual happy self. Make it four."

Jack nodded once. "Fine."

Treena stood. "You know where I live, come pick me up there. You can buy me breakfast with all the money you save on housekeeping."

They went downstairs together while Treena let Jack know he ought to have the carpet retacked because she almost tripped coming up. On the sidewalk out front she walked away without saying goodbye.

Jack started to go into Greenie's but heard, "Yo, Jackie." Eddie was in the car, sipping his coffee from a Styrofoam cup. "Who's the black chick?" he asked when Jack got in.

"Possible client." Jack started the Chevy and backed it onto East Grand. "All right, let's go talk to the assassination man. You ready?" Jack drove toward Thornton Freeway, the way downtown. Saying, "So tell me about this guy we're going to meet."

Eddie looked back toward Greenie's. "I know that face from somewheres, Jackie. What's her name?"

"You get old enough, Eddie, every face you see reminds you of someone else."

Eddie shrugged. "I guess so." He changed stations on the radio until he came to a Janis Joplin song. Telling Jack, "The feds offed her, and made it look like a drug OD. But you knew that, right?"

The Conspiracy Institute took up a small corner of a forgotten brick eight-story near the Greyhound station, about a block from the Kennedy Memorial. An awning marked the side-street entrance, leading to the kind of narrow nook where you used to find a cigar store or a typewriter repair shop.

"Check this guy's wife when we get inside," Eddie said as he opened the door. "Half Cherokee from Oklahoma. Best-looking Indian babe I ever seen, Jackie. Makes every man she meets into Chief Bulge in the Pants."

The front room was a gift shop, with books, tapes and posters. You could get a Jack Ruby ashtray for $8.95, with JFK and Jackie on a coffee mug for a dollar more. A rotating rack had Dealey Plaza postcards with a black X marking the spot of the fatal shot. Next to that were buttons and bumper stickers that said, "I believe in the Warren Commission. I also believe in the Tooth Fairy."

In one corner Jack saw a small TV showing a piece of the Zapruder film on a loop: The limo comes down the hill, the President's hands go to his throat, pieces of his skull fly, the limo comes down the hill again.

"You stand here for a minute," Jack said, "you could watch the guy die six times."

A door to the back opened. Jack turned to see a short, round, bald man with small blue eyes behind thick glasses.

Eddie said, "Hey-hey, here he is. Monroe Beets, Jack Flippo. I told Jack all about you, Monroe. Jack used to be a lawyer here in town, but now he's chasing the big dog, working with me to crack this JFK thing."

Jack shook his head. "No, I'm not."

"Whole goddamn town is talking about it, it's the hottest deal going," Eddie said. "And speaking of hot stuff, where's Mrs. Beets?"

The man looked at Eddie hard, asking, "What do you want now?"

"An hour with your wife in a Motel Six." Eddie twisted up something close to a smile. Then to Jack: "Don't get put off by him being an asshole. Monroe ain't exactly a people person."

Monroe went behind the counter and paged through some receipts, acting as if Eddie and Jack had disappeared. Eddie watched and said, "Let me try to put this in a nice way. Your attitude, Monroe, is really starting to piss me off."

Jack turned to Eddie. "I thought this meeting was all set up. You said you called him."

"I did call him, Jackie. But the short fuck wouldn't answer."

Monroe raised his gaze from the receipts. "Little instrument known as caller ID, Eddie. Well worth the monthly charge as long as they give phones to certifiables like you."

"The midget's a real laugh riot, you know it?" Eddie had some tight nods working, sticking his chin out, his burner on high. He stepped toward Monroe. "See how funny you think this is."

Jack headed him off. He grabbed Eddie's sleeves just below the shoulders and said, "Outside," giving him a push out the door. On the sidewalk Jack told him, "Go take a walk, cool off."

Eddie jerked his arms away. "Keep your hands off me, man."

"See that place over there?" Jack pointed to a sandwich joint. "Go get an iced tea, and I'll come get you when I'm through."

Eddie backed away a few steps. "Like I'm your little poodle dog? Hey, just put a leash on me, man, tie me to the parking meter."

"Forget the leash." Jack opened the door to the Conspiracy Institute. "Get a muzzle."

As he went back inside, Jack could hear Eddie on the sidewalk, yelling: "Sure, Jackie, go make your own deal with Monroe. Leave Eddie Nickles out here yanking his crank."

Inside, the little man was still at the counter. Jack smiled and said, "Eddie gets excited sometimes."

Monroe raised his head, looking at Jack through the thick glasses. "He's a psychopath."

"Part of his offbeat charm." Jack put a business card between them. "Listen, could I ask you a couple of questions? I'm a little weak on some of this Kennedy stuff, and they say you're the local wizard."

"The Conspiracy Institute is internationally known."

"Of course, hey, the world over. Anyway, if you have just a minute or two."

Monroe fluttered his eyelids, thinking it over. "Eddie stays outside?"

"He stays out of everything."

"No affiliation with you?"

"My deal all the way."

After a moment Monroe said, "Very well. Let's talk in my office."

Jack followed him through the back door. They walked past an exhibit hall that was five times as big as the gift shop. Jack caught a glimpse of some of the displays: The suspicious deaths of John Kennedy, Robert Kennedy, Martin Luther King and Jimmy Hoffa. The wounding of the Pope. The crash of the Korean Air jet that the Russians nailed.

"I had no idea," Jack said. "Everywhere you turn, conspiracies, huh?"

"They're easy to conjure and impossible to disprove." Monroe opened another door. "I don't foment them, I study them."

His office was like a big closet lined with books and pictures. No windows; put two people in the place and it was filled up. Jack took the only extra chair. Monroe sat behind his desk and started talking before Jack could ask a question.

"At its heart," Monroe said, "the Kennedy assassination is no different than the rest."

"Absolutely," Jack said.

"Your view of it depends on how you approach what you find. Related pieces of an overall chaos? Or scattered parts of a puzzle? As with anything, though, if you see a pattern there's generally a reason. Coincidence won't carry you very far."

Jack cleared his throat. "What I really wanted to ask you about—"

"I'll give you an example." Monroe talked fast, with a high voice like a sewing machine motor. "The Warren Commission said there were three shots only, all of them coming from Oswald in the schoolbook depository. Remember how they refer to the third shot?"

Jack sighed and shook his head a little. "Shot number three, maybe?"

"The third shot, they called the Magic Bullet. They claimed it took out JFK and wounded the governor of Texas too."

Monroe kept going, delivering a short lecture on ballistics and deflections. Jack gazed at one of the photos on the wall: Oswald in his backyard, holding the rifle he would use, with his shadow falling on the grass behind him.

"Many people—" Monroe paused, waiting until Jack's attention came back to him. "Many people believed that a fourth shot actually hit the governor. They did some extrapolation from his wounds, came up with a trajectory, placed the shooter on the rooftop of the Records Building."

"That's county property," Jack said. "The assassin have a commissioners' permit to be up there?"

"Nineteen seventy-five, a man's doing air conditioner repair on the roof of the Records Building, and guess what he claims to find? A spent cartridge from a thirty-ought-six rifle." Monroe Beets pushed the tips of his fingers together and appeared pleased with himself. "There are dozens of stories like that all over Dealey Plaza."

"I'm only interested in one of them." Jack leaned forward. "Something about the second umbrella man."

Monroe snorted. "More of Eddie's nonsense."

"Tell me about it."

"There's nothing to tell." Monroe rubbed his chin. "Everybody saw umbrella man number one. He was on the knoll in plain sight, sending—if you believe the theories—signals to gunmen."

Jack backhanded the air. "None of my concern."

Monroe took a pipe from a drawer and began filling its bowl. "Only one person has ever claimed to have seen umbrella man number two. That was a gent named Sylvan Dufraine, who believed the umbrella hid a rifle."

"Now you're talking."

"The late Sylvan Dufraine, by the way. Word was, he caught the whole thing on film. Which of course has never been seen."

"Think it's true?"

"It's just like the cartridge on the roof of the Records Building." Monroe lit his pipe, puffed a few times. "Fanciful story? Or piece of the puzzle?"

Jack watched him smoke, then said, "What if someone came forward today with that film?"

"Oh, come on." Monroe looked at his watch. "There have been rumors for years about this thing, all unsubstantiated. It's a Dealey Plaza folk tale. It's the Loch Ness Monster of the Grassy Knoll, but with less proof."

"Meaning what?"

Monroe had the eyelid flutter going again. "Personally, I don't believe it exists."

"What if it does? What would be the commercial possibilities?"

"Are you saying someone has it and he wants to sell it?"

Jack shrugged. "Let's play what-if." Doing the Mr. Marty weasel walk.

"Then that someone is a rich man."

"Rich like Elvis? Or just rich like a guy who cleaned up on *Wheel of Fortune?* I mean, are we talking Paris, France, or Paris, Texas?"

"If it's a film of good quality? Verifiable? Showing Kennedy and the shooter too?" Monroe tilted his head upward, like someone running mental totals. Then: "A million dollars, easy. Get some of those trash TV shows in a bidding war, a million is just the floor."

They stared at each other until Monroe said, "But I would have some serious questions."

"Me too. What are yours?"

"Secrets like this one are very hard to keep." Monroe was wreathed in smoke. "If this film really exists, how has it stayed buried all these years? And why in the world is it coming out now?"

Eddie headed up Commerce Street, his knee hurting like a mother, but he kept walking anyway. Then it hit him, the awareness coming on so fast and hard Eddie had to stop and lean against the nearest wall. A revelation with such force that for a moment he couldn't breathe: He knew her.

Ten years ago, when they sent Mineola Watts down, Eddie had spotted the woman in court. He had seen her sitting next to Mineola's grandmother, watched her get all weepy when they took the motherfucker away in cuffs.

And now, after all this time, she's hanging with Jackie, who's all of a sudden asking questions about how Mineola died. The ungrateful son of a bitch.

After a minute or two, Eddie managed to stand. He pushed himself from the wall and walked on. So maybe the two of them, Jackie and the black chick, were setting a trap. That left Eddie only one choice: set a bigger one.

20

Weldon Chaney came out of the shower exhausted. Ten minutes without his air bottle, and he was huffing like a fat man who had run a mile. He put the clear tube to his nose even before he dried himself, drawing the oxygen into his false-bottom lungs. He was suffocating, one day at a time.

Ten in the morning. Weldon sat on the side of the tub for a while, taking one shallow breath after another. Finally he managed to pull on a robe and walk to the kitchen. He made some instant coffee and had a piece of toast. It tasted like sugared mud and cardboard with jelly.

While he ate he watched through the window as Roger and Rodney got ready to play with their explosives. They were unhooking the tow chains on an old car they had bought at the junkyard, a car they planned to blow up.

Weldon figured they would wait until night, because the darkness made explosions more fun to watch. Or so Roger had said. Rodney hadn't been in the mood to disagree.

Since breaking his ankle in the fall from the truck, he'd been popping pills on the hour.

After breakfast Weldon went to the living room and sank into his La-Z-Boy. He closed his eyes and dozed, dreaming of beaches and palm trees, waking when he heard the back door slam.

There were footsteps in the kitchen. "Want a beer?" he heard Roger say.

Then Rodney's voice. "Make it two."

Weldon listened to the scraping of chairs, the smack-shut of the refrigerator door, the pop of beer can tops. "Coors Light and a Perc," Rodney said. There was the rattle of pills. "Breakfast of—shit, I forget. What's it the breakfast of, Roger?"

"Looking at you, I'd say butt-uglies who's too stupid to hang on when their truck hits a pole. Right? You're not even gonna fight back at me, are you, Rodney? Man, them pills has got you smoothed out."

"If I'd known they was this good I'd of broke my ankle long time ago."

Weldon couldn't see them but he could hear every word. Not that they said anything worth hearing. He had just about given up on the Gilliches anyway: two boys who didn't want to run nothing but their mouths. He closed his eyes again, was drifting off when he heard Rodney say, "That shit you were talking about outside? I know what you mean, man. I've had it with my old lady too."

"Who knew they was gonna get this fat?"

"Mine's always got her hand out for money. Asking every day why I don't get a job. Hey, who's gonna hire a man with a broke leg?"

"Only reason I don't haul ass and file on mine right now," Roger said, "is I think Snorkel Man's about to go down."

That sent Rodney into half a minute of snorts and girlish giggles. Weldon listened from his chair and remembered the time when he could have mopped up the room with the two of them.

Roger said, "The way's he's sucking that air, he ain't got long. So here's what I'm thinking. Old bastard's gotta have some cash put away, and Mandi says he's leaving everything to her and her sister."

"She told you that?"

"Pretty much, man."

"Hey, you and me might be rich, Roger."

"Might be."

"I see us in a hot tub with some Bossier City whores. I'm talking about after my burnt dick gets better."

"If the old man ever gets around to croaking."

"Fuck's he waiting on?"

Chairs scraped, footsteps crossed the floor and the back door opened. Roger said, "Here's my idea, Rodney. Maybe we do something to make it go a little faster."

The door slammed; they were gone. Weldon stayed in his chair.

He was thinking about Galveston, 1961. That year Weldon and his crew had a reverse con going with a shipment of untaxed whiskey. All of them knew that their close friend and associate Clubby Willis, a short man with a bad foot, had turned rat for the other side. So they fed him bad info and waited for him to pass it on. The marks thought they were beating the scam with Clubby's help. But instead of bootleg, they bought a truckload of nothing.

Weldon remembered that he and his boys walked away with ten thousand each. And that the next day Clubby had a swimming accident.

And that trusting people was good. But knowing them was even better.

•   •   •

The front door to the Glen-or-Glenda Gallery was locked.
Eddie Nickles took a quarter from his pocket and rapped
hard on the black plate glass. Saying, "Come on, come on."
Nothing happened, nobody came. His knee was throbbing
after the long walk from the other end of downtown. Jesus,
he wanted to sit down, put some ice on it, swallow a few as-
pirin. But the fire was in him; no time to waste. Eddie kept
rapping on the glass.

Finally the lock clicked and the door opened. Eddie
found himself facing a bald woman. He said, "Lola? Is that
you? Christ almighty, what happened?"

She turned and walked toward the back of the gallery,
running a hand over her bare scalp as she went. "I shaved."

Eddie followed. "I mean, sure, it was purple and green.
But it was still hair. Does Jackie know about this?"

"I did it this morning after he left."

"He's gonna freak. He's gonna think he's looking at Yul
Brynner with tits."

"My opening is next week." Lola stopped at a mirror and
studied herself from a couple of angles. "I wanted to do
something to celebrate."

"That's why they made champagne, Lola. . . . Listen, we
need to discuss something very serious."

They were inside the Nuclear Love Family exhibit. An
episode of *My Mother the Car* showed on the TV, with the
sound off. The faint smell of rotten meat seeped from the
Chamber o' Death. Lola began blowing into one of the Party
Gals that had lost air overnight.

"Lola, you listening?" Eddie sat on the couch, took a
load off his knee. "It's about Jackie."

"What about him?" she said between breaths.

"He's— Lola, honey, please. Look at me, pay attention
for just a minute." Eddie waited for her to get the Party Gal

back to full pressure. "I'm worried that Jackie is in some deep, deep trouble."

"What else is new?"

"He's in way over his head. The guy don't know what he's messing with. It could be very dangerous, and it's gonna take you and me both to get him out."

Lola stared, hand on her hip, at one of the Party Pals. "You think this one's wound needs more blood?"

"First off, you can't say a word to Jackie. Understand?"

"Like he talks to me anyway."

"Second, I'm gonna need you to get some very important information for me. Kind of a secret mission, if you know what I mean."

Lola smiled, interested for the first time. "So I get to be, like, the Girl from U.N.C.L.E.?"

Eddie didn't have an answer. He stared and thought, I'm pinning all this on a bald chick who's about two clowns short of a circus.

"It was a show," Lola explained. "NBC, 1966. Stefanie Powers as April Dancer, in a spin-off of *The Man From U.N.C.L.E.*"

"Uncles, aunts, whatever." Eddie touched her arm just above a Mighty Mouse tattoo. "So you're with me, Lola? Because you and me, we got to work together on this, completely in secret. Hey, it's for Jackie."

Weldon stayed in his chair most of the morning, trying to remember the dozen men he had killed. Actually, the total was thirteen, depending on how you counted one of them. That would be Sylvan Dufraine in 1963.

What a talker Dufraine had been: Sitting with his new friend Weldon in his little photo studio near downtown, jabbering about college football and that dumb bastard Jack Ruby, showing Weldon nude shots of some of his models.

Telling Weldon, "See this one?" He held up a picture of a young woman with no clothes. "Screws like she's hooked up to a car battery."

Dufraine shut up only once. That was when Weldon pulled his short shotgun from under his coat and said, "I'm sorry about this, but we have to go for a ride."

They took Dufraine's car. Weldon made him drive, cuffing him to the steering wheel and pointing him toward south Dallas County. Even with the gun pointed at him, Dufraine kept the motor on his mouth going. Weldon had heard men beg for their lives plenty of times, but he'd never met somebody with a nonstop, last-ditch sales pitch.

"How much you getting for this job?" Dufraine said as he steered the car away from downtown. "This *is* a job, right? I can make you a better deal. How much? What's your fee? I'll double it. Shit, I'll throw in this Cadillac. It's a sixty-one, mint condition. Well, the front end needs some work, but I'll have it down to Steakley Chevrolet in the morning for an alignment. Even put some new tires on it for you."

Weldon had a .12-gauge aimed at the man's liver. Most boys would have crapped their pants by now, but this one was talking business. A little fellow, Weldon thought, but he had some balls. You had to respect that.

"How much?" Dufraine said again.

"Only person I discuss prices with is the client."

"So you've done this before?"

"I didn't say that."

"Sure you did. Listen, let's pull over, have a beer, talk this thing out. I think we can turn this into a win-win situation, we noodle for a few minutes."

"Wish I could," Weldon said. "But I gotta be in Oklahoma City by nine." He was getting five thousand dollars to make absolutely certain a man there named Briscoe Pitts didn't talk to the police about a robbery.

"Hey, pardon me for being such an inconvenience." Dufraine's voice was getting louder. "It's just my life we're talking about. I mean, unless you're on your way to ace some Okie tonight—" He stopped and gave Weldon the eye. "I'll be goddamned. That's exactly what it is. You're killing somebody else later."

Weldon was sorry he had said anything. "Let's leave off talking for a while," he said. Watching the man. Because almost all of them, in Weldon's experience, tried something stupid at some point. Like crashing the car—that seemed to be a favorite. He had one in 1959 who sideswiped a telephone pole on Weldon's side. Weldon put two bullets in the man's head, climbed from the car through a broken window, walked a few blocks and caught a cab. By the time the cops made the scene, Weldon was in a diner miles away, having a piece of pecan pie with vanilla ice cream. So it worked out. All in all, though, he preferred sticking to the plan.

"See this?" Weldon raised the .12-gauge shotgun, an Ithaca Stakeout—thirteen-inch barrel with a pistol grip.

"I see it, I smell it, I feel it."

"Don't want you to forget it's there."

"The day I forget there's a gun on me is the day I deserve to get shot, all right? I'm just trying to work out an arrangement. What's your price to cut me loose?"

He lowered the gun slightly. Dufraine was keeping his cool. Weldon said, "Look, suppose I was to cut a deal with you, take your money and walk away. Somebody out there still wants you dead. I cross them and they'll want me dead too. You think about that?"

"Sure I thought about it. I thought about it the second I

saw the gun." Dufraine kept the car at the speed limit, signaled for turns, drove as if he were giving a friend a lift. Asking Weldon casually, "Who's the client?"

Weldon saw the face of the woman from the Gator Lounge. Saw the body too, and the tight sweater. Christmas Eve, you didn't find many knockouts like that wandering around unattached. Alice, cash up front, with no last name offered. "Client ID is confidential."

"You tell me who it is, maybe I could talk with them, work this whole thing out. And don't worry, you'll still be paid in full, my personal guarantee."

Weldon shook his head. "Sorry. No can do."

"All right, shit." Dufraine blew some air. "Try the back-door approach. Why's somebody after me?"

Weldon had a policy: Tell the men why he was killing them, if they asked. He considered it the decent way to operate, letting them know they weren't dying for no good reason.

"Only thing I can tell you," he said to Dufraine, "is you did something with a camera you wasn't supposed to."

"I knew it!" Dufraine pounded the steering wheel with his uncuffed hand. "Me and my camera, nice sunny day, minding my own damn business in Dealey Plaza. All I wanted was some footage of the presidential motorcade. That too much to ask?"

"Shouldn't be."

"These people that hired you, they're working on rumors. Rumor is, some s.o.b. with an umbrella popped up from behind the fence, started firing shots at the President. Rumor is, I got that on film. Is that what they think I got? Tell your folks there's been a big, big misunderstanding."

"Firing shots at Kennedy?" Weldon said, making sure.

"Was there another President got shot in downtown Dallas last month?"

Any asshole in a bar gave you attitude like that, Weldon was thinking, you would have no choice but to lay him out with a beer bottle across the head. But there was something about having a loaded gun on someone that calmed the nerves.

Dufraine said, "Your people, they got it all wrong. They're hearing the same bad rumors as the government. Hey, two days after the assassination, the FBI's knocking on my door. Tough-guy agent says somebody told them I was on Dealey Plaza with a camera, and they wanted to see what I got. I said, Boy, I got nothing and you can kiss my East Texas ass if you believe I do."

Weldon was thinking that he should have put a few more questions to the doll at the Gator. If she had mentioned the FBI was sniffing around, he might have said see you later. Now he asked Dufraine, "Did the feds take your movie?"

"They'd have to locate it first. I got that thing so hid there's some days even I can't find it. . . . So, see, I didn't tell the government shit, if that's what your people are worried about. Pull over, give them a call, tell them I'll show 'em everything."

"The person I dealt with didn't want a movie," Weldon said. "The person I dealt with wants you dead."

Dufraine drummed his nails on the steering wheel. "Just between you and I, it's the Cubans that's after me, am I right? Spic against hick."

Weldon blinked a couple of times. The girl had sounded American to him. "With blond hair?"

"Hey, they got bleach in Havana."

"You're telling me," Weldon said, "that the commies got the smarts and firepower to smoke the President of America, but they have to hire me to take out little old you?"

"Make sense, don't it? You think they're gonna hang around town after what they did?" Dufraine spent a couple of minutes talking about Oswald, Castro, the Bay of Pigs and Miami. All Weldon could think of was that he might be helping communists. He had worked for thieves, perverts and sadistic maniacs over the years, but he drew the line at reds.

"All right, listen, I got an idea." Dufraine said. "What if they just *think* I'm dead."

Weldon shook his head. "Something you have to understand. There's some cases where people just need to be disappeared. For example, say there's a goddamn rat in Oklahoma that's about to talk to the police about matters that nobody has no business talking about."

"You shut him up, you done your job," Dufraine said. "Proof's in the pudding."

"Exactly. But a case like yours, I suspect they're gonna want a body." Weldon looked down and surprised himself; his gun was pointed at the floor.

"I guess maybe I see your point." Dufraine drove for a while, slumping. But he perked up with, "This person you're gonna nail in Oklahoma. He's a man?"

Weldon nodded.

Dufraine licked his lips. "Now, tell me what he looks like."

Weldon started to say, What in the world you care how he looks? Then he found himself smiling. A man with a plan: he liked that.

Dufraine smiled back. He said, "Are you thinking what I'm thinking? You son of a bitch, I believe you are."

21

Lola dialed the phone. When there was an answer she said, "Jack-man, what are you doing?"

"Just walked into the office. What's up, babe?"

"I had a great time last night."

"Me too. Who knew chocolates from a motel minibar and a gift shop candle could be used for so much fun?"

"You just have to lose your clothes and keep your imagination."

"My new motto," Jack said.

"Anyway." Lola cleared her throat. "Listen, I had to stop by the house this morning to pick up some shoes—"

"Don't do that without me," Jack said. Lola rolled her eyes. He was into the lecture thing again. Telling her, "Don't go there alone. You don't know when the wack boys are coming back."

"I was there for ten seconds, Jack. Everything was fine."

"Next time let me know, and I'll go for you."

"A woman called while I was there. She said she wanted to see you right away, so I told her to try your office."

"She give you her name?"

"I wrote it down but I don't know where I put it."

Silence on Jack's end. Lola could imagine him: eyes closed, shaking his head, face doing the tighten-up. "I think maybe she sounded black," Lola said.

"Was it Treena Watts?"

"Treena Watts, that's it. Treena Watts."

"She found me," Jack said. "I'm meeting with her this afternoon."

"You're meeting with her this afternoon."

"Lola, why are you repeating everything I say?"

"Well, Jack, you get so mad at me when I don't remember things—"

"Since when?"

"—that I thought saying them after you might help."

"Whatever," Jack said. "So how are the Nuclear Loves today?"

"That's why I needed the shoes. One of them just didn't look right in slippers, so I borrowed your wing tips."

"No vinyl sex instrument should be without a pair."

"Anyway, Jack, this woman you're meeting, does she have anything to do with that old case of Eddie's?"

"Yes, she does."

"Yes, she does," Lola said.

"There you go again."

"Sorry. Does she have, like, information for you or something?"

"Lola, what is with you?"

"I'm just worried about you, that's all."

"Look, there's nothing to worry about. I'm not sure what she wants, but I'm sure it's harmless. She may want to talk about her brother—"

"Talk about her brother."

"—but she may just want to complain. I don't know."

"Okay . . . I just, you know . . ."

"Lola, are you all right?"

"I'm fine, Jack. I'm a little nervous about the show, that's all."

"It's gonna be terrific, it's gonna be great. The black-turtleneck crowd'll be slobbering all over you."

"I guess so. . . . Oh, I forgot to tell you, I did something new with my hair."

"Can't wait to see it. Why don't we have a late dinner? I gotta go, my other line's ringing. I'll call you at the gallery around eight."

Lola hung up the phone. Then she turned and said, "You sure it was all right to do that?"

"Absolutely." Eddie Nickles patted her on the shoulder. "How else, Lola, would we get Jackie out of this jam he's in?"

Lola rubbed her scalp. "But he doesn't sound like he's in any trouble."

"That's because," Eddie said, "he just don't know it yet."

Jack and Treena had a sundown dinner at an IHOP in Oak Cliff. Treena ate a lot for a skinny woman. Jack said, "You just come off a fast?"

"Suspicion of white folks makes me hungry." Treena had ordered eggs, hash browns, bacon, pancakes and a fruit cup. She asked Jack, somewhere in the middle of putting it away, "How come you're interested all of a sudden in Mineola?"

"I ran across an old file with some old questions and found myself with a free afternoon."

"That's an answer?"

"Only one I have."

Treena poured syrup on her eggs. "And you thought what? That you'd drive out to the projects and stir up a couple of colored ladies?"

"That's right. I hadn't oppressed any minorities all week, so I was way overdue. . . . Look, you're black, I'm white, I think we've established that. You want to call some kind of truce here?"

Treena gave him a long, slow look while she chewed. Then: "Hard for me to do that when I don't know whose side you're on."

"Ten years ago I was on the side of sending Mineola to prison. That was my job."

"I noticed."

"Things are different now."

"Where's a black woman heard that before?"

"I'm not on the county payroll anymore. Now I'm just a guy who's curious about what really happened."

Treena pushed her plate away. "So you decided just to come on out to South Dallas"—her voice rose—"and ask a few polite questions about my dead brother that the police killed?"

Other people in the IHOP were turning to look. Jack sipped his coffee. "Nicely put," he said, "though a little loud."

Treena took a few deep breaths, calming herself but keeping her eyes on Jack.

He held her gaze and said, "Doing the snoop on a seven-year-old shooting is no way to keep it covered up. That should say something about the side I'm on."

Nothing from Treena but a stare. Jack said, "Some guys play golf. Some drink. Me, I like to poke around."

She shook her head slowly. "That's pathetic, man."

Jack let her have that one. After a couple of beats he asked, "What did your grandmother tell you about Mineola?"

"Who says she told me anything?"

"I don't think you'd be talking to me otherwise. I'm guessing she gave you a little but not enough. So you took a chance and came to me, see if I could help you out."

The glare stayed hard but her voice softened a bit, like someone opening the door a couple of inches and peering out. "You think you can?"

"Let's give it a try." Jack stood, fishing in his pocket for tip change. "Come on, we'll see what happens."

Treena remained in her seat, looking him up and down. Asking him, "Man, don't you have some better clothes than that? Feel like I'm teaming up with Mr. Rogers."

Eddie Nickles left his apartment and stood on the second-floor walkway, gazing into the courtyard. The late-after-noon wind had picked up—from the north, with some bite to it. Trash swirled in the courtyard.

He looked down at an old roll of carpet in the pool; it lay in six inches of green water, like a ship run aground in a scummy ocean. Something was moving down there. Eddie leaned against a rusty metal railing and peered into the fading light. He waited, shivering a little in the wind, then saw it: a rat the size of a poodle.

The bastards put it there, Eddie knew—part of their campaign to force him out of the apartment. Money was changing hands somewhere, wheels turning, gears meshing. The speculators were cutting deals. All that talk of the place being a government redo? Nothing but a scam.

Eddie had seen the tear-down boys sniffing around, watching him, recording his schedule so they could strike while he was gone. He had spotted them spying on him from the street. They sat in their unmarked cars and refused to identify themselves when challenged.

One of them, a fat man in a Ford Tempo, had been out

there several times. Finally Eddie'd had enough. He had gone downstairs, wearing a bathrobe and tennis shoes, and rapped on the man's window. Asking him: You with the developers or the city? The money boys or the government? Saying, They both want me out of here, so which one's paying you?

The guy had stammered and stumbled, coming up with a story that he was just picking up a friend, and pointed at some apartments down the street. Eddie banged on the hood with his fist. Demanding to know, whose money was he taking? The guy zoomed away with Eddie still yelling. Telling him, telling all of them: Eddie Nickles don't budge till he's good and ready.

Now Eddie turned from the railing and entered his apartment. Dinner bubbled on the stove, a can of chili. Eddie walked to his bedroom and opened a nightstand drawer. In it were a pack of rubbers and his .38 Special. He'd had no use for either of them in more than a year.

When Eddie went back outside the rat was still standing on the carpet roll, claiming the place for the vermin kingdom. Eddie steadied his hand on the railing and aimed. A single shot—the sound of it banging off the stucco walls of the empty apartment building—and the world had cut its huge-rat numbers by one.

Nailing a rodent really worked up an appetite. Eddie ate the chili and topped off the meal with some Ritz crackers. When he was done he sat on his couch and stared at the phone. Wanting to call Jackie and say, The fuck are you doing? It made no sense, this messing with the Mineola case, bringing the lowlife's sister into it, hanging with her. Maybe Jackie wasn't the brightest light on the block, but nobody was that stupid.

Fucking guy, he never took anything Eddie said seriously. Eddie could imagine telling him: Jackie, buddy, you've got to lay off this Mineola thing. And the next sound Eddie would hear would be that of a lawyer tap-dancing.

Jackie was one of those people—and Eddie had met a hundred of them when he wore a badge—that you had to grab their attention if you wanted them to see things straight. Come to think of it, Mineola Watts had been another one.

Now seemed like a good time for grabbing attention. Eddie put on his shoes and picked up his gun.

22

The raggedy frame house on Abner Street stood between the Snooty Cockatoo Apartments and a vacant lot, on the fringe of South Dallas, not far from what used to be the Ford plant. Everything here had been new once, Jack thought. Trying to imagine it now was like seeing the ghost of a little boy in a sick old man.

He stopped his Chevy in front of the house and turned to Treena, who was holding a piece of paper with the address. "This it?" he said.

Without a word she opened the car door and walked across a weedy stretch of yard toward the porch. Jack said, "I'll take that for a yes."

Sundown was two hours gone, but the streetlamps had stayed off. The owners of the Snooty Cockatoo hadn't splurged on outdoor lighting either. So Jack searched beneath the front seat, pulling out an old tie and some hamburger wrappers, and found his flashlight. It was a black steel two-foot-long job that was as much club as torch. He knew this because his first ex-wife had used it on the side of his head once. Lucky for Jack, she was a small woman without much upper-body strength.

Now he got out of his car and shined the light on Treena's back. Calling to her, "Hey, you want my help or not?"

She stopped and turned toward him. "If you're coming," she said, "then come on."

He took his time. The Mineola Watts case had waited seven years; another twenty seconds wouldn't matter. Jack played the light over the house as he approached: clapboard with peeling paint, and a broken window that had been patched with cardboard. It was the kind of place where you wouldn't be surprised to find someone like Felicette Cone.

Felicette's name was the one thing Treena had been able to pry out of her grandmother. Somebody told the old woman way back that Felicette might know something about Mineola's death. That's when Mrs. Watts had written her letter to the DA asking for an investigation, the letter Jack still had in his files. Mrs. Watts had been ready to talk, until someone scared her into shutting up.

Treena had asked her grandmother who it was. A white man, that's all Mrs. Watts could remember. It was dark when he came to her door, she said, and that was a long time ago. She told Treena now, Don't go messing with this man.

"All these years later, she's still scared," Treena had said to Jack in the car. "She made me promise I wouldn't try to find Felicette. So now I've told my own grandma a lie."

"Don't say it's a lie," Jack advised. "Pretend you're a lawyer and call it a subjective application of the facts."

Treena had used her bail bond connections to pull Felicette's sheet from the county; she had prostitution and drug arrests going back a dozen years. Jack had done some computer work that tied her to a car registration at the house next to the Snooty Cockatoo.

The car, an old Bonneville, was in the driveway now. But the house looked dark. "Could be nobody's home," Jack said from the steps.

Treena was at the front door, knocking. "You don't know that."

Jack put a ragged circle of yellow on the door and watched as Treena tried the knob. "This hour," he said, "a girl like Felicette's probably out on the street, spreading her special brand of joy."

"Maybe." Treena moved down the porch to a window.

"What are you doing?" Jack said. "You going in? You can't do that."

Treena, without an answer, reached to raise the window. As she did, the porch light came on and the door opened.

Jack found himself facing a white guy as tall as he but twice as heavy, whose expression said he pegged Jack for the process server. The man wore shimmery turquoise jogging pants and a ribbed undershirt. He had long blond hair pulled into a ponytail. From the smell of things—florals and mints in the air—he had just bathed and shaved. He said, "The fuck you want?"

"We're here to see Felicette," Treena said, stepping toward the door, wedging herself in front of Jack.

"Who is?" the man said.

"I'm an old friend of hers. Tell her Treena's here, she'll break out in a big old smile."

"Felicette don't feel like smiling right now."

"She will when she sees me," Treena said. "Go tell her."

The man let his eyes crawl over Treena. Then said, "I got nothing to say about you."

"Well, I got something to say about you." She had her finger in his face. "Which is, how about working your lardy white ass to the back of the house and telling Felicette she has a visitor."

The man was looking past her to Jack now. Saying, "You want to take the bitch off this porch, or do I get the pleasure?"

Jack had Treena by the back of her shirt, pulling her away while she told the man what a piece of shit he was.

"Personal rule," Jack said when he got her to the curb. "Never insult a man who's bigger than a Buick."

"He was about to back down." She knocked Jack's hand away. "He was folding up, man, till you started dragging me away. We'd be in that house right now, you didn't cave at the first sign of trouble."

Jack opened the car door and motioned her in. Treena sat and stared straight ahead. Jack went to the driver's side, got in and started the car. Asking, "Did you catch the scent off that guy?" No answer from Treena. "After sundown," Jack said, "a man doesn't splash on cologne unless he's headed out for the evening."

"You like the way he smells? Maybe you and him can date when this is all over with."

Jack drove while Treena steamed. He made the block, then pulled to the side of Abner Street, about twenty-five yards from the Snooty Cockatoo. Felicette's beat-up Bonneville could be seen in the porch light. Jack looked at Treena and said, "My point is, why fight a guy who's about to leave anyway?"

Treena turned toward him, but Jack couldn't read her face in the dark. He told her, "We'll watch the house from here. While we wait, we can talk, get to know each other better."

"A dream come true," Treena said. "Every night I pray to

the Lord, send some boring middle-age dude my way so I can hear his life story."

". . . So I told them, I'm not a wooden-desk kind of guy. I'm sheet metal desk all the way. Linoleum floors, Styrofoam coffee cups, that's me." Jack looked at Treena. "Know what I'm saying?"

"Fascinating, man." Treena sighed. "Hey, we've been sitting out here in this car for almost an hour and nothing's happened yet. Maybe you noticed this."

Jack started to give Treena some idea of what a marathon stakeout could be like—thought about telling her some tales of twelve-hour behind-the-wheel sit-fests, of peeing in Coke cans, of the feel of vinyl car seats on brutal August afternoons. But before he could crank it up Treena said, "It's about damn time."

The big man in the turquoise jogging suit was walking from the front door to the Bonneville. "Fat boy's all alone," Jack said. "Our lucky night."

"Let's go, man. What you waiting on?"

"How about if we get him out of sight first. Think you could sit still for that?" They watched the car back out of the driveway and head the opposite way on Abner. When the car was out of sight Jack grabbed his flashlight and said, "All right, let's see if Felicette wants to talk."

Treena got out of the Chevy with, " 'Wants to' is not an issue." She reached the front door first and knocked hard. Calling, "Felicette, honey, open up."

"Like I said before"—Jack stood behind Treena—"she might not be here."

"Only one way to find out." Treena moved to the window.

"Not that again. Come on."

"Why not?"

"Texas Penal Code might be one reason. Somebody inside with a shotgun might be another."

"What I'm supposed to do, wait on the porch until Felicette comes out to check her mail?" Treena squatted and tried to push the window open. Nothing moved. "Shit, I think it's locked."

"Even criminals have to worry about crime." Jack moved to the steps. "Let's get out of here."

Treena took off her shoe and banged its heel against the glass. On the second try it punched a three-inch hole in the pane. She reached through the hole and pushed the lock free, then raised the window easily.

Jack said, "You get an employee discount at that bail bond agency where you work?"

There was no screen. Treena rolled through the window and into the dark house. She had the door open in ten seconds. "Tell you one more time," she said. "If you're coming, come on."

Jack stayed where he was. Thinking that there was no reason in the world to walk into that house, except to discover what someone who probably wasn't there might know about something that someone else might have done.

Treena snapped her fingers. "Hey man, just give me the flashlight and wait in the car."

Jack could resist anything but the chance to find out. He said, "I'm coming," and stepped inside.

The house smelled of old cooking grease, and the air tasted as if four or five people had breathed it first. The floorboards creaked under shag carpet when they walked. Jack led with the flashlight. Saying, "Don't turn on the lights in here. We could be seen from outside."

They went to the hallway and passed the bathroom. Jack caught the aroma of the fat man's soap and shampoo. A closed door was in front of them. It had children's crayon scribblings from knee level on down and, up higher, a crunched-in hole that could have come from a fist. Jack turned the knob and pushed the door open.

Another smell hit them. Piss and pus, Jack thought. He swept the room with the light until he caught a figure crouched on a mattress: a woman, holding her hands in front of her face and batting her eyes like someone who had been pulled from a sewer into the bright of day.

"Felicette?" Treena said. "That you, baby?"

Jack felt the wall near the door until he found a switch, and flipped it on. In this room even the light seemed dirty.

Cigarette butts and chicken bones lay on the grimy hardwood floor. Soiled, rumpled clothes were heaped on a rickety wooden chair. And on a flaking tabletop, a spoon, a pack of matches and a hypodermic needle.

"Our Felicette seems to have a hobby," Jack said.

The woman crouched on the bed's bare, stained mattress. She was a sack of bones in a grimy T-shirt. Her scrawny arms and legs were covered with scabbed-over sores. She had hollow eyes—blinking hard, still having trouble with light—and an expression of someone more dimly baffled than afraid. "Where's Shoogie?" she said.

"This is a mess, girl." Treena bent to her, trying to catch Felicette's gaze. "What have you got yourself into?"

"Where'd Shoogie go?" she said again.

Jack turned his head, listening. He reached for the wall and switched off the light, the room falling into inky black. Treena said, "Man, what the hell are you doing?"

"I heard something," he said.

23

Heard what?" Treena said. "What kind of something?"
The darkness in the room seemed to make the stink worse. Jack stepped into the doorway and leaned toward the front of the house, listening. "A car door, maybe. I don't know."

"What kind of answer is that? You freaking on me, man?"

Jack turned back to the bedroom and clicked on the flashlight. Felicette had moved to the far corner of the mattress, against a wall, hugging her scrawny legs. Jack told Treena, "Get up on the bed and keep her there."

"Not without a tetanus shot." Treena waved her hand in the flashlight beam. "Hey, turn the room lights on, let's get back to business. What the hell you waiting—"

She stopped talking with the sound of the front door opening. Jack thumbed off the flashlight switch. Darkness closed over them like water over a stone tossed in a lake.

Felicette said, "Shoogie?"

They heard the front door close. The floor creaked as someone moved across it.

"Shoogie, they're in here," Felicette called.

"Shut her up, Treena," Jack whispered.

"Forget her," Treena said, normal voice. "Turn on the light and let me take care of this."

One psycho on board, Jack thought, and another incoming—one called Shoogie, a bad sign. In Jack's experience, cuddly names made for warped heads.

The creaking moved down the hall toward the bedroom. With it came the rustle of nylon pants legs. Jack stood just inside the door, remembering the big man's shimmering turquoise jogging suit. He could hear labored breathing from the hallway, liquid and constricted: sinus problems. Then he smelled the big man's shampoo.

Felicette shouted, "Two of them's in here."

Jack pointed the flashlight in the direction of the heavy breathing. Switching it on, thinking he could blind the guy for a second and make his move. He saw a glimmer of steel and the big man bearing down on him.

Felicette screamed something. With Treena shouting: "Freeze!"

Jack swung the flashlight, giving it all he had, going for the guy's head. Like a kid at a piñata party: Do it right and the candy would come raining down. He connected with something solid, heard a cry of pain and tried to swing again. Next he knew, Shoogie was barreling into him, turning him around, knocking him onto the bed. The flashlight flew from his hand.

He tumbled into Felicette with Shoogie coming down on them both. The bed collapsed to the floor in a quick rush of noise.

Felicette was screaming as if someone were putting blue

volts to her earlobes. Jack was on top of her in the mission-ary position, his arms pinned beneath him. The big man lay on Jack like a load dumped by a truck, all of it happening in the dark.

Then the man's fingers were on Jack's neck. They tight-ened.

Jack couldn't move his arms. He thrashed against the bulk, trying to shout. Shoogie's fingers slid forward on his neck, going for the throat. Another inch or so, a little more torque to the squeeze, and his airway would start to shut down. It came to Jack that he was about to die, stuck be-tween a running-sore druggie and her three-hundred-pound pimp.

The room lights suddenly were on. Seconds later, the fingers on Jack's throat went limp, then pulled away. Jack heard Treena's angry voice, from somewhere above and behind him. Saying, "You know what this is, mother-fucker?"

Lola drove to Jack's house to bathe and get some fresh clothes. While she was there she thought she would grab a couple of his ties for the Nuclear Loves to wear.

She began to fill the tub with hot water and poured in some green-tea bath oil. Then she lit six candles around the tub and put a tape of monk chants into a player on the toilet tank. The chants gave her an idea: Take Jack to a Hopi sweat lodge over Christmas for a holiday purging of toxins.

Lola was pulling off her black T-shirt when she heard glass break in another room. She turned the water off and put her shirt back on. As she walked toward the kitchen she felt a breeze. A window in the dining room was open, its curtains flapping in the night wind. On the floor, in a small puddle, were fallen flowers and the clear shards of a vase that once stood on the windowsill.

Typical Jack, Lola thought as she knelt to pick up the pieces. Open windows and doors ajar trailed him everywhere he went. He kept his clothes where he dropped them and lost his keys three or four times a week. Jack was always on a tour of the world in his head. She'd once seen him drive off to work while forgetting his shoes.

Back in the bathroom, kitchen window shut now, she added some hot water to the tub and turned up the volume on the monks. The candles glimmered and steam rose from the bath. Lola peeled off her clothes and lowered herself slowly into the water. She closed her eyes and listened to the chants. The bath oil made the water feel like warm silk. She could imagine herself floating, her mind moving into a hypercreative state, opening up like a rose in bloom . . .

Until she felt someone's eyes on her. Lola sat upright and saw a man standing in the bathroom doorway.

"Hey, Lola, sorry to interrupt," Eddie Nickles said. "But I need some more help with this Jackie thing."

Felicette was crying into Jack's ear. Crying and saying, "Oh my Lord Jesus, I'm smashed flat. Please get up, please."

Jack wanted to but he couldn't. He and Felicette were entwined on the bed in some kind of sex-after-death how-to, with the fat man pressing against his back.

Now Treena said, "I already asked you once, and twice is all you're gonna get. Do you know what this is?"

"Yeah," Shoogie said, not happy. "I know."

All Jack knew was that Shoogie had stopped trying to strangle him. So whatever it was, he liked it.

Treena said, "Then get your big butt on the floor."

Slowly the weight lifted off Jack's back, like a bad ache easing. He separated himself from Felicette.

"Facedown," Treena said. "Come on, man, I don't mean next week."

Jack stood, rubbed his neck and turned. Shoogie lay on the floor, fully dressed in his jogging suit, his nose to the hardwood. Treena pinned his ponytail to the floor with her knee. She had a chrome-plated handgun pressed against the back of his skull.

"One little flinch from you," she said to Shoogie, "and you get an instant brain tumor. Understand what I'm saying?"

"Understand," Shoogie said.

Decent diction, Jack thought, for a guy whose lips were mashed against the floor. He said to Treena, "You didn't tell me you had a gun."

"You didn't ask."

Shoogie said something about a doctor. Jack saw blood oozing from one ear and remembered his flashlight swing at the man's head: decent aim under the circumstances.

"You okay?" Treena asked.

Shoogie said, "Hey, I just told you I need a doctor."

"Not talking about you, chump." Treena caught Jack's eye. First time she'd looked at him, Jack thought, without disgust. "Talking about you," she said. "You all right?"

"Better than I was," Jack said. "Tell you what, when Shoogie's on your back you feel like a wet paper plate trying to hold up the Easter ham."

He found the flashlight in a corner of the room. Near it on the floor he saw a twelve-inch hunting knife—the source of the glimmer when Shoogie made his charge. Twice in a week someone had come at Jack with a blade. He was starting to feel like the last chicken at the fat farm.

Felicette, still on the bed, said, "Shoogie, you bring my

present? I got to have it right now. Shoogie, tell the lady with the gun where my present's at."

Treena nudged his head with the barrel. "That's right, tell the lady with the gun."

"Pocket," Shoogie said.

Treena patted him down with her free hand, stopping when she found a lump in his jacket. "I stick my hand in here, something gonna bite me back?"

"Uh-uh."

Treena reached in and came back with a small, clear plastic bag containing some powder the color of dirty beach sand. "And what would this be?"

"Well, it's not brown sugar for Shoogie's famous chocolate-chip cookie recipe." Jack took the bag from Treena. "Some guys know how to treat a lady. Skip the roses, go straight to the Mexican horse."

Felicette said, "Give that to me." She scrambled off the bed.

Jack faced her. Thinking that there was nothing like the eyes of an addict whose train was running late. Felicette tried to grab the bag. Jack closed his fingers around it and stuffed it in his jacket pocket. "When the time is right," he said.

"What time?" she demanded. "Right when?"

Jack looked around the room, then swung open a closet door. A bare bulb hung from the closet ceiling. He pulled the string and got the fully lit view: a couple of skimpy red nightgowns on hangers and a pair of rubber sandals on the floor, next to a rumpled pile of towels over which four or five roaches crawled.

"If you want what I have," Jack said, "if you want your present from Shoogie, you'll go in this closet."

Felicette stared. "What're you saying?"

The expression on Felicette's face—he'd seen it a hun-

dred times as a prosecutor. It was the look people took on
when every kindness and every prayer were nothing but ash.
When they understood they were the sum of their mistakes,
and their lives had dwindled to the one choice before them,
and it wasn't a choice at all.

"I get in that closet," Felicette said, "and you give me the
bag?"

"Absolutely."

Felicette stepped to the table for her matches, a spoon
and syringe. She carried them into the closet like someone
going to the office.

"All the way in." Jack closed the door. "I said I'd give it
to you"—he took a wooden chair and braced it against the
closet's doorknob—"but I didn't say when."

Felicette pounded on the door. "Now," Jack said, "we
need a way to put our man Shoogie on ice." He studied the
boarded-up windows, then asked Treena, "You hold him
there a little while longer?"

"Shoogie tries something," she said, "I give him a blow-
hole on the top of his head so he can be the whale he looks
like."

It took Jack about ten minutes to find what he wanted,
going through every filthy cabinet in the place, finally
checking a pantry next to the oven. On the bottom shelf,
sharing the space with some mouse droppings, was a coffee
can full of nails. A hammer, handle up, leaned against it.

"What are you doing? You gonna nail that closet
door shut?" Treena showed Jack a face that said she still
wasn't sure about him. "How're we supposed to talk to her
then?"

Jack knelt on the hardwood floor and bent close to
Shoogie's bleeding ear. Saying, "I need you to lie real still
while I do my work. Because I wouldn't want this hammer
to slip and hit your pretty face. You with me?"

"Uh-huh."

"Not to mention what the lady with the gun might do." Jack found a two-inch nail in the can. He started at Shoogie's ankle, pulling the loose fabric of his pants to the side and centering the nail on the shimmering turquoise nylon.

"I know I keep asking you this question," Treena said. "But what are you doing now?"

"Nailing Shoogie to the floor." Jack drove the first nail home. "Or his clothes to the floor. Shoogie just happens to be conveniently inside them at the time."

Shoogie moaned. "That's a brand-new suit, man. Bought it yesterday. Shit."

Jack put five nails along each leg, then pounded one below Shoogie's crotch to keep his attention. When he moved to the man's arms, more moans.

"Not the jacket too." Shoogie was almost crying now. "Ain't you got no mercy, man? Fifty-four dollars that suit cost me last week. Plus twenty for the monogram."

"Hey, Shoogie? Next time, I use skin instead of cloth, and I start with your lips. Think about that."

Jack stood after he had driven twenty-five nails. Shoogie was a blue lump on the floor, fringed in steel. Felicette must have grown tired; the pounding and wailing had stopped. "Awfully quiet." Jack glanced toward the closet. "My guess is, she's ready to talk."

Treena put her gun in her pocket. "She's scared out of her mind that the fix won't come in time. Or that it won't come at all. She stays a little longer in there, she'll be chewing through the wall."

"Well, we need what's in her head, and she needs what's in my pocket." Jack removed the chair from against the closet door. "Perfect combination, seems to me."

• • •

Eddie said, "Lola, I don't mean to ruin your bath or nothing, but this thing with Jackie is really starting to shake me sideways."

She was sitting in the tub, candles all around, with some kind of strange music that sounded like a really depressed barbershop quartet. But she was showing some very nice tits, Eddie had to admit, so nice that under other circumstances he might have put a move on the babe then and there. Even with her shaved head. Any other time he'd say something like, Hey, what if I get in the water with you and we play Up Periscope?

Lola said, "Eddie, do you mind?" Giving him a look that told him he belonged in the other room. "A couple of minutes," she said. "Then we can talk."

"Sure thing." Eddie caught one last glimpse of the bazooms, then went to the kitchen. He stood by the sink and worried for a few minutes that it was all a setup, that Jackie had put Lola there naked to distract him and to get the drop. Except Jackie hadn't been around when the drop could be got. So flush that theory. Maybe her actual job was to seduce Eddie, to keep him dreaming of tang all afternoon while Jackie did some dirty work elsewhere to take him down.

Four cigarettes later, and she still wasn't out of the tub. So that was the plan: Stall him. Eddie went back to the bathroom doorway and stared at Lola in the water. She was stretched out, eyes closed, with her hands behind her head, crossed at the wrists as if bound. Eddie almost asked her, You reading my mind?

He stood in the doorway and cleared his throat. "Uh, Lola? Something occurred to me out there in the kitchen."

She sat up, giving him the tit display again but making a

good show of being annoyed. "Eddie, I told you I'll be out in a minute."

"Bear with me a sec, Lola." Eddie stepped to the toilet and switched off the tape of the depressed barbers. "Just want to run one thing past you. Now I'm thinking out loud here, all right? But let me ask you this. What if we made Jackie believe—and don't say no right off the bat, give it some thought. But what if we made Jackie believe you'd been, you know, kidnapped?"

Felicette was docile as she emerged from the closet, but with bad shakes. Jack and Treena took her into the kitchen, where all three sat at a plastic and chrome table like a family discussing household chores and homework. "I need my shit, man," Felicette told Jack. "Right now, you gotta give it to me."

"Won't be long now." Jack, feeling some guilt about locking a helpless junkie in a closet, had softened his tone. "We have to talk a little bit first."

"Gimme my shit, I'll talk all you want. We talk all day, all night, you lay it on me."

He was getting a good look at her for the first time. She had short red hair, and her sunken cheeks showed some purple acne scarring. Her neck was long and slender: A suggestion of gracefulness, Jack thought, from when she had something to be graceful about. Her eyes made him think of broken eggs.

Treena glanced back toward the bedroom. Asking, "That's where you turn your tricks? In there with the chicken bones?"

Felicette nodded. "I did five dudes today, so Shoogie owes me big."

Treena said, "Fat man keeps a girl locked in a room,

make her hump whatever loser drops by with some cash, they got jail cells reserved for people like that." She lit a cigarette and passed it to Felicette. "You had a blood test lately, baby? Seen a doctor in the last year? Bet you got some interesting stuff swimming around inside of you."

"Don't need no doctor." Felicette hugged herself but couldn't stop shaking. "Only need one thing."

"Felicette . . ." Jack leaned forward, trying to catch the woman's skittering focus. "Remember a cop named Eddie Nickles?"

"That what this is about?"

"You remember him?"

"Eddie Nickles? That what all this shit's about?"

Jack looked at Treena. Dragging a seven-year-old memory out of Felicette would be like trying to drive a junk car cross-state on bad tires. He said, "Listen, Felicette—"

"Me and Nickles used to party sometime."

"What?" Treena leaned forward. "When?"

"Back . . ." Felicette flapped one hand. "You know . . . when Nickles was doing all his po-lice shit."

"What kind of party?" Jack said.

"What kinda party you think, man?" Felicette pulled on the cigarette and blew the smoke out in a hurry. Looking at Jack with, Get my bag now?

"Did you know Mineola Watts?" Treena said.

"That what this is about?"

"Mineola was my brother." Treena put her hand on Felicette's. "Eddie Nickles killed him. I want to know why. I need to know what you know about them."

Felicette shrugged and pulled her hand away. "Long time ago." Big sigh, gaze bouncing around the room, hand rubbing a runny nose, face twitching a couple of times. Then:

"Mineola and Nickles was selling together. Everybody knows that. I need that bag now."

"Selling what?" Treena said.

"You for real, bitch?"

"Selling crack cocaine," Jack said.

Treena shook her head. "I don't believe that. Mineola came out of prison, he went straight. He was about to get a job, he just got married."

"It's true, isn't it?" Jack waited until Felicette faced him. "They had a crack operation going."

"You know all about it, why you asking me?"

"It was a lucky guess," he said, telling the truth. "Here's another one. You were there when Eddie shot Mineola."

"How I'm supposed to remember that far back?"

"Try," Treena said. "And this time tell the truth."

"Can't nobody remember that long ago."

"Not unless you have"—Jack pulled the bag of heroin from his pocket and dangled it from finger and thumb— "Dr. Flippo's amazing memory powder."

Felicette shifted her twitches into higher gear, but her stare stayed on the bag. She drew short breaths and let them out through her mouth. Jack had never seen anyone want anything so bad; it was like greed laced with rabies. He said, "Tell us what happened when Eddie shot Mineola."

"I got to have that," she said.

"And you will." Jack twirled the bag. "Soon as you tell us your story."

"Can't wait no more."

Jack leaned closer: the grave robber, back in business. "Only thing holding this up, Felicette, is you."

He gave her half a minute to chew herself up inside. Then, hammer time. Jack stood and said, "Fuck it,

Treena, she won't talk to us." He leaned over the kitchen sink. "So this smack of hers is going to make some fish high."

Felicette came out of her chair with a noise like someone whose baby had been snatched. She tried to climb over Jack's back, clawing at him and grabbing for his hands, screaming that she would kill him if he poured it down the drain. Jack hadn't even opened the bag.

Treena bear-hugged Felicette and carried her back to her chair. Jack stayed by the sink, watching. The hem of Felicette's dirty T-shirt rode up to her midriff as she struggled and kicked; she wore no underwear. Jack caught a pink flash of the product. He turned away and closed his eyes, so sad for a moment he had to lean against the sink to stand.

"Calm down, honey. That's it, easy." Treena kept her arms wrapped around Felicette, but talked softly to her until her rage cooked down to sobs and shudders. Another cigarette calmed her some more. Jack asked, "You saw Eddie Nickles shoot Mineola?"

She nodded. They waited while Felicette smoked and the leaky faucet dripped. Finally Felicette said, "We was all there in the apartment talking about, I don't know, Mineola owed Nickles some money or something. I can't remember. Nickles was yelling at him, and Mineola yelling back. Then all I know, the guns come out."

Jack watched Treena's face. "Then what?" she said. "What happened then? Come on, talk."

"Both of them was pulling guns." Felicette's cigarette slipped from her fingers and fell to the floor, but none of them bent to pick it up. "Nickles shot first, got Mineola right in the chest."

"Oh, God," Treena said.

"That's all I know."

"What about Shauntelle?" Treena said. "Mineola's wife."

"Ain't nothing more to say." Felicette kept her face on Treena's. "Because soon as Nickles shot Mineola, I ran outta that apartment, and I got my car and I didn't stop driving till I got to my sister's house in Shreveport, Louisiana. Three, four years I stay in Shreveport, just to hide from him. That Nickles is a cold one, man."

This is unbelievable, Eddie thought. Lola had the same kind of look on her face that Iris used to get. Iris would show it to him right before she announced, You're crazy, Eddie. Six years of marriage, he must have seen that look ten thousand times.

Now Lola said, "Are you out of your mind?" With Eddie telling himself, man, they're all alike. "Is this like some game between you and Jack?" she said. "It's the loopiest thing I've ever heard."

She stood in the tub, the water dripping from her, and reached for a towel. Eddie watched. Thinking, the bitch has a dozen tattoos and a *green* bush, for Christ's sake—where do you buy the dye for that?—and she's calling me nuts? He said, "Just think about it for a sec, Lola."

"There's nothing to think about."

"No, listen. We make Jackie believe somebody's grabbed you, so we can divert him. See what I'm saying? So we can get him off this Mineola Watts case he's on."

"Eddie?" She wrapped the towel around herself. "No."

He stayed in the bathroom for a moment, watching her dress. She acted as if he wasn't there.

Finally Eddie said, "You're right, Lola. And when you're right, you're right."

"Thank you."

"Hey, pretending to have somebody grab you is not a good idea. I mean, like you said, it's not a game." Eddie pulled his gun from the pocket of his jacket. "So let's just do the real thing."

24

Roger and Rodney Gillich had blown up the junk car just after sundown. Weldon Chaney had watched as Roger fastened the dynamite to the bottom of the car. And Weldon had listened as Roger crawled from under the car and said, "That'll lift this baby right off the ground and then some. Lemme have the remote, Rodney."

"Why should I?" Rodney said.

The half brothers were drunk, with Rodney deeper in the tank thanks to his pain pills. His words came out soft in the middle and blurred around the edges. He was hugging the remote control and asking Roger, "Hey, fucknut, how come you get to have all the goddamn fun?"

Weldon watched the boys have a slow-motion struggle over the remote control. Rodney tried to run away with it, limping on his ankle cast. Roger tackled him, and the two of them rolled in the dust of what used to be Weldon's goat pen.

Roger finally won. He stood and blew dirt from the re-

mote's keypad. "Next time you pull that shit," he told
Rodney, "I stuff one of them sticks of dyno up your ass and
push the button. Speaking of buttons, it's party time."

He punched the keys with his bird finger, mouthing,
"Six, nine, six, nine." The digital version of "Candle in the
Wind" came from the car, and then the blast: a shock wave
that almost knocked Weldon down. The old Chevy looked
like a skeleton within a body of orange flames. Weldon
could feel the heat from a hundred feet away.

Roger stared. "Out of fucking sight. Who's got the
marshmallows?"

Rodney limped over. "Next time, Roger, I get to do it.
And I ain't gonna beg. I'm telling you straight up, man,
them explosions is supposed to be shared."

As the fire burned down, the boys started drinking again.
It took Rodney half an hour to pass out in the dirt of the goat
pen. Roger, sipping from a bottle of Rebel Yell bourbon, fell
asleep in a lawn chair.

Weldon stood in the yard and looked at the sky. It was a
crystal-clear, cold night, with a bright round moon rising
out of the trees. He turned toward the house, its lights burning and curtains open, and saw Brandi and Mandi through
the window. They were in the kitchen, and appeared to be
making a cake. Sweet girls, just like their mother. They deserved better than these two worthless drunks.

He breathed his bottled air and closed his eyes. The wind
picked up, knifing in from the north and rattling the brown
leaves that clung to the scrub oaks. But the raw cold didn't
bother Weldon. He was busy making one final plan.

The husk of the Chevy smoldered. With Weldon thinking
that the last time he had seen a car completely in flames was
in 1963. It was Sylvan Dufraine's Cadillac, and there was a
dead man in the front seat.

• • •

"There's no meat in this spaghetti," Mr. Marty said to his wife. "What is this, noodles with V-8 juice poured on?"

"The term spaghetti refers to the type of pasta, dear." Nita Dufraine looked across the table and smiled.

"Bullshit," Mr. Marty said. "The word spaghetti is short for spaghetti and meatballs. Just like when you say Cowboys, people know you mean the Dallas Cowboys. Same damn thing."

"Your cholesterol numbers were way, way up on your last check. And your triglycerides were high."

"Just like Hank is short for Hank Williams. Ask you something else. Suppose I bought a new pair of shoes, got 'em home and there wasn't no shoelaces included."

Nita gave a weary shake of her head. "That's ridiculous."

"My point exactly."

They ate without talking for a while, watching TV, a PBS show about crocodiles. "Remember Manzanillo?" Mr. Marty said out of the blue. "Nice beach they had there. Bet it's just as pretty now as it was thirty-five years ago."

"I remember huge flies and the smell of garbage," Nita said.

"That movie *10*? Had the girl with the big jugs and the beads in her hair? Remember that?" Mr. Marty didn't wait for an answer. "That was Manzanillo. Looked pretty good in that movie."

Nita put her fork down and looked straight at her husband. "Why are we talking about Mexico?"

"Just popped into my head, that's all."

"I spent seven long years in Mexico. I never, ever want to go back."

"Dallas gets cold in the wintertime. Hear that wind whipping up outside?"

"I never heard you complain about it before."

"A man gets a few years on him, his blood starts to thin. Especially when he don't get enough red-meat meatballs. . . . So maybe Mexico ain't the answer. There's other places. I hear the Bahamas is nice and warm."

On the TV crocodile eggs were hatching. Nita Dufraine said, "You're going to do it, aren't you? Tell me the truth."

Here she goes, Mr. Marty was thinking. Here comes the Nita Dufraine fireworks show. He asked her, "What's that supposed to mean, exactly?"

Nita removed her glasses and rubbed the red indentions on each side of her nose. The heat was building. She said, "Why would you do this now? We have our life here, we have our house, we have our store."

"Selling party hats and plastic dog turds." Mr. Marty kept his gaze on the television screen. "You're right. How could a man give up all that?"

Nita put her glasses back on and looked away. "I thought you were happy."

"Like I said before, could be a lot of money out there, just waiting."

"We have some money. Not a lot, but we're doing all right."

Mr. Marty waved toward the television. "Look at that, nothing but a movie about a bunch of black boys trying to catch an alligator, and it's on network TV. What do you suppose somebody paid for that? Plenty, that's what."

Nita shoved her chair back and stood. "We talked about this just the other night." Her voice was louder than the TV now. "We talked it all out, and you said to me, Nita, don't worry. Didn't you? Well, answer me."

"They pay big for alligators, so what do you think they'd cough up for a film like we're sitting on? A bundle, that's what. Through the nose, that's what. They'd have to haul the cash over on a freight train, we cook the right deal."

"The right *deal?*" Nita slapped her hands against the table, hard enough to make the salt and pepper shakers jump. "And what if it all comes out? What if everything that you did, everything that *we* did—"

"That ain't gonna happen." Mr. Marty watched her. Thinking that any minute now she would break something.

"Well, what if it does happen? What if everything goes"—she raised her plate of spaghetti to eye level and dropped it—"just like that? When you thought about this deal you were going to make, did you think about that?"

The plate had broken in half. Red sauce oozed from the break and spread across the plastic tablecloth. Mr. Marty said, "Thirty-six years is a long time, Nita. People forget, people die. People disappear."

She was burning her stare into him. "All right," Mr. Marty said, "it's true, we all know it. Back in nineteen sixty-three, somebody was willing to kill for what they thought was on that film. No question about that." He shrugged. "Hey, Sylvan Dufraine, may he rest in peace. Sylvan Dufraine, who made me the man I am today."

"I don't think that's funny." Her voice was breaking, the storm over.

"Good-looking Sylvan Dufraine, cut down in his prime 'cause he pointed his camera the wrong way at the right time. 'Cause he thought he might make a little extra money. There's some old boy standing behind the fence with his umbrella, and good-looking Sylvan just had to roll film."

"Stop it." She was crying now.

Mr. Marty stood and walked toward the phone, shaking his head. Amazing. All these years, and she hadn't changed. She got hot, she got crazy, she cooled down. The only differences, now that her hair was gray and she had an old lady's body, were the intensity and the duration. Back when Nita was a knockout, when she was Mrs. Sylvan Dufraine, with a build that would stop traffic, it would take hours—sometimes days if she was extra upset—for her to cycle through her runaway anger. He had never seen a woman become consumed with it, moving at times into cold fury, the way Nita had done when she was young. But now she took care of it in a couple of minutes. The same thing, Mr. Marty thought, had happened to his erections.

"Look at this mess." Nita wiped at the leaking sauce with a paper napkin.

From the kitchen Mr. Marty said, "It's time old Sylvan's work finally paid off for us, hon. All this time we've had that film in the vault, and it ain't made a penny for you or me. Might as well been a hundred frames of a dead cat."

He picked up the phone and went to the refrigerator, where a business card was attached with a magnet shaped like a mushroom. "Sooner or later, you got to cash in your chips." He dialed. "Which I plan to do right about now."

The phone rang three times. When there was an answer Mr. Marty said, "That you, Shitouttaluck?"

Jack listened to the little man yammer, then said, "Keep your shirt on, I'll drop by in half an hour." He put the phone on the car seat and muttered, "Guy's something else," before turning back to Treena. "Sorry for the interruption. You were saying?"

They were in Jack's car, with Treena staring at Shoogie's house. Asking, "You believe all that stuff Felicette said?"

Jack shrugged. "You have to ask yourself why she would make up a story like that. She didn't know what we wanted to hear. All she knew was that she had to have her score."

"Tears me up to think about it. I mean, taking Mineola down for no reason. And you *know* Nickles shot Shauntelle."

"No, we don't. She was killed by Mineola's gun, remember."

"What are you trying to say, man?"

"Best guess? She went down in the crossfire."

"Mineola wouldn't have let that happen. He loved Shauntelle."

Oh, yeah, Jack thought about saying, that Mineola was one great vessel of love and compassion. "Bullets start flying, people get hit by accident."

"I don't believe it happened that way," Treena said.

"Who knows?" Jack glanced at the house. Thinking of the way they had left Shoogie, still nailed to the floor. And Felicette: cooking her dope over a candle, the belt around her arm, syringe at her side. She was pushing her fingers at the inside of her forearm, looking for a vein, when Jack and Treena walked out.

"I knew Eddie was crazy," he said. "But I never pegged him for dirty. All that stuff about running crack, that was news to me."

"What world you been in?"

He let that one pass. They sat in silence until Treena said, "You think she'll testify?"

"Felicette? Testify?" Jack laughed. "Now that I'd pay to see."

"I don't see what's so goddamn funny."

"Look, I'm sorry." Jack softened up, tried to sound earnest. "The DA can't exactly dangle a bag of smack in her face the way we did to assure her cooperation. But say for the sake of argument she agreed to talk."

"She'd talk. You get her straight, get her out of that house, she'd talk."

"Say she did. You think any grand jury in Dallas will look at a seven-year-old case—a closed case, by the way—against an ex–police officer based on what some junkie whore says?"

"If she's telling the truth they should."

"Yeah, well . . . your idealism is touching."

Treena turned toward him. In the dark of the car he could feel the anger pouring off her. "So the man who killed my brother," she said, "just walks free."

Jack started to say, Listen, the stories I could tell. Remembering how it felt to see killers and rapists dance away after cops lost the evidence, or a witness flaked, or a juror looked at a defendant and saw the shadow of his own troubled son. He said, "You spend enough time in court, shit, you spend a day in court—"

"Oh boy, here we go."

"—you learn pretty fast that things don't always turn out for the best. A lot of times, they just turn out."

Treena cranked it up. "You think I don't know that, coming from where I do? You think we sit around the projects and smell roses all day long?"

Jack waited while Treena gave him two loud minutes of lessons from growing up in South Dallas. When she was done he said, "I'm sorry you had to hear that about your brother that way. I really am."

Treena exhaled through her teeth and looked away. After a moment she said quietly, "My own doing. Not like you forced me to be in there."

Jack laid his hand on her shoulder, half expecting her to shake it off. She didn't. He said, "Best thing we can do for Felicette right now, believe it or not, is call the cops. Get her away from Shoogie, maybe she'll land in a program, get some help. Not likely, but it's her only chance that I can see."

Treena was still looking away. "You're probably right for once."

Jack started the car. "I have a client to visit. You want to ride along?"

"Sure, why not."

"We can talk on the way about Eddie, give his situation some thought."

"I know Mineola did some bad things. But he didn't deserve to get shot like a dog by some crooked cop. Shauntelle didn't deserve to die either."

Jack pulled from the curb and gassed the Chevy. "We might not be out of the game yet."

"Maybe I'll take care of him myself."

"What, you and your gun? Some kind of Wyatt Earp thing? Do that and you'll be the one ends up in prison, not Eddie. Don't go stupid on me."

"I'm not going stupid, but I'm not going soft either."

Jack drove past the back end of Fair Park, on a wide boulevard lined with trees and empty grassy lots. A neighborhood had been here once—small frame houses slowly giving way to age and termites, many of them the homes of old women who would sit on the porch breezing their faces with funeral home fans. That was before the city decided the park needed a nice green border so that the arriving opera crowd wouldn't have to gaze upon shabbiness. The locals were forced out and the houses torn down.

A mystical sort of guy, cruising the boulevard now, might feel as if he were plowing his car right through the memories of kitchens and bedrooms, mowing down the ghosts of families. That wasn't Jack. He believed in tangents, not parallels.

His father's shop had been just down the street, hanging on to a corner of the park in an old corrugated steel building, next to the railroad tracks. No air-conditioning in

Flippo Bros Welding, and on some August afternoons the
thermometer on the loading dock might hit 110. The old
man would come home with salt stains on his shoes where
he had sweated through the leather, announcing proudly to
Jack and his brother that he hadn't taken a single piss all
day. Which explained why, once or twice a year, he would
double over with kidney stones.

Jack's father spent forty years there sweating through his
shoes. One morning he had a heart attack in the middle of a
welding job, and was dead before he hit the concrete floor.
Jack's mother unloaded the business a month later, and the
buyers took about two days to knock the building down and
sell the corrugated steel for scrap. Jack imagined it now in
Korean cars or Chinese sewing machines.

That was how the past stayed in the present, he thought
as he drove: in ways you couldn't see and places you never
expected.

"Maybe the thing to do with Eddie," Jack said, "is let
him know we know something. Maybe even make him
think we know more than we really do, and see where it
leads. We have to be careful, though. A guy like him, you
don't know what he'll do. He's one of those, you press
down here and it comes out over there."

Lola said, "I played along this far just to see, you know,
what it would be like. Just to kind of check out the whole
hostage thing as an artistician, right? Which I've done. I can
access that level of consciousness now."

This bald chick, Eddie was thinking, is about to drive me
crazy. "Sit the fuck down," he said.

"Your gun added like this adrenaline-surge thing I'd
never felt before. It really shows you a completely new dimension. I mean, I got this incredible Patty Hearst flash in
my head."

"And when you sit down, Lola? Shut the fuck up too."

"So I'm not saying I didn't get anything out of this, because I did. But I need to be back at the gallery now, Eddie.
My opening is coming up and I've still got mushroom cloud
footage to edit into the video loop."

They were in Eddie's apartment. He tried to keep the gun
on her while searching a closet for a pair of handcuffs.
Eddie stopped looking when Lola said, "So are you going
to give me a ride or not?"

She bent over the coffee table and picked up the phone.
Saying, "If you're not, I'm calling a cab."

Eddie stepped toward her, the gun flat against his palm,
and swung his arm. The gun struck her on the side of the
head, just above her ear. She fell on the couch and curled
into a fetal position, covering her face with her hands. "You
think we're playing around here?" Eddie said. "That what
you think?" He swung again and caught the back of her head.

Jesus, she had gone down easy. Eddie expected more
fight out of someone like Lola. He stood over her and listened to her whimper. With Eddie thinking, and where have
we seen this before?

"Whoa, Lola, what a rush I just got." He put the gun to
her ear. "Hard to believe, but this is not the first time for
yours truly to be in a position like this."

No answer from Lola; all of a sudden the mouthy artistician was out of gas. Eddie said, "Except there's a few differences with this one. The first time, Lola, we had the small
matter of a thieving piece of monkey shit named Mineola
Watts. You listening, Lola? I can't hear a thing you're saying, you stay all rolled up in a ball like that."

Still no answer. Eddie gave her the story anyway: how
seven years ago he found out Mineola was skimming prof-
its on a business operation, so Eddie had to hunt the fucker
down for the purposes of setting him straight.

"I had to shoot his ass, Lola. Had no choice but." Lola was shaking. Eddie ran the tip of his gun barrel along the rings in her ear. "And guess what? He had his old lady there too."

Eddie pressed the gun against Lola's head. Remembering what he did with the other woman, and wondering if he should do the same with this one.

25

W e're going to see a man named Mr. Marty," Jack said.

Treena gave him a sideways glance. "Don't tell me. Old dude with goofy clothes."

"How'd you know?"

"Name like that, what else could he be?"

"He's also a client. My only client, in fact. Like a lot of people I've worked for, he's not telling me everything."

"Imagine that."

Jack went north on the tollway. The road was bathed in sulfuric light from the overhanging streetlamps. The color of it always made him feel as if he were driving through a formaldehyde spill. He said, "Actually, the guy's been a complete pain in the ass."

"But you need the money."

"Money's not the issue."

"Hey, money's always the issue, far as I can tell. Unless it's sex. That what it is? Don't tell me you're putting the bone to somebody named Mr. Marty."

Jack gave her the quick version: the umbrella man film, Sylvan Dufraine's unexplained death, the redheaded crazy coming to Jack's office, the high-speed chase in the Lincoln with gunshots. "I'm not after the money. I'd just like to know why somebody's trying to kill me. Actually"—he tapped the steering wheel with his fingers—"I'd just like to know."

"Know what?"

"Whatever there is to know." He showed her a smile. "It's a sickness."

"Uh-huh." Treena looked at him, nodding slowly. "Sounds to me like you're a dressed-up Peeping Tom. . . . This assassination movie the man's supposed to have. You seen it?"

"Haven't."

"Then how do you know he really has it?"

"I don't."

"So you got people shooting at you over something that might not even exist."

"It's possible."

"Somebody ever kills me, man, I hope it's for something real."

"I'm guessing you'll give them ample reason," Jack said. "Listen, what I'd like you to do is see if you can get Mr. Marty's wife alone. Find out what she thinks about all this."

"The man who made the movie in the first place—who killed him?"

"Don't know that either."

Treena shook her head. "When you get together with this Mr. Marty, you ever actually put any questions to him? Or you just sit there like a lump and hope he volunteers the information?"

Jack switched on the radio, see if he could find some Conway Twitty to drown the woman out. After a few seconds Treena reached over and turned it down. Saying, "And what's Eddie Nickles got to do with all of this?"

"Well . . ." Jack cleared his throat. "Eddie announces he's looking for the umbrella man film, and up pops Mr. Marty. So maybe there's a connection and maybe there's not. I'm still trying to figure that out too."

Treena looked out the window. "Good thing I'm coming along, man. Leave this deal up to you, ain't nothing gonna be found out."

Who's the colored girl?" Mr. Marty said. He and Jack sat in Mr. Marty's living room, amid the photos and the ranch-hand furniture. A gas fire was roaring around the fake logs in the fireplace. Mr. Marty wore a white turtleneck shirt, gabardine slacks in a burgundy and brown check and fleece-lined bedroom slippers. He looked like a guy out to pick up chicks at the nursing home canasta party. "She your date for the evening?"

"She's working with me," Jack said.

"Bet she works all night long, don't she?" Mr. Marty winked. "She work better on the top or on the bottom?"

Jack glanced toward the kitchen, where Treena had gone with Mrs. Marty. Treena had handled it like a pro, gushing about the loveliness of the house and asking for a tour. Now Jack said, "Don't we have some business to talk about?"

"You're right, we do." Mr. Marty looked Jack over. "Anybody tried to kill you lately?"

"Not since the last time we talked."

"Could mean the heat's off, then."

"What heat would that be?"

"Put it this way"—Mr. Marty sniffed—"if the mob was still worried about this, they'd of been all over you like flies on last week's ham sandwich. Same with the CIA, if the spookies still got a dog in this fight. The Cubans, I don't know about. They been too busy stealing Miami from America to care about anything else."

"So if I'm still breathing," Jack said, "that must mean it's safe for you to raise your head."

Mr. Marty winked. "That's why I'm paying you the big bucks. Speaking of which, I assume you did what you was supposed to and put some feelers out."

"Feelers?" Jack was looking at the ceiling above the fireplace. There was a slot about five feet long and two inches wide. "I talked with someone, if that's what you mean."

"What kind of someone? A bartender? Your proctologist while he had his finger up your ass?"

Jack stood and walked toward the fireplace, gazing at the slot. "He runs a museum devoted to conspiracies."

"All right, good. Now we're talking. The umbrella man footage—what kind of price is this boy proposing?"

"He said possibly seven figures."

"The hell's that mean, exactly?"

"He says he would have to see the film to know."

"Jesus Christ, look . . ." Mr. Marty shook his head, annoyed. "I told you what's on it. You tell him what I said?"

"He says he would have to see it." Jack was at the fireplace, staring up at the long slot. "You got a screen up there?"

"See the button next to the mantel? Give it a push."

Jack touched what looked like a doorbell button. There was a low electric hum, and a white movie screen dropped from the ceiling. "Just like a big-shot Hollywood producer." Jack pointed directly across the room at a cabinet. "The projector in there?"

"Goddamn, you're smart."

"You watch a lot of movies?"

"When I feel like it, which ain't now."

"I was thinking we could watch the umbrella man film together."

"Sure, why not? Maybe make some popcorn, show a couple of Tweety Bird shorts first." Mr. Marty stood, skittered to the fireplace and pushed the button. The screen disappeared into the ceiling. "You think I just leave that film lying around any old place? Like maybe I got it over there in a kitchen drawer, next to the spare flashlight batteries?"

The light from the gas fire shone on Mr. Marty's face from below. Jack saw fine white scars along his jawline leading to an off-angle dimple on his chin. His nose looked like a wad of putty that had fallen from the sky and landed on his face. "I'd like to know," Jack said, "what's on that film."

"Friend, the whole world wants to know what's on that film. And they will, when the price is right. That's your job, in case you forgot."

Jack leaned against a chair with wagon-wheel halves for armrests. He could hear the women talking in the kitchen but couldn't catch the words. On the table next to him was the glamour shot of young Nita Dufraine.

Mr. Marty was saying, "So are you gonna tell me or not?"

"What?" Jack turned from the picture to see the little guy's big grin and his peep show eyes. "What did you say?"

"The colored girl." Mr. Marty pointed toward the kitchen. "You never did say if you was dining on dark meat."

"You're right. I didn't say."

"Hey, don't get me wrong, I ain't criticizing." Mr. Marty held up one hand as if testifying. "First piece I ever had was chocolate. That's how every white boy in Seffner, Texas, broke his cherry when I was coming up. I got mine from a little fourteen-year-old nigger girl on a bare mattress in the back room of her mama's house. Cost me five dollars and a box of Jujubes."

"Time to go, I believe." Jack called toward the kitchen: "You ready, Treena?"

"Two pumps and a squirt was about all it amounted to."

Jack had a quick unappetizing vision of a teenage Mr. Marty humping away in an East Texas shotgun shack. Then it hit him. Mr. Marty had talked too much.

Treena and Mrs. Dufraine came from the kitchen, and they all moved toward the front door. Words and people were swirling around him, but Jack—with his mind wrapped around Mr. Marty's bare-mattress merriment—wasn't picking up much of it. Mr. Marty said something about Jack's getting back to him with an exact figure for the film. He added that Jack needed to get on this right away. Someone opened the front door, and Jack and Treena stepped out.

The two of them walked to the car with Treena saying, "What's with you? That little old man kick you in the head?"

"Something's not right," he said.

"Ain't that the truth."

"You drive." Jack handed her his keys. He got in on the passenger side and reached into the back seat for an accordion file stuffed with papers. "I think it's in here. I'm pretty sure that's where I put it."

"I'm happy for you." Treena started the car and backed out of the driveway. "Whatever the hell it is you're talking about."

"Guy I used to work with at the DA's office had his own theory of witness examination." Jack searched the papers in his file. "We called it Creighton's Interrogatory Dictum, since that was his name."

"Uh-huh. Listen, man, you want to know what Mr. Marty's wife said?"

"When Creighton retired we had it engraved for him on a brass plaque. Know what it was?"

"At the Dallas County DA's office? Probably something along the lines of, if the man's black, he must be guilty."

"Creighton's Interrogatory Dictum was—you ready? It was"—Jack cleared his throat—"'Get the key to their trunk of lies.'"

Treena drove and said, "Dude sounds like a boatload of fun."

"The key to their trunk of lies. Has an almost biblical ring, doesn't it?"

"Man, what Bible you been reading?"

"I think Mr. Marty just handed me his key." Jack kept going at the papers in the file. "If I find this clip I'm looking for, I'll know. . . . I thought I put it in here, I'm sure I did. Jesus, what a mess."

"Ask you this one more time and then I'm not gonna try it again. You want to know what the man's wife said or not?"

"Yeah, I do. Just give me one minute—here it is." Jack pulled a sheet of paper from the file: the smudgy microfilm copy of a story from the *Dallas Times Herald,* December 31, 1963. With the headline, "Slain Man ID'ed as Dallas Photographer."

"Here we go." Jack ran his finger down the page. Saying, "'Sylvan Dufraine . . . found burned to death in his car in south Dallas County . . . motive unknown.' All right, listen to this. You listening? It says, 'Dufraine will be buried Thursday in a family plot at Pine Grove Cemetery, in the East Texas town of Seffner.'"

Treena, driving, said, "Dead is dead wherever it is."

"Doesn't add up." Jack folded the paper and put it in his pocket. "Just now Mr. Marty told me he was living in

Seffner when he was fourteen. Two days ago he said he was raised by his aunt and uncle in Louisiana."

"Man can't keep his story straight."

"Takes a great memory to be a good liar."

"So he's lying about where he was raised up. So what? And what's this got to do with bringing the hammer down on Eddie Nickles? That's what I want to know."

"Not sure yet." Jack opened the glove box, looking for a map. He found it between some old Dairy Queen napkins and a tape of Buck Owens's greatest hits. "If Seffner, Texas, is where they had the family plot, I'm gonna guess that's where the family was too."

"People like to keep the bodies close to home. Unless your notion of fun is to drive a long ways to look at tombstones."

Jack stared at her. "That's a great idea."

"You're joking."

He flipped on the dome light and unfolded the map. "We could make it in two hours. We'll get some family names off the graves and make phone calls later. Dialing for descendants. Maybe find out what the deal is with this Mr. Marty."

"Ask you one more time. What's that got to do with Eddie Nickles?"

Jack smiled. "Who knows what's in the trunk of lies?"

Treena complained for a while—waste of time, wild-goose chase, better things to do—then pulled over and told Jack he would have to drive. They were ten miles outside Dallas when Jack said, "Oh, yeah—what did Mr. Marty's wife tell you?"

"She's all upset because he wants her to move to Mexico. Says they lived there long time ago and she never wants to go back."

"Mexico. She say why?" Then: "Shit! I was supposed to take Lola for Mexican food tonight."

With Treena shaking her head. "Just like all the rest . . ."

Jack reached into his pocket for his phone and dialed the Glen-or-Glenda. Whoever answered said Lola had left two hours back. Jack tried his house and got nothing there.

"Well, she probably gave up on me and went out with her friends," Jack said, putting the phone away. "I'm sure she's having a good time, wherever she ended up."

She tried singing to herself, not an easy thing to do with her mouth gagged. She sang old songs she remembered from her grandmother: "Glow Worm" and "Oh, What a Beautiful Morning." They had soothed night terrors when she was five. Now they were Lola's way of keeping panic from swallowing her whole.

She lay on her back in a dry, dirty bathtub. "You looked so good in that other tub," Eddie had told her. "What do you say we do it again?"

Her wrists and ankles were bound with duct tape. Above her, like the lid on a pauper's casket, was a sheet of plywood across the top of the tub. The darkness was absolute.

Soon the songs gave out. For a while Lola felt as if she were floating above herself, looking down. She replayed what had happened, the way she would watch it in a movie: Lola sees herself in Eddie's apartment. She is trying to use the phone when Eddie hits her. She falls to the couch and covers up, but he keeps hitting. Five or six times, maybe ten, she isn't sure. She has never felt pain like this. She passes out.

When she comes to, Eddie jerks her to her feet. His gun is pressed against the side of her neck. He shoves her from his apartment.

Outside, he pushes her along a second-floor walkway. Below them is a courtyard in dim light. Lola looks for someone who would hear her call for help. She sees nothing but the drained swimming pool and its sediment of garbage.

"In here," Eddie says. He kicks a door open. The apartment has been gutted—bare walls, bare floors, with the smell of grime still in the air. "That way," Eddie says, pushing her toward a black hallway.

They are in a bathroom. With moonlight pouring in through a window, and the stink of sewage hanging. The toilet and sink are gone, with only the tub left. Through the window, Lola sees the full moon low in the sky. It is so beautiful she starts to cry.

Eddie binds her hands behind her and goes to work on her ankles, then slaps a piece of tape over her mouth. He spins her around. The moonlight falls on his face, which is twisted in rage. "So much for you and Jackie and your big plan," Eddie says. He has peanut butter on his breath. "As if Eddie Nickles, of all people, can't figure it out when he's being grassy-knolled."

He shoves Lola. She tumbles into the tub and lands facedown. It knocks the breath out of her. She tries to open her mouth to swallow air, but it is sealed shut. For an instant, she feels as if she has forgotten how to breathe.

Eddie is above her, shouting: "What do you think you're worth, bitch? What do you think Jackie'll give up to get his bald cunt back?"

Just as she thinks she cannot last another second, air comes back into her lungs. Lola takes a dozen deep breaths through her nose and flops onto her back.

Eddie is not in the room but she hears his footsteps. He is dragging something. "Thought you might want a roof over your head," he says when he comes in. The plywood goes over the tub and everything is black.

His steps fade away, then come back. Eddie grunts, and a load falls heavily on top of the plywood. He goes away and returns again, and another load lands above her. It happens four more times. Lola feels as if she is lying in her grave and listening to dirt being thrown from above.

"That's three hundred pounds of builder's sand," Eddie says when he's done. "So don't plan on going nowhere."

For a while all she can hear is his labored breathing. Then he walks away, muttering, "Jesus Christ, my fucking knee." He doesn't come back.

26

Just before midnight Weldon looped his oxygen bottle bag over his shoulder and struggled up from the La-Z-Boy. Telling himself that when you go, you should go out with a bang. Or two.

The raw north wind was on his face as he walked across the yard to the barn. The Gillich half brothers lay passed out in the cold, right where he had left them. Weldon prodded them with the toe of his boot. Neither one moved. He started to walk away, but stopped and turned. Then spit on each of them.

Weldon went to the trunk of his car and got two identical black leather briefcases, purchased a couple of hours earlier from the Mesquite Wal-Mart. He took them into the barn. Roger had eight sticks of dynamite left, stored in a cardboard box there. Weldon put two sticks into one of the briefcases, and cut a small notch in its handle with his pocketknife. He filled the other briefcase with old newspapers, and carried both to the tool well of Roger's pickup.

He shuffled back into the house and went to his chair,

drawing hard on the bottled air. You got to a certain age, Weldon thought, and you saw how each day is made up of pieces from the days before. Spend now, have debts tomorrow. Plow a field in March and you're eating sweet corn in the summertime. Smoke unfiltereds all your life, and eventually you'll buy your air at the drugstore. Not hard to figure any of that out.

But it wasn't always that clear. Sometimes you pulled a strand of the web, and it took thirty or forty years for the other side to tremble.

Weldon remembered that first tug in December 1963. He and Sylvan Dufraine were on their way to a simple business operation. Which was: Weldon would kill Sylvan, per his agreement with the lovely woman calling herself Alice, who paid him in cash outside the Gator Lounge.

But Sylvan had made a counteroffer. First asking Weldon what the man in Oklahoma City—the man who was next on Weldon's soon-to-be-dead list—looked like. And then saying to Weldon, "What would it be worth to you to make a substitution?"

"Now you see it, and now you don't?"

"Hey, bait and switch. Works for everyone else, why not us? Go ahead, name your price."

Weldon, just for the hell of it, had pulled a number out of the blue. "Twenty-five thousand."

"Done," Sylvan had said. "Solid American, cold cash, end of story. We can wrap it up today, nice and neat, and not have to mess with each other no more."

Now Weldon sat in his La-Z-Boy and laughed at the memory. End of story, nice and neat? Even back then he knew that wasn't likely.

The trip to Seffner took two hours, with Jack doing eighty and Treena asking him why he was driving so slow. Four times Jack tried calling Lola and got no answer. "Lose your girlfriend?" Treena said.

"Temporarily misplaced. I told her to sleep somewhere besides home. Too many bullets flying around the Flippo mansion these days."

Somewhere in the sticks, just after one in the morning, Treena announced she had heard enough shitkicker music from the radio. She cut off Marty Robbins right in the middle of the second verse.

"What are you doing?" Jack had been singing along. "Now we'll never find out if he nails the señorita."

"Stuff's ear torture." Treena searched the dial until she found a faith healer with a call-in show. He was praying in a red-dirt Louisiana voice for a woman with high blood sugar. "Handle two snakes," Jack said, "and call me in the morning."

They had left the interstate and were on a curving two-lane. No more prairie scrubland. The trees were bigger, the brush thicker. "Ever drive through East Texas," Jack said, "and feel like the woods are just waiting for their chance to swallow everything up?"

"Cracker land is what it is, man, so I gotta ask myself what I'm doing here with someone like you." Treena turned to face him, arms folded. With Jack thinking, here we go again. She said, "Only one reason I'm sitting here right now. You gonna help me take care of Eddie Nickles or not?"

"Thought we covered this already."

"Since I've asked you about three times now, and you don't answer with nothing but a mumble, I'm assuming you've decided not to cooperate."

"Hear that?" Jack pointed at the radio. "The guy's healing intestinal polyps over the phone. Think he does sinus headaches? Swear to God, some mornings I think I'm having an aneurysm."

"Hey, call him up. And while you're on the line with the man? Ask him to cure your personality."

"I gotta confess"—Jack glanced her way—"your charm is starting to work on me now."

Treena said, "That shit your idea of funny, man? 'Cause after what I heard from that junkie about Mineola, I'm not in the mood to laugh. Understand what I'm saying to you? I mean, what kind of man puts someone through what I've been through tonight? And then won't answer questions. And *then* wants to yuck it up? What kind of man?"

Trying to rattle him now, lay on some guilt. It won't work, Jack thought. Nothing you can say to me, he almost told her, that a guy with two divorces hasn't already heard. Wanting to let her know that there had been days when women had to stand in line to call him an asshole. But he put all that back in the box and climbed down from the bad-marriage attic, nice and calm. Treena did have a point, he had to admit.

"All right, fine," he said. "What is it you would like to know about Eddie?"

She didn't answer right away. Scowling, burning off some anger. Then, in a voice down from boil: "Start with where does he live? How do I get there?"

"You want to find Eddie? Make a couple of wrong turns, you can't miss him. Look, let's take this one step at a time. Confronting Eddie cold won't give you anything."

"It might, if I got persuasive on his ass."

"Maybe pistol-whip the boy? Now you're veering into the crazy lane."

Treena was quiet for a while. When she started talking again, she had put the blades away, her irritation giving ground. She said, "Used to be a day didn't go by that I didn't think of Mineola. I'd ask myself what I could have done to keep him from ending up the way he did. Convinced myself for a while that it was all my fault."

"Don't beat yourself up."

"I finally got over that. Told myself, it is what it is, not a bit I can do about it now." Treena looked out the window, nothing to see but dark shapes flying by. "Then you came along, asking questions. Started the whole thing up again."

"Impeccable timing as always."

"I'm glad you showed up, man. You know why? 'Cause I finally see what I owe Mineola. That's to find out what happened in that apartment the night him and Shauntelle got murdered. I'm gonna get to the truth on that."

Seffner, Texas, wasn't much of a town, especially at two in the morning. The only sign of life was a twenty-four-hour E-Z Mart that sold cigarettes and lotto tickets to sawmill truck drivers. Jack asked the clerk, an unshaven man who looked as if he hadn't seen the sun this year, for directions to Pine Grove Cemetery.

The clerk didn't know the way, but he offered to call his cousin Budlie, who probably did. Jack pointed out the hour. "Don't worry about waking him up," the clerk said. "He ain't been able to sleep since his fiancée run off with the ex-terminator."

Budlie was wide awake and watching Home Shopping Network. His directions sent Jack and Treena to an un-marked road that ran off the main highway south of town. It was a Third World paving job that twisted for a mile or two into the woods and dead-ended at the graveyard. Even in the dark they could tell Pine Grove Cemetery needed some tending: the car's headlight beams swept across weeds and overgrowth. "The tenants have just let the place go," Jack said.

True to the name, the cemetery spread among a stand of pines. A chain-link fence surrounded it but the gate was un-locked. Jack gave Treena a flashlight he'd bought at the E-Z Mart. Then he picked up his own, which had Shoogie's dried blood on the crown.

"Time for a stone-by-stone search," he said. "Look for anything that says Dufraine."

They stood outside the car listening to the wind blow through the pines. The sound reminded Jack of sad songs.

"Full moon, graveyard." Treena pulled her coat tight around her. "Think I saw this movie. All we need now is some howling."

There were markers of granite and marble for those who had family money or burial insurance, and metal plaques for those who died broke. Jack shined his light on tombstones engraved with angels, crosses and masonic emblems. Some had vases that held mildewed plastic flowers. He went from one grave to the next. All those lives, reduced to a slab of stone and a few words: Devoted husband, loving mother, gone with God, still in our hearts, taken from this earth, at rest, at peace, watching from heaven. Jack found one that said, "He loved his dogs."

They searched for half an hour. The wind started to bite, making fingers go numb. Jack was thinking this graveyard bit might have been a bad idea when he heard Treena call out, "Here we go."

She stood near a corner of the cemetery, in a small sec-tion off to itself, shining her light down. Jack walked over as she said, "Here's your man, man."

They played their flashlights over a gray granite rectangle. Chiseled across the top: "Sylvan Dufraine 1934–1963." Jack knelt and pointed his flashlight at smaller letters near the bot-tom. Reading out loud, "Son of Leroy and Maria, brother of Martin." He added, "That would be our Mr. Marty."

"Leroy and Maria," Treena said. She had moved to the left and was looking at a pair of markers side by side. "Got them right here."

Jack stood and looked around. "That's it? That's all there is of the Dufraines? Some family plot."

"What now, man with the plan?"

"Shit, I don't know." He rose, stepped to the side of Sylvan's grave and felt something hard under his shoe. "What's this?" he said. His light, pointed toward the ground, showed him nothing. Jack dropped to his knees and poked his fingers into the grass and weeds where his foot had been. His fingertips struck smooth rock. "Come hold my light," he told Treena.

Jack pulled at weed stalks and matted brown pine needles to find a white marble slab flat against the ground. It was the size of a big-city phone book.

He leaned close and blew dirt out of the small engraved letters. "Well, now, here's some news," he said. Then read, "Martin Leroy Dufraine. Born May sixteenth, nineteen thirty-five. Passed from our lives May nineteenth, nineteen thirty-five."

"Just a baby," Treena said. "Three days old, that's sad."

"Check the epitaph." Jack leaned closer. "It says, 'He never had to suffer the world's travails.'"

"I don't care what he didn't suffer. I still say it's sad."

Jack looked at Treena, then back at the stone. "This is Mr. Marty's grave," he said. "Except he didn't get to grow up to be Mr. Marty."

"Uh-huh." She handed Jack his flashlight. "I thought we just talked to Mr. Marty."

"That's just somebody using his name."

"Using it for what?"

"See it all the time." Jack stood. "Somebody who needs a new identity, they'll look for a name to steal. Dead babies from way back are the best. Get yourself a copy of their birth certificate, which will get you a driver's license, which will get you a passport. And there you are, brand-new person, brand-new life."

"So who's our brand-new Mr. Marty?"

"I only have one guess, but I bet it's a good one," Jack said. "I'm guessing it's someone who's supposed to be dead on account of a film he made in Dallas. Someone who was believed to be all burned up in a car thirty-six years ago."

Jack shifted his light to Sylvan Dufraine's headstone and ran it down the length of the grave. "So who do you suppose," he said, "is really down in there?"

Weldon sat in his chair, breathed his bottled air and remembered:

December 28, 1963. They had driven to Oklahoma City in Sylvan's Cadillac. Two hundred miles, with Sylvan talking most of the way. Still cuffed to the steering wheel, giving Weldon his JFK assassination theories.

"First glance," Sylvan said, "you'd figure it was the Cubans who did it. They're pissed off about the Bay of Pigs, so they get this local yokel Oswald to pull the big trigger. A known Castro sympathizer. Hey, it all adds up."

"You want to watch the road?" Weldon said. The man was all over the place, with some oncoming trucks cutting them way too close.

"Except, who'd have hired that clown to wash a dog, never mind shoot the President? Oswald wasn't nothing but misdirection. See what I'm saying?"

"Not really. Speed limit here is seventy." Weldon wondered how they would explain the cuffs and the Ithaca Stakeout shotgun to the highway patrol.

"Know how a team of pickpockets'll stage a fight to get

your attention, and meanwhile they're lifting your wallet? That's what Oswald was." Sylvan nodded at his own wisdom. "And it would've worked too, if it wasn't for Sylvan Dufraine. Yours truly and his camera happened to be there, and the real killers believe they got their balls in a blender. That what's happening here?"

"I guess."

"What do they think I have? What do they think I got with my camera?"

"They didn't say."

"I could show it to them, put this whole thing to bed. One look at my film, they'll see they got nothing to worry about."

"All I know," Weldon said, "is somebody is paying to have you dead."

Sylvan turned to Weldon. "You could solve it, you know."

Weldon snapped out of a daydream about what he could do with a twenty-five-grand windfall. "Say what now?"

"The people hiring you to take care of me, they're the ones that did the President."

Weldon shook his head. "I don't know about that."

"Makes perfect sense. Don't you see it? First they ace me, then they get my film. That way they think they got this whole thing tidied up and— Shit, we gotta pull over, let me call my wife."

"No, we don't."

"Soon as they find out you've nabbed me, they'll go to my house, looking for that film. If they haven't done it already. Unless"—Sylvan cocked his head and squinted—"you wasn't supposed to do that, was you? After you took care of me."

This deal was growing more confusing by the minute.

Weldon sighed. Nothing was simple anymore. "Nobody said nothing to me about getting no film."

"So they got a team on this," Sylvan said. "That makes sense."

"Don't know nothing about that neither."

"First phone booth we see, we'll pull over and give the wife a call."

Weldon raised the Ithaca Stakeout a couple of inches. "I'll decide when we stop."

"We'll tell her to grab that film and skedaddle."

"And you might want to mention," Weldon said, "a trip to the bank. For that twenty-five thousand in cash that we discussed."

Sylvan whistled. "Undamnbelievable. You and me, just a couple of country boys going about our business, and now this. . . . Tell me the old ball don't take some funny bounces."

They made the call from a Phillips station just south of the state line. With Sylvan telling his wife to get the film, get the cash and get the hell out. Plus, be on the lookout for any suspicious-looking Cubans.

Weldon and Sylvan reached Oklahoma City well after dark. They found the man they wanted, Briscoe Pitts, in the second place they looked, on a bench outside a pool hall near downtown. A couple of years had passed since Weldon had seen him, but he looked the same: short and underfed, with limp dirty hair and bugged-out eyes. A "Born to Lose" tattoo on his left forearm, truth in advertising. Weldon glanced from Briscoe to Sylvan and thought, it might work.

"Hey, Briscoe," Weldon called, waving. "Happy New Year."

Briscoe walked over and leaned against the car. Chewing a toothpick and saying, "What's the word, hoss?"

Weldon pointed the .12-gauge at him and said, "Get in."

"He's not as good-looking as me," Sylvan said.

Sylvan drove the two hundred miles back to Dallas, mouth flapping most of the way, feeling good because the handcuffs were off him now and on Briscoe. He gave them more JFK theories, some talk about his young wife's wild temper and advice on how easy it was to coax women out of their clothes if you had the right equipment. "Something about the camera, boys, makes the girls want to pull their undies off."

Weldon didn't listen much. He sat in the back and kept his gun barrel pointed at Briscoe's head. Briscoe didn't say a word, though somewhere around Ardmore he started to cry. Sylvan, when he wasn't talking, whistled.

It was past midnight by the time they hit the Dallas city limits, with traffic heavier than usual for this time of night. "Everybody's getting ready to celebrate the new year," Sylvan said. "Just like us, huh?" He started whistling "Auld Lang Syne" and didn't stop until they were passing downtown. "Know where I'd like to be on New Year's Eve?" Sylvan pointed to the Southland Life Building. "Right up there in the Ports o' Call Club, dancing with somebody else's wife."

Weldon was thinking about the process of identifying a corpse. He asked Sylvan, "Ever been arrested?"

"I don't break the law, unless there's a statute against having a big johnson."

"Fingerprints on file anywhere you know about?"

"Nowhere, nohow." Sylvan turned to Briscoe and winked. "Boy's using the old noggin back there now. Gotta like that." He caught Weldon's eye in the rearview. "You and me, we're plucking the same goose."

"How about dental work?" Weldon said. "You had much done?"

"Me?" Sylvan opened his mouth and checked it in the

mirror. "A couple fillings, plus a gold crown in back. But here's the good news. My dentist got brain cancer two years ago."

No sound but Briscoe crying again.

"Hey, I tried to warn him all them X rays would eat him up someday." Sylvan looked at Briscoe. "Anyway, before he died he gave me my records, for when I moved on to another dentist. Which I never did. Which is looking like pretty good luck right now, wouldn't you say? I mean for me, of course."

"How about you, Briscoe?" Weldon leaned forward. "You got all your teeth?"

Briscoe, in the front seat, didn't answer. All sweaty, sobbing now, with the smell of fear from him. Weldon waited until they passed under a streetlight to catch a glimpse of the man's hands: cuffed at the wrist, but Briscoe had laid them on the Caddy's armrest. An awkward position, Weldon thought, unless you were about to try a break. He said, "Don't do nothing dumb, Briscoe. Don't make this harder than it already is." Then to Sylvan: "Take Oakland Avenue. We'll stay out of traffic from here on out."

They were deep into the warehouse district south of downtown when Briscoe made his move. He went for the door lock and then the handle, even though the car was doing at least forty. Weldon swung the barrel of the .12-gauge at his face and heard the crack of Briscoe's jaw breaking. The man cried out as he fell against the door, then slumped forward. Weldon clubbed the back of his head with the butt of the gun, coming down on him like a pile driver until Briscoe lay in a bleeding heap.

"Boy must of got some last-minute rabbit in him," Sylvan said. "Guess when you're facing the end, even this part of Dallas looks pretty good. Sort of like the women at closing time."

"No more talking, no more songs," Weldon said. "Just drive." He slumped against the back seat, breathing a little hard from all the exertion and wondering if he was about to make a big mistake. For the first time in his working life Weldon was scamming a client.

This gets out, he thought, and I'm finished, and after I'm finished, I'm dead. Even if he could keep it quiet, just the idea of abandoning his plan, of bringing someone else into the flow—someone who might not live up to his personal standards—made Weldon uneasy. He'd seen it in the Korean War, and he'd seen it in his work. Lose control, and you had to account for it somehow, somewhere down the line.

But then Weldon remembered the legal bills from his recent trial. Remaining a free man was expensive, requiring money Weldon didn't have. A twenty-five-thousand bonus would pay his lawyer off and leave enough for two weeks at the dog races in Hot Springs.

"Take a right here," he told Sylvan. Then, Christ almighty, the s.o.b. started whistling again. "Told you to shut up," Weldon said.

Another half hour of driving and they were there. Weldon had picked an old trash dump in south Dallas County for the job, half a mile off a road almost nobody used. He had looked closely at the garbage, even dropping to his knees and smelling it for freshness, when he chose the location a few days before. Nobody had dumped anything there for months, which made it the perfect spot: privacy for the deed, but not so untraveled that a single car late at night would raise suspicion in someone who happened to glance that way. In the kill-for-cash business you had to think about these things.

"Turn where you see that culvert," Weldon said. "Then just follow the ruts."

"When I see a what? Holy moly, it's dark out here." Sylvan made the turn. The car bounced over the dirt road, and brush scraped against the sides. "This ain't doing my suspension any favors," Sylvan said. "No way to treat an almost brand-new Cadillac."

They turned into a clearing, the headlights sweeping across old garbage and a shiny Plymouth. "Whose car?" Sylvan asked.

"Mine," Weldon said. "Now stop right here and get out."

Sylvan did as told. Weldon stepped out of the back, opened the passenger's door and leaned in. He had the short shotgun in his right hand. With his left he grabbed a handful of Briscoe's shirt and pulled him into a sitting position. Briscoe's bugged-out eyes fluttered and he couldn't find a focus. His broken jaw was hanging slack.

"Nothing personal against you, Briscoe." Weldon put the shotgun to Briscoe's mouth, the barrel on his lips like a kiss. "Fact is, I always liked you all right. But you screwed some people you shouldn't of."

He squeezed the trigger, and the shotgun's blast lifted Briscoe off the seat. The spray of blood and bone darkened the dome light. Weldon emptied Briscoe's pockets and walked to his truck.

"Well, I never liked that old car anyhow." Sylvan stood in the Caddy's headlight beams. "And I gotta hand it to you, partner. Ain't no dentist in the world gonna figure out them teeth now."

Weldon turned to face him. Thinking that he could take him down right now, and everything would still be according to Hoyle. Eventually somebody would find both bodies, and the cops would go crazy trying to dope a connection between Sylvan Dufraine and Briscoe Pitts. But Weldon kept thinking of those bills to pay. "Give me your wallet," he told Sylvan.

Sylvan handed it over. Weldon pulled the money from it—maybe fifty dollars in there, if that—and tossed the wallet on the ground near Sylvan's car. Saying, "You're not gonna need that driver's license anyway."

He started the Plymouth and turned it to face the Caddy, giving himself some light to work with. From the trunk he took a one-gallon can of gasoline. "Here." Weldon handed the can to Sylvan. "Soak Briscoe down, and then the upholstery."

Sylvan did it, and finished by tossing the empty can in the Caddy's back seat. He said, "Sure hope somebody remembered to bring a match."

Weldon twisted a couple of newspaper pages into a torch and used a cigarette lighter to fire up the end. He threw it toward the Cadillac and backed away. Billows of heat and the smell of burning flesh washed over him. The stink took Weldon right back to Korea. Briscoe Pitts or Chinese soldiers, they smelled just the same on fire.

"Man oh man, that's nasty," Sylvan said, hand over his face. "About time to go, don't you think?"

"Listen here." Weldon raised the gun to make his point. "Everybody in the world has to believe that's you in that car."

"Don't I know it."

"Soon as I get my money from you, I want you gone, you understand? You got to disappear."

"This person you're looking at right now? He don't exist. Man"—Sylvan winced—"that is some smell."

"They find out you're alive, they'll kill me and you both. And if I get word you're hanging around—well, you know what I'll do. I'll hunt you down and shoot you down. It don't matter if it's tomorrow or next year or ten years from now."

"Hey, don't you worry about a thing. Got it all worked

out in my head. Mexico. New identity." Sylvan pushed his fingers against his face, the car burning behind him. "Plus some plastic surgery soon as the life insurance settlement arrives."

"Congratulations, then." Weldon lowered the gun slightly. "And good luck in your new life as a dead man."

27

They were back in Dallas by dawn. Jack pulled to the curb in front of the Lipscomb Homes. Telling Treena, "Get some rest, then we'll go to work on Eddie and Mr. Marty and whoever else is at this dance."

She opened her door and looked back at Jack. "I don't care about whoever else. I only care about one man."

"Right. Grab some sack time and I'll pick you up about three this afternoon. Okay?" Jack watched her get out of the car and walk away. He said, "I'll take that for a yes."

Jack drove toward home. He was trying to put all the pieces together, not an easy task after a no-sleep night. Thinking, let's see: Mr. Marty's really dead and Sylvan's apparently not. Plus Eddie's dirty. Maybe they all run together somehow, and maybe they don't.

Traffic was a little light on Central northbound, but Jack kept to the slow lane. Fatigue had stretched the time between thought and action. Static on the line, rust in the pipes, nothing quite fitting together. He felt like a guy in a foreign movie with a bad dub job: mouth moving one way, words coming out the other.

Jack envisioned cool sheets and a soft bed, imagined how nice that would feel. Then his phone rang.

"Mr. Flippo?"

Even with his fogged-in brain Jack recognized the voice—the can of rusty nails. The last time the old man called, Jack got a visit from the redheaded fish-killing piss boy. The boy who also appeared to enjoy firing a gun at Jack from a moving truck.

"Who is this?" Jack said.

"You still interested in that Kennedy movie?"

"Maybe."

"I've got something important to show you. Your office, eight o'clock this morning." Before Jack could respond he was gone.

It took Jack about thirty seconds to patch together a plan: Stake out his own office and see if the redhead showed up looking for another aquarium to pee into, or another chance to fire some shots. And if so, no more wrestling matches for Jack, no more car chases around White Rock Lake. He would keep his distance and call the cops.

Almost seven o'clock now. He had time for a shower and coffee, and maybe a couple of minutes to scan the paper. For someone who was out of work, he had a lot of work to do.

There was no sign of Lola at the house. The driveway was empty, the door locked. Inside Jack found the usual clutter, except for the stripped-bare living room. He started the coffee, then poured himself some orange juice. An old doughnut, left in a plastic bag on top of the microwave, felt a little stale. But it had no mold yet, so it was breakfast.

In the bathroom he brushed his teeth and washed his face. While he shaved he decided on the next step regarding this Mr. Marty—straight confrontation. What Jack thought he'd do was knock on the man's door unannounced. Then say, "Sylvan, old buddy. I'm just back from the Seffner boneyard. Let's talk about why you're pretending to be your dead brother." In two seconds the man's face would tell him everything.

Jack walked down the hall to the bedroom. The bed was unmade, and clothes were scattered around the room. Dirty or clean, who knew?

He emptied his pockets, with coins, keys, wallet and pieces of paper joining other junk on the dresser top. Next he undressed and searched for clothes that didn't smell gamey. A gray sweatshirt with a picture of Sergeant Bilko on the front—a present from Lola—looked good. He was pulling it over his head when he heard someone behind him say, "And where the hell you been?"

Jack whirled to see Eddie Nickles standing in the doorway and pointing a gun. Eddie said, "Got a minute for an old friend?"

Never go into a job hungry. That was one of Weldon's rules. So he asked Mandi and Brandi to fry up some bacon and eggs and bake some biscuits. They were happy to, his beautiful girls. "You doing all right?" he asked Mandi as she laid bacon strips into the frying pan. "Your husband treating you like he's supposed to?"

"Oh, Daddy," she said. Weldon put his arms around her. Brandi left the kitchen sink and joined in the hug, both of the girls crying into his chest. Telling him how sorry they were that they'd ever set eyes on the Gillich half brothers.

"It's gonna get better soon," Weldon told them.

After breakfast he woke up the Gilliches. At some point during the night they had managed to get themselves into Rodney's trailer, next to Weldon's house. Roger was on the couch, wearing cowboy boots and boxer shorts. Rodney lay in bed fully clothed, the front of his shirt streaked with vomit. "Get up, boys," Weldon said. "We got some work to do."

Around seven-fifteen the Gilliches assembled in Weldon's kitchen. Rodney had a new shirt but still smelled faintly of puke. Roger smoked and said, "Goddamn head feels like it's been sat on by six fat ladies."

"Here's the plan," Weldon said.

Rodney moaned. "Oh, shit, not again."

Weldon looped the strap of his oxygen bottle over his shoulder. Saying, "Roger, last night I took two sticks of your explosives and put them in a briefcase."

Roger dropped his cigarette butt into his coffee cup and looked at Weldon, heavy-lidded. "That oughta do the job. Whatever the fuck the job is."

"The briefcase is in the tool well of your pickup." Weldon paused. "Now. You boys listening? We messed up the time before because one of us didn't follow instructions. Right, Rodney? But this one has got to go smooth. Right, Rodney?"

Rodney said, "That last I had was smooth."

Roger leaned across the table and thumped a finger against Rodney's head. "Shut up, shitbird. Man's talking about dynamite now."

Rodney rubbed the side of his head and gave them a goofy smile. "Gonna take more than that to hurt me, asshole. I just popped two Percodan."

"Boys, pay attention, now." Weldon checked his watch. "There's only about half an hour till I'm supposed to meet with this man Mr. Flippo."

"Say what?" Rodney sat up straight. "Firpo? The one that poisoned my dick?"

Weldon wagged his finger. "This time, Rodney, you stay with your brother—"

"Gonna dip his wick in sugar and stick it in a ant bed."

"—while I go into his office. You listening, Roger? Rodney? I'll have the briefcase with the explosives. You boys will be out front in the truck, with your finger on the button. I'll conduct my business with the man, then leave. Soon as I come walking out the door, I'll give you the high sign, and you let it rip. Follow me?"

Rodney muttered about revenge. Roger smoked.

Weldon said, "Everybody does what they're supposed to, and we'll make this a good day."

Roger smiled for the first time that morning. "Any day you get to blow something up," he said, "is a good day."

Eddie's eyes were wilder than before, as if someone had a grip on his throat. He hadn't shaved in a few days, and gave off the stink of the unbathed psychotic. He said, "You must be in love with me."

Jack stood in the middle of his bedroom, wearing the Sergeant Bilko sweatshirt and a pair of blue underwear, staring at Eddie's gun.

Eddie twisted a grin, sweat dripping from his face. "Know why I say you're in love with me, Jackie?" Talking fast, almost up to babble speed. "Go ahead, answer the question. Know why?"

"Eddie, what are you doing?"

"You must be in love with me 'cause you're trying to fuck me in so many ways. Just like when me and Iris was married, man, I was trying to put the stinger to her every chance I got, anyplace she'd let me. Not that she'd let me much, you know, but that ain't the point. The point is, Jackie, what you're trying to do to me."

"I'm not trying to do anything to you, Eddie."

"See? There you go, that's exactly what I'm talking about. You say something like that, it's just the same as if you rammed a hard one right through my back door." Eddie circled behind him. Jack felt the cold end of the gun barrel tickling the ridge of his ear and heard Eddie make kissing sounds. Eddie said, "I been hiding in the spare bedroom for hours, Jackie. Lucky for me you got a TV back there, even if I had to watch it with the sound off. Know what's pretty good with no sound? World's Strongest Man contest. Has guys lifting refrigerators and shit, seeing how far they can throw car batteries."

"You want to put the gun down, Eddie?"

"No, I don't. But thanks for asking. . . . You know, you look pretty cute there in your undies, Jackie. But you ain't my type. I like black chicks. Tall, thin ones with their hair dyed blond. You know any like that? What a coincidence, I believe you do. How about a phone number, huh? A little blind date action for Eddie Nickles."

"You talking about the woman you saw me with yesterday?"

"Sharp as a tack, Jackie." Eddie came around in front of Jack again, looking pleased with himself, licking his lips.

"She's a client, Eddie. That's all."

"Jesus, that's lame." Eddie shook his head. "I was hoping you wouldn't disappoint me, Jackie, after all I done for you."

"Eddie, put the gun down, we'll work this out."

"All I done for you, and you treat me like this." Eddie backed to a corner and sat in an armchair that was draped with clothes. He rubbed his bum knee. Settling in for a talk now, Jack thought.

Eddie said, "All the jokers lined up to take Eddie Nickles down, and Jackie Flippo's their point man."

"That's not true."

"Here's what's true, Jackie. The black chick is Treena Watts. That's Watts, as in Mineola. Now where have I heard that name before?" Eddie dropped the grin. "What you trying to do? Reopen that case? A case, by the way, where Eddie Nickles should of got a parade from the city of Dallas, for taking that piece of shit off the streets."

"You got it all wrong."

"Hey, you told Lola, and Lola told me. All sorts of things she told me, Jackie." He paused. Building up to something, Jack thought. Eddie said, "She's a nice girl, that Lola. Too bad I had to lock her down."

Jack took a step toward him. With Eddie raising the gun and saying, "Think I wouldn't do it? Try me."

"Where is she?" Jack said.

"She's safe and sound. She's in unit one at the Eddie Nickles Justice Center."

"She's got nothing to do with this. Let her go."

Eddie sniffed. "Little law enforcement tip for you, Jackie. It's the guy with the gun who gives the orders. Right now I'm ordering you to lie down on the bed. Do the snuff dive, as we say in the trade."

That meant facedown, the victim position of choice for your punk executioners. Jack had seen the crime scene photos plenty of times when he was with the DA's office: dead bodies, belly down, with bullet holes in the backs of their heads. For capital trials there were eight-by-ten glossies of unlucky drug dealers on dirty yellow shag carpet, or of scammers who had tried to swindle the wrong guy, nose southbound in a ditch now. He remembered one picture taken in the walk-in freezer of a burger joint: three workers who had been robbed, lined up side by side in their fast-food uniforms, their blood pooling, then icing over on the rubber floor.

Jack had always wondered, was it easier to shoot people who weren't looking at you? Was it too much, having their pleading eyes on you as you pulled the trigger? Or maybe it was life's final nasty joke on the doomed, a way to turbocharge the terror by throwing in some last-minute blindness too. More likely, the dumb bastards, the ones who would kill for ten dollars, had seen it done like that in the movies.

He said, "You gonna pop me now, Eddie?"

"You don't get on the bed I will. Facedown like I told you. Then I want you to tell me where the black bitch is. I'll trade you one Lola for one Treena, even up. Soon as you lie down, we start talking."

Jack lay on the bed. Thinking, if he still wants something, he won't kill me yet. Eddie said, "Simple question, Jackie. Where is she?"

"Home, I guess. I don't know."

"Where's home?"

"I don't know that either."

Nothing but the sound of Eddie breathing hard. "All right," he said. "Listen. I want you to reach over to that phone by the bed and give her a call. Keep it nice and calm, tell her you want her to come to your house. Tell her you need to see her right away, and that's it."

Jack waited. "I don't have her number."

"Jesus Christ. You're not gonna make it easy on yourself, are you." Eddie sat on the bed next to Jack and gave him a tap on the back of the head with the gun, like a polite knock on the door from a neighbor. "Hel-looo, Jackie. Always have to ride the chump train, don't you?"

"I might have her number somewhere. Maybe my office." His face was on Lola's pillow, and he could smell the bath oil she used. "You let Lola go, I'll see if I can't dig it up for you."

The mattress moved, and Eddie was off it. Jack could hear him walking back and forth across the room, saying, "Nobody's in the phone book anymore, you notice that? Including this Treena Watts. Everybody's unlisted, like they're afraid of something. What do you suppose they're afraid of, Jackie?"

"Hard to know," Jack said. Thinking, here's my guess—insane ex-cops.

"Unlisted numbers, shit." Eddie had a short laughing fit out of nowhere, the way other people suddenly cut loose a couple of sneezes. Then: "All right, here's the drill, Jackie. You help me out, maybe I don't kill you. You do what I say, we'll see about turning Lola out too. Deal?"

Makes no sense, Jack thought, setting Lola free, expecting they would act like nothing ever happened. But he said, "You got it, Eddie."

Eddie changed brain channels again. "First thing I'm gonna need is some cash. You don't mind I make myself a loan from your wallet?" Jack heard Eddie's shoes moving across the floor, then the sound of jangling keys on the dresser top. Eddie said, "When I was on the force, Jackie, I kept a little notebook with me—names and numbers, that kind of thing. It's a good habit to have, but I see you're more of a scrap paper man. Write a note to yourself, stuff it in your pocket, like a squirrel with his nuts. So maybe if I look at some of the notes, I might find the number of the black bitch, save us all some work. Chance of that, what do you think? Maybe I— Jesus H. Christ. The fuck is this? Huh? The fuck is *this*?"

He was on the bed again, astride Jack's back and grinding the barrel of the gun into his ear as if he were drilling for wax. Shouting, "The fuck is *this*?" and waving a piece of paper in front of Jack's face. It took a while but Jack finally glimpsed enough of the paper to see what had flipped Eddie's switch. He saw his own handwriting, in red ballpoint. It said: Felicette Cone, 2123 Abner.

Eddie pushed the gun harder against his ear. "You're drinking poison now, Jackie. You're a cockroach swilling Raid, man."

Jack said, "Put the gun away." Feeling his heart banging against his ribs. "Let's talk about this."

"*Talk?* Shit." He leaned close to Jack's face, and dropped his voice almost to a whisper. "All right, we'll talk. Tell you a little story, let you know what you're playing with. You wanna hear a story, Jackie?"

"Eddie, listen, put the gun down."

He ground the barrel against Jack's ear. "I said do you wanna hear a fucking story?"

"Sure," Jack said. "Let's hear a story."

Eddie sat up again, cleared his throat and began to speak as if they were two whiskey pals at the tavern. "Remember the day I come to see you at the DA's office, Jackie, about seven years back? Told you I needed to find Mineola Watts?"

"You told me you were going to save my life. You said Mineola wanted to kill me as payback for putting him away."

"Whatever. Hey, I'm sure he did if he ever thought about it. So I probably did save your bacon. The point is, Jackie, you found his grandmother's name and address for me."

Jack remembered it now, saw himself pulling the info from his file, making a copy and handing it to Detective Eddie Nickles. With Detective Eddie grinning and telling Jack he would see if he could do some good with it.

Now Eddie said, "So I send my little snitch Felicette to the granny's house while I wait in the car. Felicette sweet-talks the old lady into telling us that Mineola's hanging at an apartment in Oak Cliff. Me and Felicette pop over for a visit after dark."

Jack had the feeling of someone beginning a fall into a deep, dark shaft, of looking down and seeing no bottom.

"Ten thousand dollars that little piece of monkey shit owed me, Jackie. So me and Felicette walk in this stinking apartment—one little kick and that cheap door pops open— and he's lying on the couch drunk, watching TV. I go, 'Now where's the money, motherfucker?' That's when he reaches inside his shirt. And that's when I shot him."

Eddie shifted his weight and pulled the gun from Jack's ear. Then said, "Better believe he was going for his weapon. He had a nine-millimeter in his waistband, and if I hadn't've nailed him, he'd of nailed me. No doubt in my mind. And let's not forget, Jackie, that a grand jury saw it the same way."

"Why do I have the feeling, Eddie, that you didn't tell the grand jury the whole story?"

Eddie belched. "So the thieving fuck's gut-shot, right? He kind of tumbles off the couch and starts crawling to the back of the apartment. I pick up his nine and follow. He's gurgling up blood the whole way. That's when Felicette— this cracked me up, Jackie, I gotta admit—she says to him, 'This your idea of a getaway, man?' Then she kicks him right in the ass."

Jack listened while Eddie had another laughing seizure. All that shaking and Eddie's finger on the trigger too.

"But the little puke keeps crawling, right into this dark bedroom. I mean pitch black in there. So naturally I flip on the lights. Who do you think was in that room? Go ahead"—prodding the back of Jack's head with the gun— "throw a name out there."

"Mineola's wife," Jack said.

"Correct you are, my man. Mrs. Mineola. In bed, with- out a stitch on. She's blinking against the light and got her

mouth open like she wants to scream, but nothing's coming
out. She's scared to death, Jackie. Now the little asshole
who stole my money, he can't move no more on account of
he's bleeding to death on the floor. But he can still see, and
he's watching me. Big, scared eyes, watching every move I
make. So I go, 'Here's what happens when you try to screw
with Eddie Nickles. Here's the payout end of that deal.' And
then I let him watch, Jackie, while I use *his* weapon on *his*
old lady."

Jack remembered a snapshot of Shauntelle that Treena
had shown him—a girl with a pretty smile.

"We tossed that dump of his," Eddie said, "but all we
could find was two grand and change. Then, get this, two
uniforms show up to answer a call. A neighbor heard the
shots and punched nine-one-one. Don't you know I had to
do some fast talking? Huh? Jackie, I'm asking you a question. Think you could have the courtesy to answer?"

"The cops came, you talked fast."

"Better believe I did. . . . Then, Jesus, Felicette." Eddie
blew some air. "Two days later she ran off and took the
money with her. I hunted her for years, Jackie, but she hid
herself pretty good. And now I've found her, thank you very
much for your help. Think I'll pay her a visit this afternoon.
But first things first." He put the barrel of the gun against the
back of Jack's head again.

"You're making a mistake," Jack said.

"When I first come in here, Jackie, I was after one thing.
That was to find out how deep you was in with this Treena
Watts. If it was just a little bit, I was gonna let you walk. No
shit, I was. You and Lola too, with no hard feelings. But Jesus,
I got no choice with you now. You're too far into it, man."

There was a metallic click: Eddie thumbing the hammer
back. He said, "Like the doctor tells you before he sticks

you, this might sting a little. But after that, trust me, you won't feel nothing."

Jack played the only card he had. He said, "Eddie, don't you see it? It's all JFK."

Five seconds dragged by. "It's what?" Eddie said quietly.

"It's the assassination. Come on, man, you've got to know that. They're after you because you started talking about their film. All that stuff about the second umbrella man, Eddie, you exposed them. You put the light on them."

"Fuckin'-A right I did. Ripped the lid right off, forced the mothers into the light of day."

"You laid them bare, Eddie."

"With Eddie Nickles working this, they absolutely could not keep their secrets. Just one question, Jackie. Who the fuck you talking about?"

Jack remembered one of the rules of the con: Keep the patter coming. "That's what I've been working on, Eddie. As soon as I saw them coming after you, I tried to put the whole thing together."

Eddie rolled off Jack and left the bed. Saying, "So they got spooked when they seen I was onto them?"

Jack rolled over and propped himself on an elbow. "You were getting way too close. That's why they reached down into your past, man, and dragged up Felicette. Here's my advice. You lay low, let me handle this. Just tell me where Lola is, and I'll go get her and bring her home. I'll tell her you got a little carried away, I'm sure she'll understand."

Eddie nodded, stopped, shook his head hard and acted as if he were waiting for the pieces inside to settle. Then said, "Not till I figure out whose side you're on."

The guy was shorting out like an old toaster. "I'm on your side," Jack said. "You know that."

Eddie raised the gun again. "Here's what we're gonna

do. You said you got Treena Watts's number at your office. We're gonna go there, and you'll call her, set up a meeting with me."

"Oh, come on. We're not back to that again, are we?"

"See what she says about all this, see if she tells the same story you do, when she's facing down a thirty-eight. Bet you a dollar she tells me who's behind this."

"We don't have time for that, Eddie. These JFK cover-up guys, they're coming after you. Let's get Lola clear, and then you and I can go to work."

Eddie had the twisted grin going again. "Man, this is just like being back with the Dallas police again. Who's the good guy, who's the bad one? You never can tell, can you? I mean, shit, you might be working for the other side, Jackie. Your job might be to keep Eddie Nickles under wraps and out of the way."

"Eddie, let's go get Lola. Tell me where she is."

"Now, you don't pull no stupids, Jackie, and maybe I cut Lola loose. She gets to go back to her gallery, do all that crap with them love dolls. . . . Hey, did I tell you the bitch shaved all her hair off? Don't ask me why. Unless— Shit!"

Eddie slapped his own head. Saying, "Bet it was some kind of signal to them JFK fucks who's after me."

28

The cold rain made a mess of the morning rush hour, as Weldon had figured it would. So they left fifteen minutes early, taking Roger's truck. With Roger driving, Weldon sitting next to the passenger's door and Rodney— still giving off the smell of vomit—in the middle. Roger smoked and said, "Truck's got a bad shimmy from where we hit that curb the other night."

"Shoulda got it fixed," Rodney said.

"Shit." Roger stubbed his cigarette in the ashtray. "Took it down to the Fina station, and that Mexican? The one that runs the place? Wanted two hundred dollars to do the job."

Rodney shook his head. "Money-grubbing greaseball, man."

"I'm gonna fix it myself," Roger said. "Soon as the weather gets better. I mean, who wants to get out in the damn cold to work on a damn pickup?"

Rodney looked for a radio station he liked. Saying, "When it comes to working, only thing worse than the cold is the heat. Plus"—pointing to his ankle cast—"I'm looking at a lifetime of pain from this motherfucker. How'm I gonna get a job with that kind of agony?"

"Boys," Weldon said, "if today goes as planned, you won't have to worry about that kind of thing no more."

"Constant pain, the rest of my life," Rodney said. "I mean, I ain't even moving it, and the mother is killing me right now." He reached into his shirt pocket. "Better take another Perc. . . . Roger, I thought you was gonna stop and get some beer."

"Good idea," Roger said.

"Uh-uh." Weldon shook his head. "We got an eight o'-clock appointment. Ain't no time to stop for beer."

"Just take a minute," Rodney said.

"I said no." Weldon watched Roger cut a glance Rodney's way. It lasted half a second, and he saw the whole story in it. "Now listen to me," Weldon said. "You listening, Rodney?"

"I'm listening, Mr. Chaney," Rodney said. Then muttered, "Like I got a choice."

Weldon reached across Rodney's knees and turned the radio off. Saying, "We'll park the truck across the street from the man's office. I'll go inside with the briefcase full of dynamite. The briefcase will stay in the office. After I take care of business, once I come walking out that front door and I give you the thumbs-up—and you got to wait till I give you the high sign—you boys blow that baby up."

"Out of fucking sight," Roger said.

"Don't forget," Rodney said. "It's my turn to push the button."

"Just remember," Weldon said. "Don't do nothing till you see me with my thumbs in the air."

Roger said, "I got to tell you, Mr. Chaney. Blowing up an office has been one of my ambitions in life."

"It's my turn on the button," Rodney said.

Just before eight the truck rolled past Greenie's 24-HR Coffee Shop. "Man's office is on top of that restaurant," Weldon said. "See the second-floor windows with the blinds? That's it. Pull in across the street." He pointed to some empty spaces. "That'll give you clear sight lines and an easy exit."

Roger backed into a parking spot in front of the Ladies of Charity Thrift Store, with a full view of Greenie's. "Just like being at a damn drive-in movie," he said. "This is gonna be good."

"We all set, boys?" Weldon asked. "All right. I'm going in now."

Weldon opened the door and stepped from the truck, his oxygen bottle banging against the door as he got out. He went behind the cab and opened the tool well in the truck bed. Two briefcases were inside; he took one.

Gray rain was falling steadily from a sky so low and heavy that the clouds seemed to drag against the rooftops. With his free hand Weldon pulled his trench coat shut.

It was an old coat, with a pocket that his wife, God rest her gentle soul, had sewn into the lining. The pocket was just the right size for Weldon's midget .12-gauge, and the gun was in there now.

Weldon waved as he walked past the truck. The last thing he heard from it was the sound of Rodney laughing.

"Iris had a pretty good gig as a substitute teacher," Eddie said. "Steady work when she wanted it. So you combine that with my salary from the department, we grossed maybe fifty or sixty grand a year. Sounds like a lot of money, right? Shit."

Jack drove his Chevy, doing thirty-five in the rain down

Henderson Avenue, past small storefronts with hand-painted
signs in Spanish. While Eddie talked, Jack wondered if he
should ram a telephone pole.

Eddie sat in the passenger's seat. He had stopped sweating and brought his jabber speed down from deranged to
merely disturbed. The gun, in his right hand, was pointed at
Jack. He directed Jack along a series of quick lefts and rights,
and ordered a couple of around-the-block trips. To make
sure, he said, no Cubans or CIA boys were following them.

"Give you an example on this money thing," Eddie said
after another glance out the back window. "Iris kept bitch-
ing that everybody else had one of them minivans, why not
her? So one day she goes down to the miracle mile and
picks one out. Fucking car salesmen. Normal people like
you and me, Jackie, don't stand a chance with these bastards. They got surveillance cameras, hidden mikes, the
works. Somebody like Iris, it's like a sheep strolling into the
hyena den. I mean, it's walking meat for these guys, this is
what they live for. Understand what I'm saying, Jackie?
Excuse me, I'm asking you a question."

"I understand, Eddie."

"So she picks one out, right? Tells me I'll love it 'cause
it's got captain's chairs. *Captain's* chairs, you believe that?
I'm like, Iris, what are you after here, a van or the Starship
Enterprise? Anyway, Jackie, you see what kind of financial
pressure I was under. I mean, you know what cops get paid.
When there was a chance to fatten the eagle, I took it."

"You mean a chance to go crooked," Jack said. Thinking
that he could use the wet road to put the Chevy in a sideways slide and crunch Eddie's side into the back end of a
parked car. That might give Jack a chance to jump and run.
But it wouldn't solve the Lola problem. Same deal with driving too fast and looking to attract a cop: Suppose Eddie
went Dillinger and tried to shoot it out. If they killed him,

Lola might never be found. So Jack drove like a Baptist deacon and hoped for better odds down the line.

Eddie said, "Take a guy like this trash Mineola Watts. Fresh out of Texas Department of Corrections, right, and he don't want another trip down. He's got a street rep, he's got connections. Plus, he has the bad luck to get popped with a pocketful of crack vials one night by Detective Eddie Nickles. You see what I'm getting at, Jackie?"

"You're saying you squeezed him into dealing drugs for you."

"I'm saying we took the opportunity to go into business together. Then, later, I took the opportunity to dissolve the partnership. Happens every day in your world of commerce."

They reached Greenie's at straight-up eight. The breakfast crowd had nearly filled the parking, so Jack had to take a spot at the back of the lot. He and Eddie walked across the wet pavement with Eddie's gun against Jack's side. They were arm in arm. "Check it out," Eddie said. "Bet we look like a couple of queers out for a stroll."

They went to the front of the building and passed by Greenie's big window. Jack glanced inside. First time in years he hadn't seen a cop bellied up to the counter.

Eddie nudged Jack's ribs with the gun. "Let's go upstairs," he said, "and get this show on the road."

Climbing a flight of stairs had left Weldon gasping for breath. He had to rest for five minutes on the top step, with the black briefcase beside him like a salesman's sample case and the shotgun still in his coat.

When he finally found his wind again, Weldon had gone to the second door on the right. He studied stick-on white letters at eye level: FLIPPO ASSOC. Weldon tried the knob—locked. He knocked but got no answer.

Weldon walked down the hallway—old brown carpet on the floor, cheap brown paneling on the walls and a couple of landlord's haloes hanging from the ceiling—to an open door. It was a room no bigger than a closet, with a toilet, sink and mop bucket. Weldon pulled the door almost shut, leaving a gap of an inch or so, and waited.

The washroom faucet dripped, rain fell on the roof, and dishes banged together at the greasy spoon downstairs. Then, voices came up the stairs and into the hallway. Two men, not yelling, but not happy with each other either.

Weldon listened. Key in the lock, door opening, door shutting, men's voices gone. He left the washroom and walked back down the hall. He could hear them talking inside. Without knocking, Weldon turned the knob and pushed the door open.

There were two men in the office, one standing behind a desk and one sitting on a couch. The one on the couch said, "What the fuck?"

Weldon stepped in, closed the door and set his black briefcase on the floor. Saying, "I'm here to see Mr. Flippo." He looked at the man behind the desk. The face was the same one he had seen on the TV news. "I'm guessing that's you," Weldon said. "We have an eight o'clock appointment."

"Who's this, a customer?" the one on the couch said. "Flippo ain't in, gramps. Now turn around and get outta here fast."

"That's him," Rodney said. "Walked right up them stairs. Lemme have the remote, Roger, so he don't poison one more dick on this earth."

"Let's give it another minute," Roger said. "Snorkel Man's moving pretty damn slow today. We got to make sure he's in that office. I mean, that dyno's good stuff, but it ain't no atom bomb."

Rodney shoved his palm toward Roger. "Right now. Give it to me, 'cause it's payback time. Ain't nothing sweeter than payback, you know it, Roger?" Rodney snapped his fingers. "Come on, man, hand it over, and let's make some noise."

"Goddamn, will you stop talking so much? You're fogging up the view." Roger ran his sleeve across the windshield condensation, then rolled his window down. "Not to mention you smell like throwup."

"Hey, you keep screwing around, Mr. Chaney's gonna be back downstairs. Then what, genius? Ask him to go back up in that office for a minute so we can explode him?"

Roger stared at the second-floor office. "He's probly in there by now."

"Shit, yeah, he's there. Now give me that remote."

Roger reached into the side pocket of his windbreaker. "Man, watching that glass shatter is gonna be something else. Not to mention you and me is in for a boatload of Snorkel Man's money just as soon as they ID what's left of his remains. They'll be peeling pieces of him off the walls with a paint scraper." He took the remote from his pocket, held it in two hands and rested his arms against the steering wheel. "This is a moment to savor, Rodney. This is one for the fucking scrapbook, man."

"Well, it will be as soon as you give me that." Rodney reached for the remote.

Roger elbowed his half brother's hand away. "The hell you doing?"

"It's my turn, Roger. You promised." Rodney reached for it again and got another elbow.

Roger said, "My once-in-a-lifetime chance, and you think I'm giving it away to *you?*"

"Hey, asshole—" Rodney lunged for Roger's hands. The two of them shoved and grunted. Both of them had a grip on the remote. It gave off erratic beeps as their fingers pressed against the buttons. Finally Roger yanked it free, but lost his grip as he pulled it away. The remote sailed out the open window and hit the pavement with a sickening plastic crack.

"Now you done it," Rodney said. "Now you fucking went and done it."

Roger looked out the window, then back at Rodney. Saying, "You know what? Forget Snorkel Man. Why don't I just kill you instead?"

Jack stared at the man. Thinking whoever he was, he knew how to make an entrance, like someone who had watched plenty of old TV Westerns. He was a big guy gone to lard and sag, somewhere in his seventies, with a long gray coat hanging low and a gray Resistol on his head. He wore cowboy boots, blue jeans and a pressed white shirt. A clear tube snaked from a shoulder bag and forked into his nose. Even with the air supply he seemed out of breath.

He set his black briefcase on the floor. His gaze made the room, spent a couple of seconds on Eddie and then rested on Jack. As soon as the man spoke—announcing he was here to see Mr. Flippo—Jack snapped to the voice: the can of rusty nails from the phone.

Eddie said, "You hard of hearing, old man? I said get outta here now."

He glanced Eddie's way. "And what if I don't?"

Eddie rose from the couch. Jack watched him keep his gun next to his thigh, not hiding it but not pointing it either. As if to say, I have this if I need it but I probably won't for somebody like you.

"This is a small room, which maybe you noticed." Eddie, standing in front of the man, lifted the air tube off his belly and pinched it shut between two fingers. Saying, "So with three people in here it can get a little stuffy."

The big man was his best chance to throw Eddie off the rails. Jack said, "Maybe the gentleman should stay."

"My advice to you, Jackie?" Eddie raised the gun slightly his way. "That would be to shut the fuck up."

A mention of JFK should do it, Jack thought. Maybe the old man brought some material relevant to the case. Jack pointed and said, "What's in the briefcase?"

Roger knelt on the wet pavement, picked up the remote and cradled it in his palm. "Got a crack in the casing," he said, "but it don't look like it's hurt too bad. It don't look fatal."

"Make you a deal," Rodney said from the truck. "You punch in the first two numbers, and I do the last two."

Roger thought it over, then said, "I do the first one, you get the middle two, and I do the last."

"You do the last one," Rodney said, "but I'm holding the remote while you do it."

They stared at each other until Roger said, "All right."

"Get in the truck, then," Rodney told him, "and let's rock and roll."

"This is gonna be primo," Roger said as he settled into his seat.

Rodney nodded and licked his lips. "That last I had was primo."

"Here we go now." Roger pressed the 6 key and handed the remote to Rodney. "Your turn."

"And a nine," Rodney said. "And then a six. Roger would you do the honors?"

"Love to. Adios, motherfuckers." He pressed the 9 key.

The Gilliches heard the faint sound of "Candle in the Wind," digital version, from the tool well behind them. "Something ain't right here," Roger said.

•   •   •

The blast rattled the windows and gave the building a shake. "Jesus Christ," Eddie said. "What was that?"

Jack raised the blinds and looked. "Got a truck in flames across the street. Fully involved, as the fire boys say."

Eddie stepped to the window for a glance. "All right, the shit's starting to rain down now, Jackie." He scanned the street. "Could be a diversionary move. That's the way they do these things. Same deal they pulled with Oswald, Jackie. Get you looking one way while they're coming at you from the other. We're gonna get out of here right now."

"Let's have a little talk first," the old man said. Jack and Eddie turned and stared into the barrel of a shotgun.

29

T he big man ordered Eddie to put his gun on the floor,
slide it over with his foot and return to the couch.
When Eddie didn't move fast enough the man said, "See
that burning truck? They's two boys down in there, got it by
messing with me."

"You did that? From up here?" Eddie looked impressed.
"Tip of the hat, grampa."

"I don't have no grandkids." The man glanced toward the
window. "Don't believe I will anytime soon neither." He
turned toward Jack. "The name is Weldon."

"My pleasure," Jack said. "Just a suggestion, but why
don't we all put our guns down?"

"I'll decide when to do that," Weldon said.

Eddie said, "Exactly what I tried to tell you back at
my place, Jackie. Guy with the gun makes the rules." He
started to stand until Weldon swung the shotgun his way.
"Piece of advice, Weldon. Jackie don't always listen like he
should."

Weldon waited until Eddie had settled back onto the couch. Then to Jack: "I'll get to the point real fast. This umbrella man movie. You know where I could get it?"

"I might," Jack said.

"You *what?*" Eddie gripped the hair at the sides of his head, as if he were holding himself on a hot seat. "Jesus Christ, Jackie, how many knives you gonna put in one man's back?"

Weldon nodded. "All right, Mr. Flippo, here's what I want to talk about. Answer this next question and give me nothing but the truth."

"Hey, lotsa luck," Eddie said.

"It might be"—Weldon paused, locking eyes with Jack— "that I hear what I want to hear from you, I turn around and walk out of this office, let you boys get back to your business."

Eddie said, "The business of Jackie screwing me in the ass, you mean?"

"Other hand," Weldon said, "I might require some further assistance from you."

"The business of stealing a major score right outta my pocket?" Eddie still had two handfuls of his own hair. "That business?"

"What I need," Weldon said, "is a name. Anybody connected with this movie that goes by Sylvan Dufraine?"

"You know him?" Jack said.

"Maybe."

"Man's supposed to be all burned up long time ago."

"That's what they say." Weldon looked like a tired old rattler with enough venom left for one more rat. "Is it him or not?"

"You want to find him if it is?"

"I might."

Jack stared at Weldon. Thinking, get the payment up front. "There's something I want first," he said.

"Son"—Weldon raised the barrel of the .12-gauge—"I'm setting the conditions here."

"What'd I tell you, Jackie?" Eddie said. He turned to Weldon. "Like talking to a fucking wall, this guy."

Jack waited until the man's eyes came back to him. "It's not something I want from you," Jack said. "Eddie, here, has kidnapped my girlfriend—"

"You're blowing this way out of proportion, Jackie."

"—and I want to know where she is. Make him tell me, let me call the cops to go get her, and I'll give you everything you want to know."

"Nobody's calling no police," Weldon said.

With Eddie nodding fast. "Guy knows how to do business, Jackie. Weldon, you know how to do business, my friend."

"Number one, unless Lola goes free," Jack said, "and unless I know she's all right, I don't say anything. Number two, Eddie has to be turned over to the police. Those are my terms, gun or no gun. And I should point out that none of it, Weldon, comes out of your hide."

Weldon pointed the shotgun at Eddie. "All right, let's hear it," he said. "Where's the girl?"

It was a piece-of-cake arrangement, Jack thought, using Weldon to hammer Eddie. A can't-lose deal, and he had fallen right into it. He would get Lola's whereabouts, lock Eddie down, then send Weldon on his way to deal with Dufraine as he wished.

He thought that until Eddie said, "Weldon, how'd you like to put your hands on a million dollars?"

Weldon took a couple of shallow breaths from the hose and said, "Do what?"

"Did I say one million?" Eddie had a big grin going. "Fuck, that's the lowball. Two, three million is more like it."

"Shut up, Eddie," Jack said. "Weldon, don't listen to him. The guy's a nutcase hustler."

"Maybe even four million," Eddie said, "we play our cards right. Ask you a question, Weldon. Who you with?"

"With?"

"Who you working for on this deal? You don't mind my asking. The Cubans? The feds? I'm gonna bet the feds."

Weldon said nothing. Eddie said, "Hey, it don't really matter. Main thing is, I don't get the impression you came in here gunning for Eddie Nickles. Am I right? I mean, despite the crap Jackie tried to lay on me."

"You mentioned four million."

"At least," Eddie said. "So right now, whoever your backers are, you might want to think about your own deal, know what I'm saying? We could be talking five mil, just for one little film."

Weldon blinked. "You mean for that umbrella man movie?"

"I like the way you do business, Weldon." Eddie winked and pointed. "You get the facts first. You and me, we're both straight-ahead guys. You and me, we don't stab friends in the back. You and me, we—"

"That's enough." Weldon looked at Jack. "What about this?"

Jack waited. He felt like someone diving into black water. Maybe he would find himself among mermaids, maybe sharks. "Eddie's right about one thing," he said. "You want to make money off the umbrella man, you can do it. Couple million sounds about right, if the film really does deliver the goods. But you don't need Eddie. I'll give you Dufraine, and you can cut your own deal."

Nobody talked until Eddie said, "Sure, Judas—I mean

Jackie—he could do that." Eddie stood. This time Weldon didn't make him sit down. "You could do it by yourself, Weldon, but how would you know what you're looking at?"

Weldon said, "What do you mean?"

"He doesn't mean shit," Jack said. Thinking Eddie might be nuts, but he could still slither with the best of them.

"All due respect," Eddie said, "you consider yourself an expert on JFK conspiracy theory?" Eddie smoothed his hair. "What I'm asking, Weldon, is could you look at that film and tell if it's the genuine chops? If the answer's maybe not, let me tell who you need at your side." Eddie patted himself on the chest. "That would be Eddie Nickles, premier assassinologist."

Weldon nodded. "I remember you now from the TV news."

Jack said, "Oh, for Christ's sake."

"So let me ask you this"—Eddie straightened his collar—"if being on Channel Four ain't proof that I'm the top JFK man, what is?"

"Boy's got a point," Weldon said to Jack.

"Boy's got a woman's life at stake, is what the boy's got." Jack waited for Eddie's eyes, then said, "Anything happens to her—*anything*—you bleed."

Eddie sent Jack an air kiss and turned to Weldon. "Did I say five million?" He sniffed. "I'm starting to think six. Maybe seven, once you factor in the overseas market, Weldon. Or should I call you partner?"

"While you two are counting your money," Jack said, "you're forgetting one thing. I'm the one who knows where the man with the movie is. And I don't talk until Lola walks."

"Jackie, I didn't lay a finger on her, all right?" Eddie showed him a palms-up shrug. "She's got her a nice, cozy place where she's probably taking a quiet nap right now. Swear to God."

Jack looked at Weldon. "You heard my terms."

Weldon took some short breaths from the hose, then said, "Soon as you lead me to Sylvan Dufraine, I'll get you what you need on your girl. You have my word."

"Hey, she's *fine*," Eddie said.

Jack didn't answer. He felt as if he had his hands on the wheel of a speeding car whose steering was out.

Weldon's eyes had gone cold and flat. He said to Jack, "Will it take a hurting to convince you?"

"Piece of advice, Weldon?" Eddie stepped forward. "This guy Jackie never makes it easy on himself."

Weldon stared at Jack. "Son, is pain what it takes to make you act?"

Jack didn't have a chance to respond. Weldon moved to his left, faster than Jack thought he could go, and swung the butt end of his shotgun.

It caught Eddie on the jaw. He staggered, fell against the wall, bounced off and went down. He tried to rise, moaned and flopped onto his back.

"Take me to Dufraine," Weldon said to Jack, "and you'll have what you want from this joker on the floor. One way or the other. But you don't help me out, I have to kill him." Weldon pointed the shotgun at Eddie's head. Asking Jack, "How you gonna find your ladyfriend then?"

The truck explosion had drawn half a dozen police cars to the front of Greenie's, so Jack, Eddie and Weldon took the fire exit in the rear. Jack drove the Chevy with Weldon in back, holding the shotgun. Eddie slumped beside Jack, bleeding into a hand towel.

Jack caught Weldon's glance in the mirror—like looking at the Marlboro Man gone to seed and emphysema—and said, "There was this crazy bastard with red hair and gold teeth came to see me a while back. He one of your boys?"

Weldon waited. Then said, "Used to be. But he got too close to a fire this morning."

"So you're working solo now."

"Best way to do it. Cuts down on the unknown factor."

"Speaking of fires," Jack said, "that one back in sixty-three appears to have missed Sylvan Dufraine, though it was in his car. Maybe you could tell me why."

"Sometimes it's best not to ask too much."

Jack tried to read the man's face in the rearview. It wasn't telling him much except that Weldon didn't enjoy the line of questioning. "Well," Jack said, "here's my guess. One reason or the other, you're not too thrilled that old Sylvan's popped back up."

Weldon grunted. Jack drove up North Central, the most direct route to Dufraine's house. Wondering if he was delivering the executioner, and not pleased with the thought. Even if Dufraine was a lying little prick, Jack wasn't in the mood to provide limo service for his killer.

"No matter what happened," Jack said, "that was a long time ago. More than thirty-five years back. The mists of history and all that. Maybe we ought to forget about it, let bygones be bygones."

"Son," Weldon said, "it don't work that way."

Jack nodded. "I know," he said.

Weldon checked the .38 Special he had taken from Eddie. Each chamber had a round in it. He put the gun in the left side pocket of his raincoat. It balanced out the .32 he had in his right pocket. With Weldon thinking that you could never have too much firepower. Because who knew how many people you might have to shoot.

The car was on an overpass now. Weldon glanced at the rainy streets below, and thought of Timmy Skinnet, a man he killed in Dallas in 1962. Timmy Skinnet, who called himself a financial adviser, wore white shoes and had capped front teeth. He was a homosexual who was always chewing cinnamon sticks, which he claimed kept him from smoking. Apparently Timmy Skinnet desired a long, healthy life. If so, he shouldn't have bilked one hot-tempered client out of nearly half a million. A client who happened to know Weldon.

Weldon had done the job for his usual fee. He came in the back door at night and waited in the kitchen for the dead-to-be.

Timmy Skinnet, surprised in his underwear, had tried to run. It took two blasts from Weldon's shotgun to put him down on his kitchen floor. Weldon was just about to leave the house when he heard something in the next room. The place was dark; Weldon turned on a light and found a naked man cowering behind the couch.

The man begged for his life, got on his knees and cried. I'd like to let you go, Weldon told him, but you've seen my face. Because he hadn't brought extra shells or another gun, Weldon had to use his knife on the man—a messy piece of business that ruined his jacket and stained the soles of his boots. From that point on, Weldon vowed always to pack an extra gun.

Now the Chevy was pulling off North Central, at the Park Lane exit. Used to be nothing but fields out here, back when he disposed of Timmy Skinnet, but the place was full of shopping centers now. They could put up all the buildings they wanted, Weldon thought, but it was still the same ground underneath.

In the front seat Eddie had a coughing fit, spit up some blood and muttered something about a broken jaw. It got

Weldon thinking about the question Eddie had posed back in the office: Who was he with on this deal? Only thing he could say for sure was that the good-looking woman at the Gator Lounge had handed him some cash in 1963. But who really had paid to get Sylvan Dufraine dead? After all these years he still hadn't figured that out.

All he knew now was that he would have to make the job right, no matter how much time had passed. He had told Dufraine to disappear, and there was no expiration date on that.

But now a bonus might be riding along: the chance to make some good money, if what they were saying about the Dufraine movie was right. Problem was, some extra people had wandered into the scene. That could be fixed.

You never leave witnesses alive, Weldon reminded himself, even if it's your last job.

30

J ack pulled his Chevy in front of the house and wondered how soon the shooting would start. Weldon said, "You go first, Flippo. Mouth man, you follow him. I'll be right behind."

They walked through the cold rain single file, and stood on the porch in a line while Jack rang the bell. Dufraine answered the door in his bathrobe. Asking Jack, "Don't you ever call first, Shitouttaluck?"

Jack glanced back at Eddie and Weldon. "Sylvan," he said, "you got some 'splaining to do."

"I'm busy," Dufraine said. "I got things to—" He narrowed his eyes at Jack. "What'd you call me?"

"I've been to the cemetery," Jack said. "The one in Seffner. Some fascinating gravestones there in your family plot. But that's the least of your problems right now." He pointed over his shoulder with his thumb. "Remember your old pal Weldon?"

Dufraine stared through his thick glasses past Jack. He

looked at Weldon, blinked a few times; then his face passed slowly from bafflement to fear. It was like dawn breaking over an ugly land. "Oh, no." Dufraine's hand, all boniness and liver spots, rose slowly to his face. "It's him."

"See what I mean about problems?" Jack said.

"We got some unfinished business," Weldon said.

Dufraine's wordless gaze dropped from Weldon's face to something about hip high. From the fright in the little man's eyes, Jack would bet he had just seen Weldon's shotgun pointed his way.

"Gets your attention, doesn't it?" Jack said. "Why, thank you. Yes, we'd love to come in."

Dufraine stepped aside. He had the look of someone watching the repo man haul his life off with a tow truck.

"The fuck is this?" Eddie said, checking the Western decor as he came in. "Hopalong Cassidy's secret bunk-house?"

All the old photos were still hanging on the wall, and the framed glamour shot of young Mrs. Dufraine remained on the lamp table. A fake-log gas blaze was going in the fire-place. Eddie said, "Where's Trigger?"

Weldon motioned with his shotgun toward the wagon-wheel couch. "Mouth man, you sit down over there. Flippo, you're right beside him. Dufraine, why don't you take the easy chair."

"I know what you're thinking." Dufraine sat, facing Weldon and talking fast. "But you got it all wrong. You got to hear my side of the story. Everything was on the up-and-up as far as our agreement goes. I disappeared just like you said. Didn't come back till I was legally dead. Changed my name, even changed my face. I mean, Christ, look at this nose. It's a Mexican quack job. You think I would of done that if—"

"Shut up," Weldon said.

The walk into the house had left Weldon short of breath. While he drew on his air hose, Eddie dripped blood onto the carpet.

Dufraine looked pale and shaky. He leaned over a metal trash can—one decorated with depictions of cattle brands—and threw up.

"And that's not the plastic joke kind," Jack said.

Dufraine wiped his mouth on the sleeve of his bathrobe. Weldon managed to slow his breathing. Jack said, "All right, Weldon, you've got what you wanted." Then to Eddie: "You gonna tell me where Lola is, or does the big man have to get persuasive on your ass?"

"Hold on," Weldon said. "We're not done yet."

"Far as I'm concerned we are."

"We got a few things to talk about. Then you get yours."

"Stabbed me in the back," Eddie muttered. "That's what I got."

"Hang around and gab awhile?" Jack shook his head. "That wasn't our deal."

"It is now," Weldon said.

With Jack thinking, bad sign.

"I mean, did you get a look at this nose?" Dufraine pointed to his face. "The local butcher could of done a better job in the dark. Ain't that proof I did what I was supposed to?"

Weldon pointed his shotgun at the nearest wall and pulled the trigger. The blast filled the room. When the noise settled, plaster dust swirled in the light of the lamps.

"What you do that for?" Dufraine said. "Ain't no call for tearing up a man's house."

"Look at the size of that hole." Eddie stared. "Man, you could throw a wiener dog through it."

"That's to get everybody's attention," Weldon said.

Jack, ears ringing, added up Weldon's firepower:
Probably four shells left in the shotgun, plus Eddie's gun in
his pocket. Likely another handgun in there somewhere too.
Enough to put multiple vents in everyone. Jack said, "Let's
take care of business here and I'll be on my way."

"Why?" Eddie said. "You got another friend to screw up
the ass?"

"I know this looks bad." Dufraine coughed a couple of
times and spit into the trash can. "But it ain't what you
think. I got a whole new name and everything."

"You're here," Weldon said. "You wasn't supposed to be.
Ever."

"See, this ain't me you're talking to." Dufraine held up
both hands like someone being robbed. "It's somebody else.
I'm my own brother now, see."

"Weldon, can I make a suggestion without you clubbing
me in the head again?" Eddie pulled the towel from his face
to show a nasty gash on his cheek. "So that we don't forget
the grand prize here?"

Weldon waited a moment, then gave him a short nod.

Eddie turned to Dufraine. "We hear you got a film."

"A film?" Dufraine's eyes went from side to side. "What
film?"

"What film?" Eddie said. "Listen to this guy. From the
grassy knoll, chump. Shows the second umbrella man."

Dufraine looked as if he was about to throw up again.

Eddie said, "Cough up the film, or we turn the place inside out. That hole in the wall? That'll be a decorating touch
before we get through. Not to mention what happens when
Weldon gets in the mood to start conking people on the noggin. I'm here to tell you, it ain't a love tap." Eddie glanced
at Weldon. "Okay I mention that?"

Dufraine turned toward Jack and rasped, "Son of a bitch,
you sold me out."

"Hey, welcome to the club," Eddie said.

Dufraine put his head in his hands. A woman's voice said, "For God's sake, give it to them."

Mrs. Dufraine stood in the doorway to the kitchen, holding a grocery bag and a ring full of keys. She wore a green work-out suit and white tennis shoes, with a green band in her white hair. Short and plump, as forgettable as Jack remembered.

"Just give it to them and get them out of our house." She set the groceries and the keys on the floor and came to Dufraine. The woman put one arm around his slumping shoulders and dabbed at his mouth with a tissue. "Let them have it so they will leave us alone."

"It's not theirs," Dufraine said. "It's mine. I was the one with the camera, not them. I'm the one who caught lightning in a bottle. *I* did, nobody else."

Jack watched Weldon, who was staring at the woman like someone trying to decipher bad handwriting.

"This your old lady?" Eddie said to Dufraine. "Better do what she says."

The woman dropped to her knees and put her face a few inches from Dufraine's. "Listen to me. Give it to them and get them out of here," she said. "And if you won't do it, then I will."

Dufraine kept his movies in a refrigerator in his garage. "Constant thirty-eight degrees," he said. "Best way to pre-serve film."

They all crowded into a space between the old Frigidaire and Dufraine's Cadillac. The light was dim, with the sound of rain on the garage roof. Only Weldon, holding the shot-gun, kept some distance.

"You shitting me?" Eddie said. "Blockbuster of the cen-tury, and it's out here in the spare cooler with the leftover potato salad?"

Dufraine opened the door, crouched and peered in. He could have been a guy after a midnight snack. The refrigerator light made his Mexican-quack nose look like a statue's first draft on a day when the sculptor had whiskey shakes.

On the refrigerator's wire shelves were several gray metal file boxes. Dufraine pulled one of the boxes toward him and raised its lid. "Here we go." He shook his head sadly. "Never thought it would happen like this."

Eddie leaned over him and looked into the box. "Think you could move any slower, old man?"

"Leave him alone," the woman said.

"I was hoping maybe this year," Eddie said.

"Here it is." Dufraine took a manila envelope from the metal box. "Number twenty-two. Labeled for the day on which it was shot."

"What's it show?" Eddie said.

Dufraine stood and puffed himself up for a moment. "Well, it puts goddamn Zapruder to shame, I'll tell you that."

"Second gunman?" Eddie said.

"You think people would of wanted me dead if it was anything less?"

"You got a projector?" Weldon asked.

"Of course I have a projector." Dufraine looked offended.

Weldon motioned with the shotgun toward the door into the house. Saying, "Let's take a look, then."

In the living room Dufraine pushed the button that lowered the screen from the ceiling. Then he opened the cabinet that housed the projector. "All those years in Mexico, I kept this by my side." Dufraine held the clear plastic reel of film, about the size of a coaster, in his palm. "All those years of selling plastic dog turds, this was my retirement plan. One print only, never made another one. This original, noth-

ing more. Now you sons of bitches gonna steal it from me.
Aren't you?"

Nobody answered. Eddie was warming his ass at the fireplace. Weldon tried to watch Dufraine and the woman too.
Jack thought of Monroe Beets at the Conspiracy Institute,
remembered the man telling him: There's a reason for
everything, and coincidence won't take you very far.

"So who wanted me dead back there in sixty-three?"
Dufraine said, talking loud now. "At least you can tell me
that, you're gonna steal this from me."

"Honey, please," his wife said. "Let's just get this over
with."

"Go ahead, let's hear it." Dufraine placed the reel on a
spool and threaded the film into the projector. "Don't you
think it's time I knew?"

Eddie wandered over from the fireplace. "Good question."

Weldon breathed through his tube and said nothing. He
was still alternating an unsure gaze from Dufraine to his
wife and back.

"I think it's the least you could do," Dufraine said.
"You're gonna rob me blind? At least let me know who kept
me on the run all this time."

While Dufraine talked, Jack tried to figure out a way to
escape the place alive, and take Eddie with him. The question was, if he went for Weldon's gun, what would Eddie
do?

"Don't you think you owe it to me?" Dufraine was near
bellowing now. "Don't you think you should tell me just
who in the hell wanted me dead? Huh? You gonna answer
the question or not."

Jack watched Weldon shift in his seat. As Weldon
moved, his air hose snagged on one of the framed pictures

on the lamp table. Weldon turned slightly to free it, and caught a glimpse of the photo: the glam shot of young, beautiful Mrs. Dufraine.

Weldon's mouth fell open slightly, and he stared at the picture. Then he turned to Mrs. Dufraine. Their stares met head-on.

"Good God almighty," Weldon said, almost a whisper. "The Gator Lounge . . . Christmas Eve . . . The woman named Alice . . . That was *you*."

31

J ack watched: Weldon looked as if he had been clubbed in the forehead with a mallet. The woman seemed ready to reach over and rip out the big man's tongue. If it had been dark enough, Jack thought, you could have seen the charge arcing between them.

Dufraine was so busy demanding to know who wanted him dead that he missed it all.

Finally the woman stood and told Dufraine, "Turn that goddamn thing on. Let's get this over with."

"All right, fine," Dufraine said. "I see that nobody's gonna answer my question. Steal the greatest piece of film ever made, but don't let me know who tried to fry my ass. Fine. Kill the lights, Nita, so these thieves can cart our livelihood away."

Weldon recovered enough to say, "Don't do them lights all the way down."

The woman mowed Weldon down with a glance, then reached for a dimmer switch on the wall. The wattage dropped by half, giving the room a dusky mood, with wa-vering firelight from one end.

"Should have sold my work the day I shot it," Dufraine said. He turned on the projector with, "All right, shit, here we go." There was some whirring, and then an illuminated square with rounded corners on the screen. Scratches and dust flickered through the square. Next came the images: grainy black-and-white shots of what looked to be some-one's living room.

"What the hell is that?" Eddie said.

"Got about a minute of home movies on this first," Dufraine said. "Few things I shot around the house before I went down to the grassy knoll that fateful day."

"What are you doing?" Nita Dufraine said to her hus-band.

On the screen two elderly women sat at a table playing cards. "My aunts," Dufraine said. "If anyone cares."

"I don't," Eddie said. "You care, Weldon?"

No answer from Weldon.

"What is this?" Nita Dufraine said. Gazing at her hus-band as if he had begun to bark.

"Minute or two of these gals," Dufraine said, "then you'll see the presidential limo coming into Dealey Plaza. After that you'll have umbrella man number two, behind the stockade fence, and then a muzzle flash."

Eddie whistled in appreciation. "Oh man, I'm about to cream."

Dufraine nodded. "With everything in focus, by the way, the way a pro does it. Unlike Zapruder. But who gets all the damn credit?"

The aunts on the screen kept playing cards. Jack could make out a televison in the same room as the old ladies. It was in the background, a little fuzzy, but he could see a shot of Eddie Albert on a tractor: the opening credits of *Green Acres.*

Lola had made him sit through reruns dozens of times; by now he knew the theme song by heart. The way Lola saw it, *Green Acres* was no mere TV comedy, but was one of the seminal prefeminist documents of the sixties. Jack agreed to watch it because he liked to look at Eva Gabor's tits.

"What about Lola?" Jack said to Weldon now. "You got what you wanted, so give me mine." Then to Eddie: "Where is she?"

Eddie, eyes on the screen, waved him away. "Like I said, Jackie. She's fine."

Jack turned back to Weldon. "I'll say it again. We had a deal."

Eddie said, "Whoa, mama."

The film had jammed. The image on the screen was half framed and jumpy, the way Jack remembered projector problems from eighth-grade social studies class. Dufraine had caused the jam by putting his fingers against the rollers.

Weldon said, "What's happening here?"

"This ain't right." Dufraine flipped the projector off and pulled the film reel from its spool. "You boys taking what's mine? That ain't justice."

Weldon tried to stand. But the low chair and the weight of his air bottle seemed to hold him down.

Eddie said, "The fuck you doing?"

Dufraine stepped toward the fireplace. Shouting, "If I can't have it, nobody does."

He threw the film into the fire.

Eddie screamed as if it were his own liver that Dufraine had tossed. He leapt toward the fireplace, grabbed an iron poker from a stand and tried to rescue the reel.

Dufraine said, "Try and steal *that,* you bunch of shriveled-up squirrel dicks." The smell of burning plastic wafted through the room. "Only copy in the world, and I destroyed it." He turned to face Weldon with, "Now what you gonna do, big man?"

Weldon had managed to make it up from the chair. He was pulling hard on the air hose. "I'm gonna do"—two breaths, three—"what I should of done in the first place."

"Fine," Dufraine said. "Ask me I give a hoot in hell."

Jack stood and edged toward Weldon.

"Don't surprise me one damn bit you're here," Dufraine said. He had one hand on his hip, and the other pointed at Weldon. "Chicken shit always comes back to the roost."

Eddie looked up from the fireplace with the face of someone who had lost his mortgage at the dice tables. Shaking his head and saying, "We're fucked. The whole thing melted."

Dufraine gave him a thin smile. "That's what fire does, you dumb bastard."

Weldon pointed the shotgun at Dufraine. "Never should of let it go this far," he said.

Jack jumped for the gun. It roared just as he reached it. He had his hands around the barrel as he plowed into Weldon. The two of them tumbled over a couch and onto the floor. Weldon hit the rug like a sack of meat.

Jack pulled the shotgun free, rolled and stood. Weldon, still on his back, had lost his hose. He gasped, "Need air." Ten feet away Dufraine was crumpled on the floor, moaning, bleeding from the mess that used to be his knee. His wife lay over him, wailing. By the fireplace, Eddie knelt as if to tie his shoe.

"Air," Weldon said again.

Jack pressed the shotgun against Weldon's ear. Saying, "Maybe. But first, get Eddie's gun out of your pocket. And any other weapon you might have in there. Hurry up."

Then came Eddie's voice from the other side of the

room: "A good cop, Jackie, never goes into the jungle without a backup piece. And mine is pointed right at you."

Jack kept the shotgun on Weldon. But he turned enough to see that Eddie, for once, was telling the truth.

"Put it down," Eddie said. "Else I'm gonna have to start shooting people. My guess is you're first in line."

It was the second time in one day that Eddie had the drop on him. Jack felt like shooting himself in the head.

Eddie stepped closer. "Come on, Jackie. Act smart for once."

Jack put the shotgun on the floor.

"Believe it or not, I ain't killed that many people." Eddie came across the room toward Jack. "Just a few, but they all deserved it."

Jack watched him approach, saw the little gun in his hand: a .22 that must have been pulled from an ankle holster. Eddie said, "No shit, Jackie. Every one of them I popped, they deserved the hell out of it. Just like right now. Talk about a motherfucker that has it coming."

Eddie was just a few feet away when he thumbed the hammer back, leaned over and shot Weldon between the eyes.

"Take it from me," Eddie said, "he'd kill everyone here, maybe even yours truly. Big guy was a maniac. So, what do you know, Jackie. I saved your worthless life."

Eddie reached into the dead man's pockets and found the .38 that Weldon had taken from him. "Here's what I'm gonna do." He aimed the .38 at Jack while he emptied ammo from the backup. Then he dropped the smaller gun on the floor and kicked it toward the Dufraines.

"Tell the cops you killed Weldon in self-defense," Eddie said. "They go for that kind of shit. Or make up whatever kind of story you want. But you mention me to them? Even whisper a description? Do that and I tell everyone who you are. You got me?"

Terrified nods from the Dufraines. With Eddie saying, "Can't believe I'm cutting a break for somebody that sent my big payday up in smoke." He stepped closer to Dufraine and watched him bleed into the rug. "You are such a fuck- ing asshole, you know that? Lucky for you, chump, I got other fish to fry right now."

Eddie turned to Jack. "That fish would be you."

They went out the front door and got in Jack's car. The rain had stopped, leaving everything wet, gray and cold, like the underside of a slug. Eddie glanced at the outside of the Dufraine house. "Okay, the umbrella man film's toast. But there's still some excellent blackmail opportunities there." He held the .38 on a line with Jack's head. "I'll deal with that later. First, though, let's drop by my place."

Jack started the car and pulled away, his body driving while his brain tried to sort out the mess he had fallen into.

Eddie had a cigarette going. "Gotta hand it to you, Jackie. Here I am, premier assassinologist, and I had no idea that little guy Dufraine was around. Much less that he had the film. I mean, I'm big enough to admit that."

No answer from Jack, but Eddie kept talking. "Thing I don't understand about you, man? We could have made ourselves rich with this, and you go mess it all up. You keep the whole umbrella man deal a secret, and meantime you're nosing around the Mineola Watts thing. Throw a mil- lion bucks out the window, man, so you can dig up Mineola."

Jack navigated the neat North Dallas streets. He looked at other drivers in other cars, imagined them listening to music or the news, while he had to hear the story of the germ that infected him.

"What is it?" Eddie said. "You banging Mineola's sister? That it? You backstab me so you can jump some coon poon?" Eddie killed his cigarette in the ashtray. Saying, "I guess that's the lesson here, Jackie. You dig shit up, you get stink. Which is something, my friend, that maybe you should have learned a long time ago."

They were deep into the old, decaying blocks of East Dallas now, with Jack finally seeing it all clearly. He had learned years back that the more time he spent prying into the lives of others, the less time he would have for looking at his own. That was the way he liked it. Better to peep through keyholes than peer in the mirror.

No justification needed. Just to know, to find out, that was enough: Who was killed? What did he steal? When did she leave? Where did they screw? Why was it done? As long as Jack had questions, he had something to do.

Now, once more, he had found the answers. Who had led everyone down this path? He had. Whose fault was it? His. Who was about to die? He was. And he was taking Lola and Treena down with him.

Jack had plucked the ring off the corpse's finger again, only this time he had stolen it from himself.

"Right here," Eddie said.

Jack parked at the curb outside Eddie's abandoned apartment complex. The shabby block was deserted, as if a big storm had swept through, taking the people but leaving the garbage.

"Scoot this way." Eddie opened the passenger's door and stepped out. "We'll take a stroll upstairs." Like someone inviting a date in for coffee.

Jack did as told. They walked toward the apartment courtyard, with Eddie's limp giving him trouble on the broken pavement of the sidewalk. He kept the gun poked against Jack's side as they went.

Eddie said, "Problem here, Jackie, is you boxed me into a corner on this Mineola Watts thing. I mean, bringing in the black bitch? His sister? No telling what she's gonna do. For all I know, she's down at the police building right now, making a case."

"She doesn't know anything," Jack said.

"Jesus, Jackie, you can't lie no better than that?"

"She's got nothing on you, Eddie. Leave her alone."

"Can't do that." Eddie tripped slightly as they climbed three concrete steps. He caught himself with a clutch of Jack's Sergeant Bilko sweatshirt, and kept the gun against Jack's ribs. "Can't take that chance. So we're back to the same old problem."

The apartment courtyard hadn't changed since Jack had last visited: construction debris, heaps of empty boxes and the stray, wet pages of old newspapers. Jack looked at the kicked-in doors and broken windows and said, "Where's Lola?"

"Knew you'd ask that." Eddie pointed to the second floor. "Got herself a little bird's nest up there. You want to get her out? Deliver the black bitch."

They skirted the pool, with Jack telling himself: Should have known Eddie would stash her here. He glanced down at the junk carpet roll and scrap lumber that lay in several inches of dirty rainwater. "Let Lola go," Jack said, "and you and I can work this deal ourselves."

Eddie cleared his throat. "Here's what I'm thinking. Make it worth your while. I don't get cooperation from you, I do something as an incentive. Like maybe I shoot off one of Lola's—I don't know—toes, how's about. That work? And I keep shooting off toes, Jackie, until you do what you need to. We run out of toes, we move on to something else."

"I'll tell you again," Jack said. "You hurt her and I'll kill you."

"Then save us all a lot of trouble, Jackie, and deliver up Mineola's sister."

Someone behind them—a woman's voice—shouted, "Freeze!"

Eddie turned, swinging Jack around with him. Treena Watts stepped from the dark doorway of an empty apartment.

"Now *that's* service," Eddie said.

Treena was halfway across the courtyard, maybe fifty feet away. She held her gun hip-high.

"Talk about getting it on a platter," Eddie said. Then called, "Hey, honey. Put your weapon on the ground or your pal Jackie here finds himself with a new hole which he don't need."

Treena took a few steps forward. Eddie said, "Say this so you'll understand it. Like Tarzan used to tell the jigs, Oongawa."

Jack looked down. Eddie stood at the lip of the pool, with his right foot on a tile that had been painted with a black 10. Ten feet down. That might hold him for a while, keep him busy for a minute or two while he crawled out.

"Gonna give you five seconds, bitch," Eddie said. "Here's the deal. I count to five while you drop the gun. One . . . two . . ."

Jack shoved. Eddie teetered on the lip, windmilling his arms. Jack reached out to shove again. Eddie grabbed the tail of Jack's sweatshirt as he fell.

Jack bent forward, and the shirt rode up his trunk as if he were being skinned. He lost his balance; the shirt covered his head as he went over the edge. He was falling blind.

He landed on top of Eddie. The sound when he hit was a sharp crack like the snap of kindling wood.

The fall knocked the breath out of him. Jack lay gasping the way Weldon had, wondering if Eddie would pull the trigger. But Eddie wasn't moving.

The shirt was still over his head. When Jack could breathe again, he pulled it off, rolled away from Eddie and stood. He was in cold green water to his ankles.

Eddie lay belly down in the water, with his face mashed against the roll of carpet. His head looked like a bulb screwed in crooked: his neck twisted, his chin touching his shoulder.

Jack felt for a pulse and found none.

Treena leaned over the edge and peered down. "Well," she said, "there's one who definitely ain't coming back."

32

The doctors kept Lola in the hospital overnight for observation, then sent her home with a jar full of sedatives. She recovered fast, more or less. By the end of the second day she was talking about a new gallery show based on her experience: chilled, dark isolation booths with custom-made video loops of personal memories. "I'll call it the Training Grave," she told Jack.

"It'll be a smash," he said.

Lola spent the week in bed. Jack fixed her meals and rubbed her back. He cleaned up the house. He made late-night runs to the store for ice cream, and he told her he was sorry every hour or so.

Seven days after the incident, for the first time since Lola's release, they made love. The sedatives took the air out of Lola's arousal, but it was a nice glimpse of normal life. Jack hadn't known how much he would miss that.

Afterward, as they lay in bed, Lola reached for the remote and turned on the TV. She found some old comedies to watch, and Jack heard her laugh again. While Lola drifted into sleep, Jack thought about what she found funny. He got as far as Arnold the television-watching pig when the truth charged through him. It was like sticking his finger in a wall socket.

Jack bolted from the covers and stood naked next to the bed. Almost shouting, "The slippery son of a bitch."

He reached for Lola's shoulder and shook her. "Wake up!"

She turned over. He shook her again. "Lola!"

Finally she surfaced to half-awake, eyes barely open, and gave him a drowsy, "Huh?"

"I have to know this," Jack said. "Are you awake? I need this answer now."

"*What*, Jack?"

"Are you awake? Here it is," he said. "When did they first broadcast *Green Acres?*"

"All right, about the other day." Treena Watts looked at Jack. "Maybe I take a shot, and instead of nailing Nickles, I hit you. Think that makes the world a worse place?"

"Yeah, for me."

"You didn't have anything to worry about." Treena took a mirror from her purse and checked her hair. "Could have saved yourself that whole falling-into-the-pool thing. Because I had the mother cold. You think after waiting in that empty-ass apartment for three hours that I'd let him walk away? Think I'd shoot and miss after that? Uh-uh. He was going down."

"You done?"

"You didn't even ask how I found him."

Jack sighed. "Does it matter?"

"Man had a felony assault charge pending, you know that?"

"No, but it doesn't surprise me."

"One call to a bondsman, I had his address. One call, man, that's all it took."

"Congratulations," Jack said.

"Just wanted you to know the facts."

"Can we go in now?"

"Sure, man."

They got out of the car and walked across the yard. Jack knocked. The door opened, and Nita Dufraine faced them. She said, "I knew you would be back."

Nita asked them in, invited them to sit down, offered them some tea. When everyone had sipped from their cups she sent a half-nasty look Jack's way. "You brought those people here," she said. "To my home."

He nodded. "That's true, I'm sorry to say."

"On the other hand, you saved my husband's life when you grabbed the gun. So I have to say that I hate you and like you all at once."

"Been there, done that," Treena said.

They sat in the same room where Dufraine and Weldon had been shot. The bloody carpet had been replaced. Dufraine was back at the hospital, where the surgeons were trying to rebuild his knee.

Jack looked around, thought about what had happened and said, "I have a couple of questions."

Nita put her cup on its saucer. "I didn't think you came by just to chat."

Jack remembered the big man sitting where he sat now, remembered an astonished Weldon saying to Nita, That was you. He shot a glance at the photo of the young Nita on the table, then brought his eyes to the face of the old one. He said, "In nineteen sixty-three you tried to buy the murder of your own husband."

"She did?" Treena leaned forward and dropped her jaw,

giving a big show. "Whoa. You didn't tell me that. You did that, Nita?"

Nita was quiet for a while. Then: "I was very young. I got angry. I made a mistake. That's the way I was in those days." She gazed at the floor. After a minute or so she took a deep breath and said, "I found a film he made. A film showing Sylvan and a young woman. It—" She stopped, raised her head and looked at Jack. "It didn't leave much to the imagination."

Jack nodded. "But instead of a divorce lawyer you hired Weldon the friendly hit man."

Treena said, "You go, girl."

"I read about Weldon Chaney in the paper," Nita said. "He wasn't that hard to find. Dallas was a fairly small town then."

"Except Weldon didn't do the job."

"God, I was so happy when I found out Sylvan was alive, I dropped to my knees. I was crying and I was praising the Lord." Her eyes went moist. "Do you know what it's like to do a horrible thing and be given a chance to undo it?"

"Wait a minute," Treena said. "Your husband didn't know you did it?"

"Sylvan thought it had something to do with his Kennedy footage. He thought the people who killed the President were after him." She almost smiled. "I swore to myself then and there that I would stay with Sylvan and protect him the rest of my life. If that meant leaving Dallas in the middle of the night and spending years in Mexico, so be it."

"Living off life insurance," Jack said.

She didn't answer. He pushed on: "And somewhere along the line he stole his dead brother's identity."

"My father died," she said. "He had a novelty store in

Dallas. . . . We decided to come back and run it, and Sylvan
needed to be somebody else. . . . Everything was fine until
all this happened just now."

The room was quiet until Nita said, "Nineteen sixty-
three." She closed her eyes. "That was a long time ago."

Jack put his cup next to her photo. "All these years, and
Sylvan never had the faintest it was you. That's amazing."

She met his stare again. "You want money? Is that what
you want? You want money not to tell my husband, don't
you?"

Jack shook his head. "That's not it."

"Then why did you come here?"

"I'm still interested in the movie Sylvan took on the
grassy knoll."

She gave a little laugh and waved him away. "You saw
what happened. He threw it into the fire."

"Uh-uh," Jack said. "You were watching the screen
same as everybody else. You catch the TV behind the card-
playing old ladies? The one showing Eddie Albert on that
tractor?"

"Do what?" Treena said. "Eddie which?"

"What are you saying?" Nita said. Sounding to Jack as if
she didn't want the answer.

"That's nineteen sixty-five vintage. Or later." Jack laced
his fingers and tilted his head like someone who had just
laid down a winning poker hand. "There's no way JFK's
on that film your husband burned. Believe me, I asked
the *Green Acres* expert. That reel was a ringer, and you
know it."

She didn't say anything. And she can't, Jack thought.
Because he was back to his old tricks. It was just like the
days in court, pinning someone on the stand and laying
them bare. Strip them to their last secret, and they would do
whatever you wanted.

Jack leaned forward and took Nita Dufraine's hands in his. "Do you want the secret of what you did to your husband to stay with you?"

After a moment she nodded yes.

"Then you know what you have to do," he said. "You have to give me the film of the umbrella man."

33

Nita Dufraine pulled a rope hanging in the hall. A hatch in the ceiling opened and the attic stairs dropped down with a groan of springs. "Come on," she said as she went up.

Jack and Treena followed. They stood on a plywood platform in the attic, beneath a bare lightbulb, while Nita pushed a key into the lock on a small refrigerator that looked like a hotel minibar.

She opened the door, and the refrigerator light came on. Jack looked over her shoulder to see maybe a dozen reels of film, each one the size of a coaster. One had a blank label. Others bore dates or names. Only one said 100-X. Nita took that one and handed it to Jack. "He's going to be very upset that I did this," she said.

"He'll get over it. And believe me, he's better off without it." Jack studied the reel's label; it had been marked in blue ink. "One hundred X," he said. "Accept no substitute."

Treena bent to look. "What's that mean?"

"Secret Service code for Kennedy's limo." Jack palmed the reel. "I thought everybody knew that."

"I knew it." Treena sniffed. "Just checking to see if you did."

Nita kept her sad eyes on the film. "God, I wish he had burned that one years ago. I always knew it would be nothing but trouble and grief for us. It was like keeping a cup of poison around."

"Know what I would have done?" Treena said. "First day it bothered me, I would've dropped the sucker right in the trash."

"It was Sylvan's." Nita looked wounded. "That would have been stealing from my own husband. And after what I had already done to him . . ."

"Uh-uh." Treena shook her head. "Right in the trash."

"It's different now," Jack said. "Now you're doing it to save Sylvan."

"Save him from what? Hey, if I was you?" Treena stepped between Nita and Jack. "I'd take it out and sell it. Right now. Get lots of money, do something good with that. All sorts of poor people out there could use a little help. Ever heard of the Mineola Watts Scholarship Fund?"

Jack said, "Treena, you want to keep your mouth shut for a while?"

"No, man, I don't."

"Just so we understand each other, Nita." Jack stepped sideways so he could see her. "Your giving me this film guarantees my silence about your husband."

"Silence?" Treena talked louder. "I ain't saying a damn word about it. So she's got my silence for free."

"Well, mine has a price," Jack said. "And it's in my hand."

"Dude is a cold one, Nita."

Nita pulled another reel, the one with the blank label, from the refrigerator. "I should have thrown out this one too. It's the one that started all this in the first place . . . Sylvan and the young girl."

"Same deal, huh?" Treena said. "You wanted to chuck it but it wasn't yours. All right, I'll make it easy on you. Hand it over to me or I'll do mean things. How's that?"

"Thank you," Nita said. She gave it to Treena with a look of relief. "I can't tell you how good it feels to finally get this away from me."

"My pleasure." Treena shot a look at Jack as she dropped the reel into her purse. "Check it out. I'm almost as good at extortion as you."

They went downstairs. In the living room Jack pushed the button to lower the screen and opened the cabinet that held the projector. When he had the film threaded he said, "Showtime."

Nita sat on the couch and folded her hands. "Can you believe I've never seen it? Sylvan's talked about it for years, but I can't truly tell you what's on it."

"Just want to make sure we got the right one this time," Jack said, and turned on the projector.

The film was grainy black-and-white, with no sound. First there was a pan of Dealey Plaza: the broad lawn and the crowds, men in boxy suits, women with below-the-knee dresses and sixties hairstyles. They wore sunglasses and cast the short, sharp shadows of a sunny midday. On the grass a family of four was enjoying a picnic lunch.

The camera swung up Elm Street, toward the top of the gentle hill, and the motorcade rolled into view. It was led by five cops on motorcycles, lights flashing, followed by a white Ford carrying the police chief.

Behind it, quicker than Jack would have thought, the

presidential limo came down the sweeping curve. The Secret Service Cadillac followed close.

Jack watched the Lincoln convertible move down the hill. He saw JFK and his wife and the governor of Texas, all waving. Flags flew above the headlights. The front bumper gave off a flash of reflected sunlight. Even from this distance Jack could tell Kennedy was smiling.

"Look at that," Jack said. "He's in the last seconds of his life."

A shadow crossed the frame, as if someone had walked in front of the lens, and the camera began to move. The view tracked up the grassy knoll, past some trees and shrubs to a wooden fence. A dark-haired man in a white shirt stood behind the fence. He was holding an open umbrella above his head.

"The star of the show," Jack said.

The focus blurred and sharpened, but the camera stayed with the man. Someone in his thirties, Jack guessed. Maybe a Latino, maybe someone with a deep tan. Hard to tell, because the shade of the umbrella fell on his face. He might have had a thin mustache.

After a few seconds he closed the umbrella. He lowered it, put the handle against his shoulder and rested the other end—the barrel, if he was firing a rifle—on the top of the fence. He dropped his head as if sighting a target, and put his hand where a trigger would be.

"He's gonna do it," Treena said. "Watch him. He's gonna shoot the President."

That was when Jack turned off the projector.

Treena jumped from the couch. "What you doing, man?"

Jack ran the ribbon of film between his fingers, feeling for knowledge, like a blind man reading the Bible.

Finally he said, "I think we've seen enough."

• • •

When they were in the car Treena said, "The way you did that? I bet that's what it's like having sex with you. I bet you pull out just before the guns go off. Not that I want to find out."

"It was all you needed to see." Jack drove his Chevy on the park road along White Rock Lake. Late afternoon on a weekday, cold and cloudy, they had the place to themselves. The umbrella man reel was on the front seat between them. "It was all anybody needed to see."

"You're not making any sense, man."

"You'll have to take my word for it." Jack pulled into a picnic spot on the lakeshore. The water was gray and choppy, the trees bare. It wasn't far from the hairpin curve where Eddie had told him the story about sinking into the soft lake bottom.

"What are we doing here?" Treena said.

"You know," Jack said, "Nita Dufraine was right. It's like poison, poured into a cup, waiting for someone to drink it."

"Hey." Treena tapped the reel with a fingernail. "For all you know the dude just had an umbrella, nothing else. You didn't hang around long enough to find out it was a gun."

"What difference does it make now? Say it was a gun, and that you could see him shooting it. It's not going to undo what happened. So what's it going to change?"

"Change somebody's wallet, that's what."

Jack shook his head. "Money's not going to be an issue here."

"The only people that say that about money? People that already have it."

Jack got out of the car, leaving Treena behind but taking

the keys, and felt the cold wind on his face. He took a dozen steps on brown grass to the lake.

People had gone swimming out here when he was a kid, but no more, not for years. The water was too dirty now, the bottom too silty. Things changed.

Treena sat in the car, looking at Jack's back. Watching him do some deep thinking out there in the cold. Telling herself it would be a fatal shame to waste a chance like this.

She picked up the film marked 100-X. Then she pulled the other reel, the one Nita Dufraine had given her, from her purse. She held one in one hand and one in the other. Except for the label, they looked just the same.

Which led to the money question: Did she have a pen with blue ink?

She rifled her purse but didn't find one. When she opened the glove box, wads of paper and a couple of cassette tapes spilled into her lap. She shoved her fingers into the mass of junk—maps and more tapes—and came out with two pens. One had red ink. But the other had blue.

Treena wrote 100-X on the blank label of the second reel, and placed it on the car seat. The umbrella man film went into her purse. She snapped the purse shut and looked up to see Jack walking toward the car.

If he had been watching her he would have seen the entire business. But he was looking at the sky.

Jack opened the Chevy's door, leaned in and grabbed the reel off the seat. He glanced at the label, 100-X, as he walked toward the water. Then he threw it as far as he could.

There was a splash and it was gone. The ripples lasted only a few seconds in the chop. The lake had swallowed the film as if nothing had ever happened. Jack envisioned it falling slowly through the cloudy water and settling into the muck for good.

When he got back into the car Treena was shaking her head. She said, "I knew you were going to do that. I would have bet a million dollars you were going to toss that thing."

Jack started the Chevy. "This whole mess was my fault. Two men are dead because of what I did."

"Like that was some big loss, those two."

"Doesn't matter. Now I've done what I can to make sure nobody else dies because of this. It's the first smart thing out of me in a long time."

"Whatever you say, man."

Jack went north on the winding park road. There was a good song on the radio about falling in love for the first time. He said, "You know, I feel great."

"Goody for you."

"Remember what Nita Dufraine said about getting a chance to undo a bad move? It's true. There's a real washed-my-sins-away quality to it."

Treena gave him a look. Jack turned up the radio. "I'm going to go home now," he said. "How about you?"

She shrugged and held her purse tight. "I don't know," she said. "Maybe I'll take in a movie."

Jack laughed. "That's a good one."

He drove along the lake and studied the gray water. Rain had started to fall. There seemed to be no one in the park but them. Jack pulled off the road and stopped beneath a leafless hackberry. He waited for Treena to look at him, then said, "You switched them."

After a while she said, "Just trying to save you from yourself."

"Trying to keep me from making a stupid mistake."

"That's right, man."

Jack held his palm out. "Give it to me, let me show you something."

Treena held his stare for a few seconds before opening her purse. She said, "You throw away a deal like this, you'd be sorry later. That's what I was thinking. I was gonna come clean when you cooled down and stopped washing away sins."

"You know, I believe you. I really do. But check this." Jack began to pull the film from the reel, holding it to the light, and pulling some more. Then said, "Run your touch right along here."

Treena drew a fingertip across the film. "It's got a rough spot," she said.

"That's a splice," Jack said. "Meaning we've got two pieces of film here, not one. And it comes right at the spot where the camera moves away from the limo and up the grassy knoll."

Treena blinked three times. "You're telling me," she said, "that this thing's a fake."

Jack nodded. "You can imagine how it happened. Sylvan Dufraine was going to make a little money off the assassination, so he decides to phony up a second gunman. Stages the shot and grafts the footage to his stuff from the motorcade. But before he can make a decent copy of the film and peddle it, Weldon the hit man comes knocking."

"Comes knocking real hard," Treena said.

"Scares Sylvan to death, which you would expect. So all those years, he keeps his scam in a vault, until one day he picks up the paper and finds out someone wants to buy it."

Treena stared at the film, running her finger back and forth over the splice.

"So the umbrella man killed Weldon, and he killed

Eddie," Jack said. "He almost killed Lola and almost killed me. But he didn't kill Kennedy."

They both looked at the lake until Jack said, "You want to throw this one in?"

From the *New York Times* bestselling author of *An Instance of the Fingerpost*

IAIN PEARS

The Titian Committee
__0-425-16895-6/$5.99

The Last Judgement
__0-425-17148-5/$6.50

The Raphael Affair
__0-425-16613-9/$5.99

Giotto's Hand
__0-425-17358-5/$6.50

"Elegant..a piece of structural engineering any artist would envy."—*New York Times*